HOLT COLLEGE

An Oxford Novel

BRIAN MARTIN

A

Arcadia Books Ltd
139 Highlever Road
London W10 6PH

www.arcadiabooks.co.uk

First published in the United Kingdom 2018
Copyright © Brian Martin 2018

A catalogue record for this book is available from the British Library.

ISBN 978-1-911350-25-5

Typeset in Garamond by MacGuru Ltd
Printed and bound by TJ International, Padstow PL28 8RW

ARCADIA BOOKS DISTRIBUTORS ARE AS FOLLOWS:

in the UK and elsewhere in Europe:
BookSource
50 Cambuslang Road
Cambuslang
Glasgow G32 8NB

in Australia/New Zealand:
NewSouth Books
University of New South Wales
Sydney NSW 2052

HOLT COLLEGE

1

What an irony! 1286. As long ago as that, the college had been founded by Elias de Holt as a chantry for the souls of the departed and as a fraternity for the Christian education of its members. He ordained in its statutes and ordinances that the college should provide for the instruction and education of twenty poor students or commoners and house for the proper purpose of study, prayer and scholarship, twenty fellows. The fellows were to constitute its governing body, one of their number should be elected their Principal, another his deputy the Vicegerent, and the collegiate governing body should be answerable during his lifetime to Elias, the founder. Thereafter, the college would be subject to the periodic visitation of the Bishop of Winchester who would oversee the administration and general discipline of the institution.

All members of the college were to be "sufficiently instructed in grammar", and in logic and rhetoric. They were then to proceed to the learning of arithmetic, geometry, music and astronomy. Then they would master philosophy and theology. Such was the achievement of several of the college's early fellows and students that it quickly attracted powerful and wealthy patrons. Walter Grimmond, Archbishop of York, and William, Earl of Chester, were both minded to give money and land to the foundation in acts of piety that were intended to secure its long-term stability. As the college grew through the centuries in size, reputation and accomplishment, it attracted other gifts and benefactions, most notably the patronage of its Visitor in 1649, the then Bishop of Winchester, who enabled an expansive building programme that included a capacious chapel, the size of an abbey church, and a tall, dominant bell tower. He laid down an endowment for the provision of singing clerks and choristers.

It was in this way that by the beginning of the twenty-first century Holt College had grown to become one of the wealthiest, most fashionable, and most successful of Oxford colleges; but it was infected by the various evils of ambition, greed, and corruption. I found myself in what I came to believe was a basket of snakes, a pit of vipers. Yet that description is too extreme. Most of my colleagues were plausible rogues, self-seeking and wily, products of a British political education that comprised a combination of egocentric Thatcherism and Blairism. Far from a dedication to the promotion of good learning and intellectual discipline, the men and women who occupied the present day fellowships were mostly intent on furthering their own careers and wanting to exercise power over others.

Thus it was when, after a year or two in post as Fellow in Economics, I was assailed by manoeuvres of political intrigue. The college, it appeared to me, mirrored the nation; it was a micro state. The Principal seemed to regard himself as the equivalent of the Prime Minister, elected into a position of almost unlimited power. That was an enigma for me; I belonged to an old tradition that saw him as elected to be chairman of a collegiate body. Willoughby Morris's principalship had developed, been transformed by him, into an autocratic rule. The majority of fellows had lost their capacity or will to hold him to account. I witnessed his gradual accumulation of power, his disdain for collegiate discussion and decisions, his diktats, his cronyism, and exploitation of the generosity of the original foundation. That's what I mean by drawing attention to the irony of the situation. Our founder and benefactors, "entombed in the urns and sepulchres of mortality", I felt, must have been ruing the day of Morris's election.

2

Walking towards me across the quad, she came, poised, beautiful, elegantly tall, like a model on a catwalk. Estelle taught English; she had written definitively about Dean Swift, his poetry and prose, but particularly about his letters. She had publicised his terms of baby-like endearment to his mistress, at odds with his hardbitten satire of society and its mores. She was in her early thirties and at once in conversation with her you knew that she was sophisticated, charming and, above all, manipulative. Her attraction to all but a few was magnetic. Those who knew her called her Est; by the verb to be she was known. I was always reminded of the fine Italian wine, *Est! Est! Est! Di Montefiascone*. Legend has it that a twelfth century German bishop on his way to the coronation of the Emperor in Rome, sent ahead a scout to discover houses and inns with the best wine; where the servant found it, he was to write on the door of the tavern, *Est!* So good was the wine in Montefiascone made from a fusion of grapes, Trebbiano, Malvasia and Roscetto, that he emphasised the endorsement thrice. My association of Estelle with the famous wine was appropriate. It was light, dry, straw coloured. It matched both her temperament and the colour of her hair.

Before I had a chance to greet her she called out, 'Johnny, lovely to see you,' and she had kissed me on both cheeks. Instinctively I put my right arm round her and felt her warmth. She never failed to excite me. Her presence engaged all of my senses. It is what I mean about her magnetism. She was someone you wanted to be with. To part from her was to experience a deep feeling of loss. Of course, that particular magic made her a highly successful tutor. Her students wanted to be with her and they listened to her mesmerised by every word.

'What about coffee later? Are you free later on? I'm doing eleven thirty to twelve thirty. Eleven for coffee?'

She always organised her tutorials that way, three in the morning from nine to eleven, then eleven thirty to twelve thirty, and two in the late afternoon, five until seven. That was on the days when she taught, two and a half days each week during term. The rest of the time she devoted to her research and, of course, the machinations of college politics. She had resisted administrative positions, the equivalents in my analogy to offices of state, cabinet positions, and preferred a backbench position, a sort of power behind the throne.

'That's great,' I said. I held her hand briefly. It was the most natural thing to do. There was no self-consciousness about it either on her part or mine. 'In the common room then. See you there.' We went our separate ways, she to her rooms, and me to the plate glass greenhouse box of the Social Sciences Library in Manor Road, a building whose architecture I detested but by force of circumstance I had to use.

By five to eleven I was back in college. I liked the walk; it took less than ten minutes and the fresh air enlivened my mind. There was nothing like the incentive to see Est; it was a spur that quickened my life force. I felt alert, eager and excited. I don't know if she knew that she had that power over me. In a way, I hoped she did; but if she did, she hid it well and appeared to be indifferent. I usually managed to convince myself that she thought I was just run-of-the-mill, a person she worked with, a colleague, no one special. Yet the prospect of seeing her and just being in her presence enabled me to work in concentration and to great effect. The certainty of seeing her at a particular time always made me work hard.

I went towards the chapel and then into the cloisters. Staircase 4 was the gloomy approach to the common room. As you were embraced by its shadows, you felt that you were entering Hades. On your return to ground level, coming down, you were relieved by the open view through ancient arches to the cloisters' green lawn in the middle of which there stood a sundial on a stone plinth. In different times and different settings, you could imagine playful monks with their skirts tucked up into their corded belts, stringing a makeshift net across the grass and playing the royal game of tennis.

At the top of the stairs I met our butler, a Spaniard, who had been in the service of the college for forty years. I knew all about his family, his grown-up children who were totally anglicised. He had never lost his heavy accent. His wife had recently died. The college was everything to him, and now that his wife was no longer with him, he devoted all his waking time to the institution and to us.

'Is Est here, Antonio?'

He replied formally. He adhered to old-fashioned manners and did not believe in familiarity. 'Good morning, sir. Miss Treisman is not here yet. She did say she would come. She spoke to me earlier.'

'Good. I'll get myself some coffee.'

'Let me bring it to you, sir.'

Although I was unhappy to be waited on in such a way, I knew better than to rebuff Antonio. He enjoyed his role. He relished being a facilitator, being helpful, being useful. His years of service had set him in his ways and if he could not perform his perceived way of doing things properly, he was offended. My feelings, and most of my colleagues', gave way to his. Thus we always enjoyed being looked after by him in a most lavish way. It was as though we were back in the eighteenth century, or at least, in the Edwardian era.

I went across the panelled common room to a broad, high window that looked out and down on to gardens that fell away towards a colonnaded neo-classical building. I sat down on the cushioned window seat and swivelled to look out. The garden beds were mostly herbaceous borders, but at that early summer time of the year they were full of clumps of late flowering tulips, primulas and primroses. An Old Member of the college had established in the twentieth century a college garden fund. It endowed a gardener's post and allowed for an amount of money each year to be spent on stock plants for the beds. With the college's maintenance resources boosted by such generosity, the gardens always looked superb. The head gardener, with an extra hand added to his team, kept to the highest of standards.

In the half distance stood an ancient oak, some of its lower limbs, so huge and heavy, supported by iron crutches. I wondered who had, over time, sat in its shade. Then, in a moment, I experienced a frisson, a slight shudder of excitement, run down my spine. Immediately Keats's lines came to memory, 'He knew whose gentle hand was at the latch/Before the door had given her to his eyes.' Half turned as I was to look out of the window, and dreamily far away pondering the beauty of the scene, I suddenly felt a hand on my shoulder. 'Johnny, you're here before me. Let me get you some more coffee.' Est was standing there. I felt a privileged thrill; her touch, familiar, comfortable and casual in its gesture, somehow made me feel intimate with her, as though we shared something that others did not. On the other hand, it immediately occurred to me that maybe I was cherishing an ill-founded illusion, and that she treated everyone like that. I could not be sure; and that meant that I was unsettled, slightly insecure in my relationship with her, and therefore nervous.

'Thanks. I should be getting it for you. Let me. Sit here.' I indicated the window seat. 'Admire the view. It is, as usual, just fantastic.'

She sat down. I went to the coffee machine in a far corner of the room. Typical of the new regime in the college, Principal Morris's new broom approach was to economise. Our fresh coffee had been replaced by a machine that could offer from an electronic lit-up menu on its facia, espresso, double espresso, regular with milk, decaffeinated, and, remarkably, even hot chocolate. The only remotely drinkable potion was the strong espresso. The reformed coffee provision was a constant source of complaint, which the bursar sought to extinguish by ignoring any criticism. Nevertheless, Est and I thought that pressure was building up that would inevitably see the old coffee-making procedure reinstated. It was another example, though small, that contributed towards dissatisfaction with the college's ruling elite. The machine had been introduced without consultation. It had been a coup; but minor irritations develop into major confrontations.

I went back to her with our coffee, my cup refreshed by a single espresso, and her double espresso with a dash of milk. Est took hers.

'Thanks, Johnny. Why do we put up with this? It's our choice, not Morris's, not the bursar's. Why does Eedes go along with it?'

Jeremy Eedes was the bursar, the financial officer in charge of expenditure and economy. Est added, 'He can't like it any more than the rest of us.'

'He doesn't take coffee here,' I said. 'Needless to say, he has it percolated in his room. This is for the rest of us. Therefore it doesn't matter to him. Anyway, he's Morris's man. He allies himself with what he sees as the governing party. If the Principal thinks it a good idea, Jeremy will implement it.'

Est sipped from her cup and grimaced exaggeratedly. 'We must occupy the kitchens, sit in the hall, march on the Principal's lodgings. What are we doing? We're supine. Let's rise up. We have a just cause. The coffee's lousy.' She giggled, put down her cup and rested her right hand on my arm. I felt the warmth of her touch.

'Well, one day something will happen, something will snap. But it's not time for revolution yet. Too many of our colleagues are uninvolved. They want a quiet life. They have to be fired up. What happens here has to affect them radically and beyond endurance. That has not happened yet.'

'I know,' Est replied. 'It almost certainly will; it will. The time is not yet ripe. The pot of turmoil must came to boiling point, unlike that coffee machine which never will; hence the lukewarm-ness.'

Again, she giggled, put down her cup and patted my arm.

Meanwhile a number of people had been coming and going. Rodney Bennet, a nuclear physicist, waved to me across the room.

He rarely appeared in college in the morning; he was usually to be found in the lab in the science area. Often he was away at some institution abroad such as CERN; much of his teaching was covered by post-graduate and post-doc students. That was a pattern among scientists. It was more difficult for tutors in subjects like mine, although I did have the assistance of a part-time college lecturer.

Rodney came across. 'Morning, Estelle. Hi, Johnny. How are things? What's it like this term in the People's Democratic Republic? Is the generalissimo behaving himself?'

'If you are referring to our glorious enlightened leader, Willoughby, he continues to act unilaterally. He simply doesn't realise that he is accountable to the governing body. So, there's no change there.' Est sipped her coffee and glanced at the carriage clock positioned on a sideboard where some of the magazines were laid out.

'It's time you came to a governing body meeting, Rod. You should air your views. After all, you can give an objective view, someone looking in from the outside, as it were.'

He registered my satirical barb. 'I know you think I should be around more often, but work in the national interest and all that. Where would you lot be without me and nuclear weapons?' He looked at Est. 'I rest my case, madame judge.'

'Will you be here much this term?' I asked him.

'Most of the second half of term. I'll try to make sure that I attend the fellows' meetings. Still, I'd better be off. I'm flying to Frankfurt this evening.'

He put down his cup and saucer on a small Jacobean side table. Antonio, ever watchful, immediately collected them and took them to another table by a service door to the pantry and placed them on a tray. Rodney picked up a leather document case and left.

I said to Est, 'That's good news. We need him. He has the right view and he's not afraid of speaking his mind. I think this term will be crucial. If we don't do something now, the Principal and his cronies will absolutely dominate this college. It'll be the usual story of nepotism and petty corruption, acceded to by the silent majority who want a quiet life to get on with their research. Anyway, you know what I mean.'

'I'd better go,' Est said. 'It's odd. Willoughby seems to see himself as a CEO, the boss of some sort of company, when in fact he's just the elected chairman of a collegiate committee. I think with him it's a power jag; and he loves dispensing patronage.

'Look, we must continue this anon.'

I took the prompt. 'Shall we meet later?' I suggested. I was a little tentative, slightly nervous.

'Yes, why not? I've got to go to a Faculty meeting at five, but from seven onwards I'm free.'

I panicked mildly. I could not remember what I was supposed to be doing later that day. Did I have any promised engagements? Was I meeting anyone else that evening? It did not matter; I decided that it was an opportunity not to be missed. Never before had the initiative come from Est. I had once asked her to have dinner with me but she had declined.

'OK, where shall we meet?' she asked.

'Why don't I come to your room? We could go up the High to Quod and have a drink, a cocktail or something.'

By this time she was by the door. 'Good. See you then.' She turned and touched her fingers to her lips and gently blew me a kiss. Once again I felt extreme elation. She had never done anything like that before. It occurred to me that we were into a new stage of a rapidly developing relationship.

3

It is difficult to describe the exhilaration I felt. For a long time I had wanted to get closer to Est. I had dreams, fantasies, of an intimate relationship with her; but somehow she always seemed unapproachable. She was friendly enough but everything was on a professional level. We were merely colleagues at work. There was a neutral distance between us, a sort of no-man's-land where nothing happened. Now there was a change. She had made the first move. At least, that is what I thought. In fact, I kept stopping myself and thinking that I was deluding myself. I was misreading the signs perhaps. What she was saying was just that she would have finished work and that on her way home she would simply have a drink with a colleague about whom she had no particular feelings. On the other hand, she did blow me a kiss; that had never happened before.

That morning I returned to my rooms and met my young French student. He had been educated in English schools; his parents were, unusually, Anglophile. He was extremely bright and aimed to go on to postgraduate work. For that he needed a first class degree. I knew that he was capable of that and so did he. The teaching was therefore easy. The hour passed quickly and the tutorial went on until five to one.

I looked on my desk at my diary and pondered my afternoon's schedule. I could work in the Social Sciences library until four and then give another tutorial from four thirty to five thirty. I could then relax. At around five past one I went to the senior common room dining room for lunch.

The Principal was there, self-important and expansive as usual. On one side of him there was Eedes, on the other Knowles, the senior tutor. Knowles was Morris's most powerful acolyte. He was an Australian, an academic lawyer and an MBA. Somehow he had worked his way into academic administration. We liked to think that he was not good enough to earn himself distinction and a prestigious professorship in law and so had changed course. A couple of years previously, Morris had insisted on creating the senior tutor's position and had found Knowles through a contact in Sydney. Knowles came with the recommendation of the head of the law faculty and we subsequently thought that the high praise was a device to get rid of Knowles.

Knowles was gay. There was no objection to that. Oxford has always had a distinguished array of colourful homosexuals; and Knowles was, superficially at least, pleasant and accommodating. At the same time he was manipulative and Machiavellian. Within a year of his appointment he had a favourite, a companion, a young fair-haired research student, who accompanied Knowles everywhere on social and even on some official university occasions. Ordinarily, not even that would have proved a problem, a cause of complaint and annoyance, but when it involved precedence, there was immediate resentment.

An example had occurred just a week ago when the college had entertained the Mayor of London to a lavish lunch, and who, after a suitable interval, had gone on to the Sheldonian Theatre to give a lecture on cabinet government of a large city. There had been a procession over the short distance from college to the Sheldonian, an official affair, the beadle carried the mace, the Vice-Chancellor wore robes, the Principal followed, and then the college fellows in order of seniority. Knowles was placed number four after the Principal, the Vicegerent, and the senior fellow. As the procession reached the approaches of the Sheldonian, Knowles's catamite inserted himself into the proceedings next to Knowles in front of the rest of the fellows. He accompanied the senior tutor into the auditorium and took his seat next to him. Needless to say, there were some very cross fellows who resented the presence of this upstart who had no right, in their view, to be in the party at all.

Nevertheless, Knowles was capable and efficient. So far as I was concerned, he served the college well in the detail of his work. Yet I could see that his mode of operation might annoy the majority. He was no diplomat. He did not recognise, no more than the Principal himself did, that in order to secure his position, he had to carry the majority of the fellowship with him. It was a collegiate body that he was part of; voices were equal and, in the final analysis, it was the vote that counted.

Anyway, that lunchtime, Morris was seated with his chief supporters, one either side of him. I took a seat opposite them.

'Johnny, dear boy,' Morris called out as I sat down, 'how are you? I trust all is set fair in the economics factory. You must give us some advice.' He gestured towards each of his acolytes. 'Remember there will be a finance committee meeting on Thursday.'

'I shall be there. I have it marked,' I assured him.

It would be true to say that the Principal customarily ignored me unless a finance meeting was in the offing or he needed advice on his personal investment portfolio, advice which I usually managed not to give. I found his greeting patronising.

'The senior tutor is going to need a personal assistant. We've got to find resources to pay for him or her. We'll have the bursar on board.' Morris looked over the top of his glasses at Eedes. 'You're happy with that. Aren't you, Jeremy?'

Eedes nodded his assent.

'Do you think that you can go along with that?' Morris continued.

Antonio had come to the table with a jug of tap water. I helped myself to a glass. I hesitated to answer.

'You're not going to drink that awful stuff, are you? It tastes of chlorine, positively lavatorial.' He beamed at what he considered to be a witticism and went on, 'Have something better.' He offered me a bottle of Hildon sparkling water.

'No thanks. I prefer this,' I said raising my tap water to my lips.

Morris cut into a lamb chop, forked a piece with some salad into his mouth, and spluttered, 'What about Timothy's PA?'

'Good point,' I said. 'Thanks for alerting me. It needs thinking about. Let's discuss it at the meeting on Thursday. There's quite a long agenda. I reckon expenses will take up a lot of time.'

'Precisely, dear boy. That's why I thought I'd do some groundwork beforehand. Maybe we could fix this without having to waste time in committee.'

I immediately saw what his game was. He hoped to pass this measure without reference to the control and scrutiny of the finance committee.

'Well, I think it will probably have to be discussed on Thursday. We are going to have to keep track of expenditure more and more in the present climate. Don't you agree, Bursar?'

Jeremy Eedes did not look at me but made an evasive answer. 'Yes, it's true; but I'm sure the Principal has thought about that and the money spent can be justified. So perhaps we can just get the committee to rubber-stamp it.'

Eedes knew as well as I did that the move would be highly irregular but then he was one of Morris's men, a placeman.

'We can rely on you then?' Morris added.

'Not exactly,' I said. 'It will need some thinking about as I said. I think the bursar will agree, we are in for a period of financial constraint. We must do our accounting carefully.'

'Oh, Johnny, you're such an old stickler. Flow with the tide, dear boy. If you do that, in the end it's so much easier to get what you want.'

That remark really annoyed me. Morris was clearly pointing out that my compliance with his present wishes would make matters better for me personally when in the future I might need his support. Again, he was being patronising and exposing his scheming streak.

I retorted rather icily, 'I'm sure that whatever I might want in future will be decided on its merits; and I would not expect the college to overstretch its finances on my behalf.'

Morris noted my tone. 'Come, come, dear boy. Nobody's being held to ransom. You're far too sensitive.' He tried to cover his tracks with blusterous bonhomie.

Fortunately, at that moment, my immediate colleague, the politics fellow, came in and joined us. The seat next to me on my right was empty and she sat down. Antonio was at her elbow and poured her some water. Jane Templeman taught the politics course for the PPE degree. The initials stood for politics, philosophy and economics; thus we saw much of each other and cooperated in our teaching. What was particularly crucial at that lunchtime was that she sat with me on the finance committee, and she was puritanical about accountability and transparency. Willoughby Morris changed the subject.

'Will you be at the drinks party on Friday evening?' he asked Jane.

'I shall try to be there,' she replied. 'It's an awkward time for me. Six is not good. I have a tutorial from six to seven. I'll have to try to move it. If I can, I'll be there; if not, sadly not. Thank you for asking me.'

I had already replied to Morris's invitation and declined it: I had to be in London that night and planned to leave Oxford at around four. In a way I regretted missing the party. The Principal's parties were always good fun. Throwing parties, entertaining, was what he was really good at. As well as being a leading scientist at the top of his discipline, he was an irresistible social animal. He loved mixing with people and on such occasions mixing them around. I thought I saw beneath the veil which hid his real milieu, that where he was able to fix and arrange bits of business confidentially and amiably between different people who were feeling well disposed towards him. He was adept at manipulation and a master at disguising his motives. I knew of so many deals of one sort or another, academic, administrative, business, fundraising, that had been made in those circumstances but all of which had been to his personal advantage. They boosted his position, embellished his profile, or even increased his wealth. Nevertheless, the parties were always great.

Morris was first to finish lunch and leave. Rather insidiously, he rose and said, 'Can't delay. I've many things to do. I'll leave you all to your leisure. I know Oxford afternoons are not conducive to work.' He nodded to me and remarked, 'Don't take it seriously, Johnny. You know that if there's anything you want, anything pressing, a word in my ear…' He went, around the long table, across the room. As he approached the door, his shadow followed him reducing at an angle to nothing, and he vanished, as it were, through the oak panelling. Why he should have imagined that his last remark to me was either mollifying or encouraging, I failed to understand. It simply made me think that he misjudged me, and, at the same time, reinforced my view that he achieved what he wanted by manipulation, secret deals and unilateral decisions.

When he had gone, I turned to Jane and said, 'Jane, you'd better try to go on Friday. You need to keep an eye on him, otherwise there's no knowing what he and his cronies will get up to. I'm sorry I can't be there. If I were, I'd have my pocket tape-recorder and hidden camera with me.'

'You're absolutely right. I'll do my best; but it's annoying when you have to alter your teaching schedule to keep an eye on the guy who's supposed to be in charge.'

'Make damn sure that you're at the finance meeting Thursday afternoon. I get the feeling that Morris, Eedes and Knowles are up to something. And you know that Bradshaw has put travel expenses on the agenda.'

'Oh, don't you worry. I'll definitely be there for that. We have to appoint new auditors as well. We don't want anyone Willoughby recommends. He's just the sort who would take a backhander.'

'Who's the Old Member who runs an accounting firm in the City? He was here at the last Gaudy.'

I was trying to remember the name of a Holt College graduate who had attended the last reunion. The dinners on such an occasion are called Gaudies deriving from the Latin 'Gaudiam', 'merry-making', 'rejoicing'. The idea is to celebrate the good fortune of the college by feasting and entertainment. Always supplementary to that purpose is an implied continuing support for the institution by generous giving, that is to say the day or weekend becomes a fundraising device.

'Eliot I think you mean. A very nice chap. He told me that he makes sure his firm makes a donation to Mencap each year. He has a son who was afflicted in his teens, so he has an interest there. He would be fair and efficient. Roy Eliot. An old pupil of old Mayhew, the mathematician who retired the year before you joined us.'

'Good. We might suggest that soundings should be made. We can be pretty insistent. The Principal and his party will be outnumbered in a vote. Morris is bound to have some crony he wants to appoint.'

I made my excuses and left. I needed to escape into the real world, if that is what you would call it. I left the common room with the sun low in the sky illuminating the central Persian carpet and casting shadows on the panelling. I descended the narrow stairs into the dark, gloomy cloisters of the chapel.

To the right, the cloisters gave out on to the first quad of the college, the one that you first came into when emerging from the lodge. The head porter, a man from Iffley village who cycled in each day, was on duty with a new recruit whom he was training. He called through his window, 'Afternoon, sir. The sun's come out. It should be good for a walk in the fresh air.'

'You're right, Archie. I think I'll take a stroll.' I could never tell whether Archie Rook was being sarcastic, ironic, gently satirical, or not. There was a general feeling that he felt we did not do much work. He belonged to the general majority who viewed a don's life as one of ease and idleness. I knew he believed that because on more than one occasion I had light-heartedly discussed his prejudice with him. He was not to be shifted in his opinion; and he was not aggressive about it. Rather he was amused by the way of life we led. He was good at his job. He was hard-working, conscientious and loyal. It might sound as though I am writing him a job reference, but he does not need one. He was well off in the college's employ, a pillar of its establishment, and we all valued him enormously.

I stepped out through the lodge to the pavement that one way led into town, and the other led over the bridge towards the suburb of Headington and thence eventually to London. The High was fairly busy with traffic. Once past Holywell, vehicles were largely confined to buses and taxis. A re-organisation of road plans had banned private cars and commercial vehicles from the High during the day; the aim was to keep the city centre less polluted and to preserve for the discerning eye the beautiful architectural sweep of the High and its bordering buildings, the skyline spoilt only by the central heating chimneys of St Edmund Hall.

The low sun shone on the range of houses, shops and colleges that stood on the northern side of the street. The view was magnificent, enhanced by a tree here and there whose buds were late in breaking into leaf. I walked briskly and as I passed the church of St Mary the Virgin, the official university church, I saw crossing the road, an old friend, Malcolm White. He had retired a year ago from being a top civil servant to a life of contemplation and perambulation in Oxford. He was a tall, fair-haired, upright man, despite the years he must have spent crouched over piles of paperwork on his various desks. In fact, over the years, he had maintained his prowess as a good sportsman, a cricketer and tennis player. He had started out as a diplomat, but in the latter part of his career he worked for the Cabinet Office as chair of the Joint Intelligence Committee. He had been knighted for his trouble.

He was preoccupied in his walk, his head was bowed, his eyes down. I hailed him. 'Malcolm, how are you? Good to see you.'

He looked up somewhat slightly bemused but immediately registered my call. He was alert at once and his eyes sparkled.

'I'm fine. OK,' he said. 'And you? I was a bit lost in thought. They want my advice about whether we should use military force in one of the southern Caucasus states. Can't tell you which one; but use your imagination. Usual story: the Yanks are gung-ho. The Russians say they are complicit; but you never know. Can't see it doing any good, to tell the truth. Just mess things up a little bit more. Anyway, they ask and never listen. I could tell them anything and confidently know that I've wasted my breath, or rather my pen and ink, as it were.'

He enjoyed these verbal rambles and I always enjoyed listening to them. He liked teasing too. He never told you the whole story but seduced your interest with hints and clues. You had to work out the rest for yourself.

I did not feel like a long chat. Malcolm was prone to digress into long biographies of anyone he knew who cropped up in conversation. You had to be in no hurry when you met him. I felt it was a reaction to his years of clipped, efficient decision-making.

'Look, I must get on. Lovely to see you. Let's meet for lunch. Perhaps next week, say Wednesday. Pencil it in.'

'Can't do Wednesday, I'm afraid. In London. Let me call you. It's time we discussed matters of grave import.'

He went off through to Radcliffe Square where the side of the church bordered the southern edge. The crypt and spacious vestry room had been turned into a vegetarian restaurant. Outside, in the small churchyard, a few tables had been set up, some disturbingly on ancient tombstones laid flat. I tended to avoid that little area; a close friend, a manic depressive, had jumped to his death from the top of St Mary's tower.

I continued up the High. Tourists mingled with shoppers. In the Cornmarket representatives from a Palestinian organisation solicited signatures for a petition against Israeli settlements on Arab land. Bundles of literature were laid out on a wooden trestle table. A neatly dressed young girl, aged in her middle twenties, sang an operatic aria accompanied by music from a CD player. A little crowd of curious and appreciative onlookers stood around her and one or two put money in a box on the ground in front of her. In the closed service doorway of a bank, a West Indian evangelical preacher expounded the good news of the New Testament and exhorted sinners to recognise their waywardness; Jesus loves and Jesus saves.

How different was all this, I thought, as I went into the HMV store, from the secluded precincts of the college and the internal politics driven by the machinations of Willoughby Morris.

There were two CDs that I wanted to buy. First, I went upstairs to the classical music section. I sorted through the Chopin disks and found what I was searching for, Preludes played by Evgeny Kissin. I had recently listened to Prelude 19 in E flat while I was driving back to Oxford from London and had been entranced. That was the usual prompt for me to buy such music; listening, by chance, to something on the radio.

Then I headed for the Indie Pop department. An old student of mine had given up academic pursuits and established a band called, for some reason I had never fathomed, Foals. It had succeeded and he had just won the *New Musical Express* award for the best single track, 'Spanish Sahara', from the album *Total Life Forever*.

I presented the two CDs to the assistant, a long-haired semi-Goth male in his mid-twenties, dressed in black T-shirt and low-slung black jeans, with the obligatory logo-branded waistband of his underpants visible. 'Eclectic taste, mate,' he commented.

I countered with, 'Incongruous vocabulary. Not what I would expect.'

'Part-time. Trying to write my doctorate.'

That, I suppose, was no more nor less than I should have expected in a university town. I walked out into the cool sunshine.

As I had half planned and anticipated, I spent the best part of the afternoon in the library. Then I gave my tutorial, run-of-the-mill, rather uninspiring. My thoughts were mostly preoccupied with the prospect of meeting Est a little later. At around twenty-five to six, my tutorial undergraduate left me alone with my own thoughts. I took the cellophane wrapping from the Foals CD and listened to it for about thirty minutes. 'Spanish Sahara' was the only track I liked. The rest did nothing for my sense of appreciation or enjoyment. The Chopin was much more acceptable at that particular time.

I cannot explain why, but I felt nervous. At a quarter to seven I felt an immense urgency to urinate. I went to the lavatory and did so. By five to seven I felt I had to do so again. I knew, of course, it was all on account of meeting Est. Subconsciously I set great store by liaising with her and everything being a success. I did not want the beginning of this relationship, which I had so much wanted for such a long time and which had customarily been gently rebuffed, to fail. This time it had been instigated by Est. It was important not to misjudge or mishandle the situation. That was the reason for my nervousness.

I allowed a few minutes to elapse after the tower clock had struck seven so that Est's student had time to disappear, and then went to the staircase where her rooms were. The stairs were narrow and wound up. She was at the top on the third floor. I felt like one of her students and by the time I reached her door, I was ready for her tutorial interrogation. I knocked gently on her door. There was an immediate response. I knew she was expecting me. My attendant worries about her forgetting the arrangement, about her not being serious, were banished by her quick call, 'Come in.'

'Hi, Est. Sorry; I'm very much on time.'

'Don't worry, Johnny. I'm just in here, reinforcing the make-up. Touching up, if you know what I mean.'

With that, I at once relaxed. She spoke from behind the door of her bedroom in that set of rooms. She was on good form, bantering, and easy in her conversation.

'Take your time. There's no hurry.'

'True. The whole evening lies ahead. I intend to do no work. I hope you propose the same.'

I relaxed even more. That, it seemed to me, was the invitation to the dance, as it were. Then, I began to feel nervous again; a whole evening with Est. It was going to be a test. What would we talk about after the first few minutes? Would she change her mind halfway through and remember she had other things to do? I was haunted by self-doubt, uncertainty, a lack of confidence.

My silence prompted her.

'Are you still there, or have you gone on ahead?'

'No, sorry. I'm still here. I was just thinking. Of course I'm free all evening. Let's discuss what to do when we have a drink over the road.'

'Good idea. I thought you might have tried to get one in before me and I'd have to run to catch up.'

I knew from the tone of her voice that she was determined to enjoy herself.

We walked the short distance from the college, up the High, to Quod. Through the double-fronted glass doors I could see that about a quarter of the tables were taken. Inside it was quite noisy. There was a party of ten or so people, some sort of office outing, drinking champagne, laughing and shouting. Est and I turned left in the restaurant and went to the area where the bar was. We settled ourselves into a corner on a leather sofa with a small table in front of it. Behind us on the wall was a huge painting, a close-up of three girls on a beach, Nice perhaps, St Tropez. The proprietor, whom I knew, was quite an art collector. Surprisingly, all his paintings that hung in his three restaurants were noteworthy and ought to have commanded more than a sidelong glance which most of his clients gave them. There was one collage picture of an African township that, he told me, attracted lots of offers from discerning people who stayed at his adjacent hotel. So far, he refused to sell. Yet like all good businessmen, he said he was waiting until the price seemed right. There were always other paintings to buy, investments to make. He had been recently looking at a Julian Opie in a Bond Street gallery, £75,000, or something in that order.

'What will you have?' I asked Est.

'A dry martini, please, with green olives.'

I went to the bar and ordered from the Scottish bartender who, at the same time, seemed that evening to be in charge of the waiters and waitresses. I had decided on a double malt whisky, a Jura.

Inevitably the conversation turned to the Principal. I had been telling Est about the small music PR firm in London that the daughter of a friend had started. Over the past five years she, together with an old school friend, had established their company in Commercial Street, in the East End, a couple of hundred yards away from Brick Lane. It had not been the orthodox location for people in the music industry; that would have been in west London, Notting Hill or Shepherd's Bush. Yet the enterprise had succeeded. I had been one of the first to put up some money for the business, along with her father and her brother.

I liked the way she ran the outfit. She and her business partner were the bosses. No one was left in doubt about that. The gradually expanding company had grown to employing eighteen individuals. It was because Quod hosted a band on Friday and Saturday evenings that played outside on a landscaped wooden deck, and under an awning if it rained, that the subject came up. The band was advertised, chalked up on a large blackboard mounted high on the wall by the entrance to the kitchens. My friend's daughter had mentioned that particular band the last time I had met her.

I mused to Est about the major difference between running a company and being head of a college. 'Some of these college heads think it's the same sort of thing. It's not. As a college head, you've been elected by the collegiate body of fellows, who themselves have been elected. The Principal, Rector, Warden, what have you, presides so long as he or she enjoys the confidence of the fellows. He's a glorified chairman. Willoughby Morris has got ahead of himself. He thinks he's a CEO, or, worse than that, an equivalent of the Prime Minister.'

Est agreed. I knew anyway that I was talking to the converted. 'Yes, I know. He's heading for trouble. At the moment, he can rely on apathy and the connivance and support of his few supporters, mostly his creatures.'

She was right. Like many people in similar positions to his, Morris made sure that those he appointed during his tenure so far were sympathetic to his rule; and it was not surprising that they should go along with him. After all, they owed their positions largely to him. Thus it was with Eedes the bursar and Knowles the senior tutor.

'Of course, what happens in the end, is that the apathetic major-ity begins to lose its apathy and decides to do something about the situation; but it takes a long time and there needs to be a spark that leads to the conflagration which then consumes the leadership. The coffee machine, of course, is not a big enough spark, although it is a burning issue.'

I realised that I was speaking as though dictating a chapter of an academic book.

'Sorry. I'm being a little pompous,' I said rather self-consciously.

'No, you're right. That's just how it is. Willoughby should listen to his constituency. He's mad not to. I suppose he can rely on the bursar; but Knowles is different. He's entirely self-interested. So long as he sees there's advantage for himself, and perhaps for one or other of his acolytes, then he will remain loyal to the Principal. But who knows what will happen when the mood changes and Willoughby loses momentum, if he ever does.'

'You're quite right. Knowles reminds me of one of Colonel Nasser's generals who said in an interview, "I am 110 per cent loyal ... until the time for treachery arrives."'

We continued to talk about various people in the college and where their loyalties and affiliations might lie. It was clear that Morris's inner core of close support numbered no more than about five fellows. Yet such was the character of the man, his confidence, his determination, his dominance in debate and conversation, his assumption that he knew best, that he usually got his own way. Eventually I wearied of the topic; it was like talking shop. I wanted to know more about Est and her life, which was much of a mystery to me.

'Anyway, enough,' I said. 'Tell me about you. Morris is a bore.' The Jura started having its effect. 'What have you been doing all your life? Why have you been avoiding me?'

She took a sip of her martini and looked at me somewhat askance. 'What do you mean? You know very well. And I don't like mixing my social life with my work. If possible, I like to keep them separate.' Then, flirtatiously, she added after a little pause, 'Mind you, in your case I might just make an exception.'

I have to admit that I thrilled at that, although I thought that it might have been the martini talking. I had told the barman to make it strong, three parts gin, one part vermouth. She delicately stabbed an olive and speared it in one try.

'I admire your skill,' I commented.

'As you might imagine – years of practice.'

'Shall we find a table?'

She swirled her drink in its glass and nodded. She sipped and threw her head back revealing the brightness of her eyes. They were shining, almost gleaming, an intense liquid green. I instinctively wondered what was going on behind the mask of beautiful face. She reminded me of the concerns of the metaphysical poets who saw the eyes as the windows of the soul. I wanted to look inside, view behind the mask.

I went across to where the floor manager was welcoming diners. I pointed to a small table for two at the back of the restaurant, behind a substantial pillar that partly shielded its occupants from the rest of the company. He signalled a waitress who escorted us to the table. We could see out to the raised deck with its topiaried boxes and the fountain that sprung out from the Cotswold stone wall. To the side, we could see through some double doors into the vestibule and reception area of the hotel. Perfect. We were sufficiently private not to be disturbed by other guests, you could not be overheard, and there was the faint, but realistic, chance of intimacy that I was hoping for.

The waitress left us and quickly returned with a couple of menus. I asked her for a bottle of sparkling water. Again, she left us and we discussed what we should eat. I caught the waitress's attention as she finished delivering an order to another table, and asked her to bring us each a glass of Languedoc white wine, a Picpoul de Pinet, Duc de Morny, and meanwhile we would consider what we wanted after that.

Outside on the deck, a mother and father paused with two small children before entering by way of the rear hotel door. The children, one a boy of about four and the other a girl of about two, were fascinated by the fountain. They lingered and splashed their hands in the fountain's pool of water. The father finally decided that they had played enough, made his way through the box topiaries, and shooed them in through the door. I could see the receptionist welcome them and point out the double door of the restaurant. They went in and a waiter showed them to a table across the floor by a window that gave out on to the High.

'A nice enough family,' Est remarked, 'but I'm glad they're sitting over there.'

As she said that I noticed someone approach the receptionist's desk. The figure was not immediately clear through the double glass doors. The reflection of light blurred and slightly impeded my vision. I shifted a little and caught a different angle and recognised the outline of Timothy Knowles's back. He was leaning over, talking to a charming, professionally pleasant, blond receptionist who I knew from previous conversations was Estonian.

'Est, that's Knowles.'

'Where?' Est looked around.

'No. Out there through the doors. At reception.'

She looked round.

'What on earth's he doing here? I suppose he might be meeting someone.'

'Probably. Maybe it's someone he doesn't want to put up in college.'

Knowles turned round away from us and disappeared.

By the time our waitress returned with our drinks, we had decided on what we were to eat. Est ordered Jersey crab with chicory and fennel, followed by goat's cheese, thyme and olive tart; I asked for ham hock with piccalilli and then roast pollack with capers, anchovies and olives. We both preferred red wine with our main course, regardless of the customary accompaniment to fish, and had chosen a bottle of Italian red, Sangiovese di Puglia from Ancona.

The waitress noted our order on her pad and went off to the kitchens. I stretched back and glanced through the doors to reception. There was Knowles again, but this time he was accompanied by his young, fair-haired companion. They stood close at the desk and it was clear that they were signing into the hotel. Knowles was making the arrangement. He handed over a credit card and signed a single sheet document. As he did so his friend touched familiarly his hand as he laid down the pen. Knowles turned, smiled, and put an arm round the young man's shoulders. They moved away and out of sight.

Est had been watching too, her interest captured by my total involvement in the observation of that curious event.

'Well,' she whispered, although there was no need to: they were beyond the doors and out of sight. 'What do you make of that? You might have thought they were fixing a dirty weekend, except it's not the weekend and, added to which, it's too close to home. What on earth's going on?'

'Haven't a clue. Perhaps they're reserving a room for someone. That must be it. They can't be using it themselves, can they?'

'You never know. The affairs of the heart. The one thing the study of literature does for you is to make all possibilities possible. Human nature, behaviour is wonderfully diverse. It could be a celebratory tryst. A birthday, an anniversary, or something.'

'Hmm, very intriguing. Well, let's watch this space.'

We both enjoyed that evening in Quod. The time went quickly. Every so often the conversation veered back to Willoughby Morris and college or university politics, but when it did, one or other of us would pull up sharply and change tack. Mostly we talked of music, literature, the world scene, or friends whose behaviour had surprised us; the latter was inspired by the vision of Knowles through the glass.

It was not until the end of the evening there that Knowles cropped up again. As we left, went out of Quod on to the High, we saw Knowles and his young friend coming from the direction of the college towards the hotel. They were talking animatedly and laughing, totally preoccupied with each other. So immersed were they in each other, they did not glance at the one or two couples emerging from the restaurant. I was quite prepared to greet Timothy Knowles cheerily without registering any surprise, just to see what his reaction would be. Would he be embarrassed, would he be evasive, or would he carry it all off with accustomed and practised nonchalance?

In the event, he did not see us; but we saw him. He and his friend, lover perhaps, went into the hotel.

'Well, there we are. How romantic,' Est said.

'I don't get it. Why don't they just shack up in college?'

'Who knows what their thinking is. Anyway, enough of Knowles.'

'I agree. Though I wonder what credit card he's using. Perhaps it's his college expenses one. I'd like to find out.'

We left the subject of Knowles at that, in the limbo of a possible potential financial scandal.

At college the night porter was on duty. 'Evening, sir. Evening, madam.' Ever respectful, the lodge staff were universally efficient and polite, and revelled in the role of serving the fellows. The job attracted all sorts of different people. There were one or two from old Oxford families that had generations of college servants in their histories, white-collar workers who had been made redundant, and a few retired servicemen. A neighbouring college had employed as a day porter, a retired army major who clearly enjoyed his new role. He was a well educated, well spoken man who had immaculate manners and when you rang the college and he answered, you thought you were talking to the Principal. I always thought that the reason the college appointed him was because he exemplified the college motto, Manners Makyth Man.

'Shall we go to my rooms for a nightcap?' I suggested.

'No, I don't think so. I need to get to bed. I've a busy day tomorrow. Have to get up early. Faculty committee papers to read first thing.'

That was disappointing. Naturally I had been cherishing the prospect of an advance along the romantic front. To tell the truth, I am not sure what I expected. Realistically, such an early development in Est's overture to me should not have made me anticipate falling into bed with her that night; but an eager lover is ever hopeful. It did not happen. Est went to her rooms to collect various things before she went home and I went to mine for the want of anything else better to do. Half an hour later I was walking quickly back to my bungalow in the North Oxford suburb.

My house had become available when house prices had become static in Oxford at a time when virtually everywhere they were plummeting. The bungalow was an anomaly. It was a piece of late twentieth century socialist inspired in-filling, built on half a huge garden of a late Victorian five-bedroomed house. Nevertheless, it was well designed and fitted in with the ambient architecture; the roof pitch was appropriate and so was the brickwork. It had a paved garden space with flower and shrubbery beds bordering, and a high brick wall that closed the property off from the road. It was satisfactorily private; and, as I say, it was an anomaly, a bungalow amidst its surrounding substantial three-storey houses with basements.

Anyway, I had not even kissed her. It was early days.

4

All that had so far happened had taken place on the Tuesday of the second week of the university term. Nothing was to develop further in any respect until the Thursday when the finance committee was to meet. It was scheduled for two fifteen.

When I took lunch that day, I sat with my like-minded colleagues on college affairs, my own opposite number, Jane Templeman and the philosopher, Professor Jacob Black. Black, who was known universally as JOB because of his initials, was distinguished by worldwide fame and occupied an established chair. His professorship was not one of any number that had been conferred recently on any Tom, Dick or Harry of the academic scene. His historic chair rested on highly original thinking and an uninterrupted line of publications. He took his share of duties in college offices and because he had private experience of managing considerable family wealth, both inherited and earned, the latter mostly by his wife who was a famously successful novelist, he had volunteered for the finance committee. So far as I was concerned, he was a welcome addition because he was eccentric and unorthodox, and yet he gave to our discussions shrewd and inspired judgements.

'Jacob. How good to see you. Are you looking forward to the meeting?' I asked him as I sat down next to him.

'Well, I-I-I suppose I am in a way. A-always a pleasure to be entertained by Willoughby. I-I-I like the p-puzzle of h-having to work out w-what to believe or not.' JOB suffered a slight hesitation, a stammer in his speech that he had endured since childhood: on occasions he could use it to good effect, delaying and disconcerting his opponents in discussion. He had the measure of the Principal and viewed him with caution. JOB was an important power to have in the ranks of those with reservations about the regime.

Jeremy Eedes was sitting by himself. In most colleges bursars are never found sitting alone. They usually find themselves being lobbied about some concern or other, being asked to write a cheque for some project, some improvement, or some fellow's proposed trip for alleged research. It was not long before Eedes was joined by company, but it was notable that they all belonged to the same clique. First the Principal came in and sat opposite Eedes. I heard him say, 'By yourself, I see. Ostracised by your colleagues.' He gestured widely around him. 'Don't take it to heart. I'll keep you company.' He leaned towards Eedes and muttered something which I lost in a hubbub of chatter and laughter.

A few minutes later Timothy Knowles arrived, paused, looked around, and then sat next to the Principal. Jacob Black commented, 'Ah, I-I-see the f-forces of d-darkness assemble.'

I observed, 'Yes, unsurprisingly. We'll see what they have to say later.'

Tacitly, we all agreed to leave college politics at that. I reckon everyone felt that there would be enough of that sort of thing during the afternoon's meeting. We talked of other matters. Jacob was keen on the Turf. He had been, if you like, a racing man since his days at Eton. He liked to tell newly introduced people of his betting activities and subsequent scandals while he had been at school. Jacob reckoned that he had a certain winner in a mid-afternoon race at Newbury where he insisted he had inside knowledge from a particular stable. Jane wanted to know what films we had seen recently. She extolled a film then showing that had been directed by an undergraduate she had tutored ten years back and who had just won an Oscar for best director.

'You must go and see it,' she said to no one in particular but to all of us.

'Well, it's a pity he wasn't at this college,' I remarked. 'He must be a millionaire by now. That film's a huge box office success and what with his Oscar he must be able to afford a generous donation to his old college.'

Frank Bradshaw, a bio-chemist and plant scientist, who had come to the table and was sitting next to Jane, said, 'Yes, but you know, these people like to bide their time, quite reasonably. The next film might be a flop. He'll need to consolidate then perhaps give something. Where was he, Trinity?'

Jane assented. Bradshaw continued, 'Well, they don't need it anyway.'

I remarked, 'There's nowhere that doesn't need good hard cash. It's just that some need donors more than others.'

Around twenty to two I left the common room and walked quickly to the Cornmarket. I needed fresh air before the finance meeting and I thought I would take a chance on JOB's fancied horse. At the bookmaker's in Cornmarket I placed ten pounds to win on Rogue Male in the two thirty at Newbury. It was a modest bet without backup or insurance policy but I did not have time to cover my bet. In any case that was always my way of investment. In the share market, so far as I was concerned, risk was king; it was all or nothing. I always invested for capital return, capital gain, not for dividend income. I occasionally backed each way on the horses but only if I had time. Otherwise I bet to win. Over my monthly accounting period I usually made a profit.

I walked briskly back down the High to college and once again in the distance I saw Malcolm White crossing the road. I slowed and allowed him to pass on the opposite side of the road, head down and oblivious of anyone else. There was no time to stop and talk with him.

Back in college, I went straight to the common room staircase and arrived at the meeting room just as Knowles did. There was an awkward silence which I broke.

'We're just on time, Timothy. I wonder if we're the last.'

He replied, 'The Principal will be a little late. He went off to his office to get some papers he'd forgotten.'

The meeting room was spacious. In the middle was a long table with about thirty chairs around it, a sufficient number to seat the whole governing body of the college. It was where the weekly college meetings of fellows took place. As a small committee of seven, we were rather swamped by space and chairs. One end of the table had been laid out for the meeting. In front of each seat there was a pad of paper, a pencil, and a glass and bottle of water. The Principal's place was at the head of the table as chairman: three places were laid on either side of him. It was unusual and exceptional for the Principal to chair the finance committee but a year ago while I had been on sabbatical leave, he had manoeuvred himself into the chair. The incumbent at that time, our mathematics fellow, had to stand down for reasons of ill health and Morris had taken over at short notice. He then assumed the role and had it agreed at a governing body meeting, largely because no one else wanted the job, and there was the usual indifference and then acquiescence from the silent majority. On my return I thought it unsatisfactory but again no one seemed to be prepared to do anything about it.

By a minute past two fifteen everyone was there except the Principal. We took our places. Eedes quickly took the seat to the chair's right. Knowles followed his lead and sat down to the chair's left. Thus, because no one else was quick enough off the mark, Willoughby Morris was to be flanked by his lieutenants. Next to the bursar sat Jacob, and next to him Jane. On the other side, I sat next to Knowles and then Bradshaw next to me.

At twenty past two Morris hurried in. He banged the heavy door shut with some force. He was a burly man, stout and strong without, I reckoned, being in good physical shape. He wore his gown. The rest of us, apart from Knowles, did not. We had all sat down. When he entered, Jacob, Jane and I stood up; it was a token of common civility. The others remained seated.

He waved his hand impatiently for us to sit down.

'Don't bother to stand. Sit down. Sorry I'm late. May I remind you that you are supposed to wear gowns for college meetings.' He sat and slapped his papers down on the table in front of him.

'Have we a secretary, a minute taker? Bursar?'

Eedes tapped his pencil on the tabletop. 'Shortage of staff, Principal. Two in my office off sick. I'll take minutes myself, if that's acceptable.'

'Thank you, Bursar. Any objections?'

It was certainly not ideal. There was the possibility of spin in the writing up of the minutes and even though they would have to be read and passed by vote at the subsequent meeting, it was not a good idea to have someone who might be partial to a particular cause write the minutes. I therefore interjected, 'It's not ideal. Is there no one on the secretarial staff who could be used? Timothy, haven't you someone you could spare?'

'I'm afraid not. It's a busy afternoon.' He left it at that without being specific about the tasks that his staff had to fulfil.

Morris commented, 'There we are. Nothing to be done. Thank you, Bursar.'

I had made a token objection and that was that.

Morris asked Eedes to read the minutes of the last meeting. They had been recorded by the college secretary, a very reliable, competent woman who had worked at the college for years.

'Is everyone satisfied?' demanded Morris. 'I note that expenses were referred on to today's business. They are on the agenda but I'm sure we don't want to waste much time on that item. I'm sure everyone's honest. This meeting shouldn't take long.'

I did not like the way he was trying to pre-empt the expenses issue and it was typical of him that he wanted to hurry through the meeting. He would only take matters slowly if there was some tactical reason on his part to do so. I began to feel that we were all being set up to waive business through quickly and I did not like it. I was fairly confident others would feel similarly. I looked across at Jane. She looked up from the agenda paper and we clearly registered a common antipathy to what was obviously going to happen. I could not gauge what Jacob felt but I knew he was no one's fool and would almost certainly see through the devices of Willoughby Morris.

'The minutes, then, as read? Proposed and seconded?'

Eedes proposed acceptance; Bradshaw seconded.

'Item two on the agenda. Do we accept the estimate and budget for the refurbishment of the Lady Coleman Memorial Building? I don't see any problem with that. The bursar's summary, and the surveyor's report attached, lay out the analysis of expenditure. It's a lot of money but necessary. Ackrill and Co will do the work – best bid.'

Jane interrupted, 'Principal, have we seen other quotes for this work? We do seem to give Ackrill's a monopoly on our commissioned work.'

We certainly did. I knew that and it was because Eedes was a close friend through golf and Rotary of Johnson Ackrill whose firm it was.

Morris glanced crossly at Jane, 'No need. The bursar has scrutinised the whole preparatory business. I'm sure we can leave this sort of thing to him. He's the expert.'

I backed up Jane. 'Nevertheless, I think for the sake of transparency and good practice we all should look at the offered estimates of costs. I must say the quote looks to be on the expensive side from a first pretty cursory look.'

'Well, it would delay things. Are we really questioning the bursar's judgement? Can't we get on with this?'

'It's not a matter of questioning Bursar Eedes's judgement,' I persisted, 'it's just that we should all be part of the process, not just one person, or two, of course, with you, Principal. Otherwise, what are we here for?'

Jacob then spoke. 'Yes. I-I agree with that. L-let's see the other quotes.'

'How very annoying. Is that the general view?' the Principal complained. 'How do people feel? We shall have to delay – a wretched nuisance. Who wishes to delay proceedings and look at other estimates?'

Jacob, Jane, Bradhsaw and myself, raised our hands.

'Against?'

Knowles alone signified his opposition. Eedes quite rightly abstained. Morris gave the impression that he was above the voting process.

'Item held over to the next meeting. Right, let's move on and hope there are no other obstacles to progress.' I thought he was referring to me. Jane looked over at me. Her eyes signalled triumph.

'Next item: the junior common room has asked for a subvention to support its charitable work in the East End of London. They want one thousand five hundred pounds. The bursar suggests we concede one thousand two hundred and fifty. Shall we agree that?'

Jane immediately cut in. 'It's hardly a concession. There are two points: in principle do we support the JCR in this way? Secondly, can we afford a thousand five hundred? Personally, I think we should support them. This college has a long tradition of good works in the East End, and quite rightly so. We are a charitable foundation and we should, if we can, support others. Judging from the last set of accounts, we can afford it and so we should give them the money and not some compromise figure.'

Morris, clearly irritated by the way she had so quickly picked him up on his proposal, riposted, 'On principle, we should not give them what they ask for. Trim the figure down. That's wise management. Bursar, what do you think?'

'I agree with you, Principal. I'm always cautious in this sort of thing. I don't think it's our job to give away our income. We have to be guardians of our resources. That's part of the conditions of our charitable status. Maximise our investments and our income.'

Jane said, 'Well, that's all very well but at some point we have to spend. We can't just sit on our profits; and in any case there's more to this business than that. It's right that the JCR should be involved socially and morally in charity work. It would look very poor indeed if the governing body did not support them.'

At that point, I joined in. 'If we are in a healthy enough position, then I think we should do it and give them totally the whole amount. I think we can do it and therefore I propose that we donate one thousand five hundred to the JCR East End fund. I know the work is in support of the college's youth club and each vacation some of our students go and work there.'

'Yes, that's all very well,' Morris said, 'but I think the bursar should have the last word on this. He is our financial officer. What's your view, Bursar?'

Jeremy Eedes looked dolefully down at his papers and muttered that he thought it best to give them less than they asked for.

'Quite right. I fully agree. If we so easily give them what they want, they'll simply ask for more next time. That's sound reasoning. I think we should leave it at that. Shall we pass on?' Morris tapped his pencil impatiently on the table.

'No, I'm sorry but I don't think we should. I have proposed a motion to this committee,' I said, 'and we should proceed for or against. And Jeremy might be our finance officer, but we are the finance committee. And so far as asking for more next time, we shall, of course, judge each request on its merits. We do not make ourselves a hostage to fortune.'

'Right, I can see we are not going to get anywhere without a vote. Have we a seconder?' He stared grimly around the table giving the impression that anyone who might have felt so inclined would face immediate execution. Bradshaw raised his hand.

'Proposed and seconded then. Those in favour of giving a thousand five hundred?'

Jane, Jacob, Bradshaw and I raised our hands in approval.

'And those against?'

Eedes and Knowles signified their opposition.

'Very well, motion carried. This is not satisfactory,' Morris commented, 'executive officers must have executive power. Let's get on to the next item. The chaplain has written to me and asked formally that all claims for expenses should be detailed and published for the information of all members of the governing body. His drift is that all college officers and fellows on official college business should itemise their claims so that every penny and pound is correctly accounted for.

'Needless to say, I think this is quite unnecessary. The system has worked well as it stands and doesn't need to be interfered with. It is also, in a way, impertinent to think that our claims are in any way suspect. It's a matter of honour and conscience which we can confidently leave to our fellow colleagues. Can we wrap this up without further discussion?'

There was quite a long pause. Everyone seemed to be happy to leave the question hanging in the air. Then Jacob spoke.

'I-I think the chaplain's g-got a p-point; and I-I'm sorry, P-Principal, I simply d-don't agree. Receipts and r-records of payment should b-be kept and recorded. Th-that's my view. Th-then there's no room for evasion or deceit.'

Morris interrupted, 'Exactly my point. There isn't any evasion or deceit. Such a measure, if we demand it, will be seen merely as bureaucratic, and evidence of the fact that we don't trust our colleagues or ourselves.'

As I expected, we lined up as before with Eedes and Knowles supporting Morris and the rest of us opposing and supporting the chaplain. The tone of the meeting was growing combative. I thought it might be time to defuse a potentially explosive situation. I said, 'Why don't we refer this on to our next meeting and in the meantime we can sound out our colleagues' views. Then, if necessary, we can debate the issue at a governing body meeting.'

My suggestion was supported by our group and oddly enough by the bursar. Eedes said, 'I think that's the way to go. I don't think we should decide now. This concerns everyone in detail. If we are going to do it, there are various different ways of ensuring a clear accounting system. I would recommend each fellow being issued with a college credit card. Then expenditure on college business can be checked, itemised on monthly statements. Anomalies can be queried easily. Anyone else claiming expenses on college business has to produce receipts. In case of dispute, the bursar has discretion. I know one or two colleges follow this pattern.'

It was most unusual for Eedes to be so constructive and I immediately felt that he must have some ulterior motive in mind, which I could not appreciate. The Principal did not look best pleased.

'Well, if that's the general feeling, then we'd better hold it over. Thank you, Bursar, for your ideas. I think it wholly unnecessary but we shall have to consult our colleagues.' The Principal shuffled his papers. Bradshaw leaned towards me and whispered that his expenses subject that he wanted to bring up had been pre-empted. 'It's just as well,' he said, 'it's going to be a necessary reform in view of what I've heard has been going on.'

Morris tapped the table. 'Next. This is the item about charges to non-members of the college for entrance. Two of our colleagues have brought this up. What views?'

He sat back in his chair and gave the impression of not being interested in this particular subject.

Eedes spoke first. 'It's not so much about raising money. I know Professor Wright and others want to lessen the disturbance of college life by tourists. There's noise and litter. Even undergraduates have complained. We could start by making a modest charge by entrance through the lodge, say two pounds, and see how it goes. Initial expenditure wouldn't be great and would, I think, soon pay for itself. We'd need to put such a proposal to the whole governing body.'

I agreed with Jane who said that morally and on principle she was opposed to entry charges. She regarded the colleges of Oxford as national institutions, buildings and grounds, which belonged to the people, rather like national museums and art galleries. We, the fellows, were the temporary guardians of long historic tradition. On the other hand, she sympathised with the view that college life should not be upset by tourists. In the end, the bursar's view prevailed and it was agreed to recommend to the fellowship that a two-pound entrance charge should be tried for a period of six months over the summer period and thereafter reviewed.

'That leaves us with cost of ground maintenance and the recently added item about the prospect of a large donation. First then, the state of the grounds.'

While it was true that the college quads and gardens were immaculately kept, financed by an Old Member's generosity, the gardens of outlying buildings were neglected. There had been complaints. A graduate block of apartments in the northern residential area of the city had caused many complaints from neighbours. The truth was that our one gardener and his two assistants, one added thanks to the benefaction, could not keep up with the seasonal demands of the gardening and maintenance work. They needed at least one more member of the garden staff. The question was, could we finance an extra person?

Again, the bursar surprised me. 'I'm in favour of employing someone else. It does the college's reputation no good to have our neighbours complain about us; but this has happened in north Oxford and at our new residential block just in the Marston Road. We must do something about it. Judging from the state of accounts so far this year, I think we could afford another employee. Perhaps, too, we can economise elsewhere.'

There was no comment from Morris and everyone agreed that it was fundamentally necessary to maintain good order and appearances.

Then came the fraught issue of a potential donation of a considerable sum to the college. It was by no means a certain gift but it was there in the offing.

Naturally and predictably enough, Morris was very much in favour of accepting a donation under any terms. He had been elected as Principal partly because the majority had been persuaded by his backers that he would be good at fundraising; and although the college was well off from the point of view of ancient endowments, ownership of property that brought in rent income, and latterly, in the last century, investment income, it was important that during harsh economic conditions college funds were boosted whenever possible. Morris had so far failed to deliver any major donations. He was eager to redress the disappointment of those who had promoted his cause.

Increasingly, those fellows who had voted for him were growing disillusioned. Willoughby Morris was conscious that the hard core of support was dissolving, at the least fragmenting. He needed a substantial gift from a wealthy lead giver.

Eedes explained the position. 'The problem here is that the donor wishes to remain anonymous. Questions arise. Everyone knows that the university and particular colleges have had trouble over various bequests and gifts. For instance, our neighbour college was forced to turn down a gift from a German industrialist because his grandfather's firm used slave labour during the Third Reich. The LSE has refused a donation from the family of the dictator of an African country. So, there are ethical considerations.'

Morris at once gave his opinion. 'Thank you, Bursar. I don't think we need worry on this account. I think we can trust our source to be legitimate and ethically acceptable. I've looked into this matter and you can rest assured it will pass muster.'

Morris used curious expressions of speech which were not always appropriate. Jane looked at me. We both understood that he was trying to steamroller debate again. He wanted no discussion and wanted to hurry us into a decision.

Jane said, 'In the present climate, I don't see how we can easily accept an anonymous donation. We need to know where the money comes from. That's reasonable. It would be irresponsible otherwise. There might be serious repercussions if we accepted it blind.'

'My dear,' Morris said which I knew at once would annoy Jane intensely; she could not stand him when he tried to patronise her, 'of course, one or two of us would have to know the provenance; but that would be under strict agreement. You would have to trust me.'

I noted that he said "me" not "us". He was like one of those megalomaniac prime ministers who always talks about "me" and "I" as if his cabinet colleagues did not exist. In any case, the idea that at least three of us sitting round the table should trust him was laughable.

I added, 'I just don't think that would be good enough for the rest of our colleagues, our students, the press, and the general public. We would have to know more about where the money comes from. Presumably the donor could still remain anonymous but the provenance would need to be laid bare.'

'For goodness' sake, if we nit-pick we'll lose the gift. It'll go somewhere else where there are fewer scruples. We have to make up our minds and quickly too.'

Jane and I had opened the discussion. It went on for some time, about half an hour in all. Willoughby Morris grew impatient and irritable. 'Well, we can't go on like this all afternoon. What does anyone suggest?'

Frank Bradshaw proposed that it was a matter for the whole fellowship to discuss. There had to be a full ethical debate. Reluctantly and crossly, the Principal agreed. Eedes suggested that in the meanwhile Morris might negotiate with the donor or his agents about being able to supply assurances over the integrity of the money's source. Grudgingly Morris agreed. 'I can't help feeling that you're all being far too sensitive. You cannot look a gift horse in the mouth. Still, as you wish. I wouldn't be at all surprised if we lose this gift. The horse is quite likely to take fright and bolt.'

He paused, hitched up his gown in irritation, and said, 'Now, I hope we don't have any difficulties with the next item. I've mentioned it before. You all know about it. Can we do this quickly? It's the matter of the senior tutor's PA. We just need your assent for the appropriate funding. Bursar, have you the leeway for this?'

Eedes looked down at his papers, shuffled a few sheets, and responded. 'Yes. We can manage this. The senior clerk of accounts is retiring at the end of this term. He's relatively expensive. We can replace him with someone younger at approximately half his salary and then we can afford another youngster as PA to Timothy. What with National Insurance and one or two other more minor expenses the whole business will be marginally more expensive, but we can manage it.'

Jacob objected, 'B-but, P-Principal, w-what about c-cumulatively, o-over the years?'

Jeremy butted in. 'I don't think we need bother ourselves with that. Year on year, the increase in expenditure will be small and anyway circumstances change. We have another senior position retirement in another year's time.'

Morris looked round the table quickly and said decisively, 'Well, if the bursar's satisfied, we should approve it. Everyone in favour?'

'Not quite,' I said. 'We haven't debated the necessity of this extra position. Why does Timothy need an assistant? He's managed well enough until now without. He has his own secretary. Is there really any need for someone else? Oughtn't we to be economising?'

Morris said sharply, 'Look, this is beginning to be tedious. The senior tutor wouldn't be asking if it wasn't necessary. Can we proceed to a vote?'

It was typical of Morris. He wanted to convey to us that he was satisfied and that there was no need for further discussion; but what his style of chairmanship did was to convince most of us that what he was proposing, or supporting, was a stitch-up. I felt I had to protest.

'Well, on the little evidence I've seen and heard, I'm not convinced. Still, if the bursar is satisfied, I suppose we should proceed to a vote.' Jacob nodded his assent.

That appointment was approved. Jane abstained. I opposed. The rest passed the measure.

With that Morris asked, 'Any other business?' He looked around distastefully as though he would rather none of us had turned up for the meeting, collected his papers together, pushed his chair noisily back, got up, hitched his gown, glowered and said in retreat, 'Bursar and Knowles, a word in my study.' He marched out.

Jacob said, 'I-I must r-rush. A lecture to g-give l-later on.' He left the room. Frank Bradshaw, Jane and I remained. Jane commented, 'At least we didn't let him get his own way. I think we've done right. The really important issues must go to the governing body. Morris wants to keep as much as possible away from them.'

I wryly observed, 'Knowles, Eedes and Morris, all together – the junta meets. I must say, I don't trust Willoughby Morris one little bit. Why on earth did we elect him?'

Bradshaw pushed his chair in to the table. 'Easy to answer. He came highly recommended. His scientific reputation and admin abilities were second to none. Our science lobby supported him; that was crucial.'

'What's gone wrong then?' Jane asked.

'I think he thinks the college is small beer. He can do what he likes with us. Compared with what he was used to, we are in a parochial backwater. He thinks he knows best. He doesn't want to listen to anyone. Now, my science colleagues are withdrawing their support. You've probably noticed, many stay away as much as possible from college, Gail Hardwick, Osborne, Rodney Bennet for instance. They don't like the atmosphere. It's a pity. Something will have to be done.'

'Ah,' I commented satirically, 'revolution. Do I hear dissent? Have we arrived at a time for plots and devices? The dark shadows of political manoeuvring begin to envelop us. Jane, this is your field.'

'I think you exaggerate,' she responded tartly. 'I must go; but I do think someone should have a word with the Principal. The present situation should not be allowed to get any worse. I'll leave you with that thought.'

And so the rump of the finance committee meeting finally broke up. I walked with Frank Bradshaw down into the cloisters and then into the main quad. The sun which was low in the sky to the west was shining in a cloudless sky. The dull clouds that had threatened to bring rain had fled. There was a roseate glow on the soft yellowing stone of the buildings as the sunlight illuminated the west facing walls of the college. It promised to be a glorious evening.

'OK, Frank, we must think on these things. Maybe you and one or two of those who brought him in should talk with him. If you want someone to represent a wider spectrum, I'm willing to join the party, stick my neck out.'

'Yes, it's a good idea. Leave it with me for a bit. I'll talk to them, fork over the ground a bit, prepare the way. Tony Gill particularly is important. He knows Morris better than anyone. He worked with him at the Ministry of Science and Technology. And Rodney, of course; but Tony was instrumental in persuading Morris to let his name go forward for the election of Principal. I'll report back. Bye, Johnny.'

Frank walked away briskly to the lodge.

5

Everything went quiet for a day or two after that. I did not see Est around college when I was there. I knew she was busy. The day after the finance committee meeting, the day of the Principal's evening drinks party, I had to go to London at four in the afternoon. I did see earlier on in college Timothy Knowles with the young man Est and I had seen him with in Quod. They were walking across the front quad towards the chapel and seemed very familiar with each other. The young man was fair-haired, almost blond, blue-eyed and athletic. He looked very Germanic, a perfect example of the *volk*. I estimated his age at around twenty-four or -five. I imagined that he might have just finished some research degree, a master's or even a doctorate. They walked close together and at one point, as I watched from the shelter of the lodge, the young man put his hand on Knowles's arm, and Knowles responded by grasping his hand; for a moment they walked hand in hand like two lovers. I thought that strange; so far as I knew, Knowles had not to my knowledge come out publicly. Anyway, it was something that had not until then seriously crossed my mind.

I caught the 4.16 p.m. fast train to Paddington and I was walking through the Burlington Arcade at a quarter to six towards St James where I was meeting an old colleague and friend for dinner. As an academic, and particularly an academic economist, I thought it important to keep up with people who worked in the real world of finance and not just with those who theorised about the science. It was successful. I learnt that evening much about the market's view of the crisis over the future of the euro.

It was not until late Saturday morning that, back in Oxford, I

45

heard about the Principal's party. I met Jane as I was going late into college. We stopped and spoke for more than twenty minutes.

'So, go on. Tell me. What was it like? What happened?' I asked facetiously, 'Did Morris announce his resignation?'

Jane frowned censoriously. 'Don't be ridiculous. He was at his ebullient best, expansive, extravagant, provocative. There were a few undergraduates there: they think he's wonderful, a real party animal. He took great delight in baiting some of his enemies, the dissidents, though, of course, most of them didn't go. Who pays? Does the cost come from his entertainment allowance, or does the college pay on top of that? Do you know? We should find out.'

'No, I don't know. I must see if I can find out from Eedes. I've always assumed he pays for those parties out of his entertainment fund. Anything spectacular happen?'

'Oh yes, I suppose so. Two things. Morris's wife had a little too much more to drink than she should have done. She was in a small group, talking away; she turned and as she was doing so, Knowles's catamite turned at the same time. She was knocked away from him, couldn't keep her balance and fell into the arms of Knowles. It was hilarious. She played up to it and gave Knowles a kiss full on the lips. Morris roared with laughter, slapped his wife on the bottom, had his glass refilled and toasted the happy couple. Some of our more serious colleagues were scandalised. Frank didn't like it and the chaplain thought the whole incident vulgar.'

I interrupted her. I assumed an ignorance of Knowles's affair. 'You say Knowles's catamite. What's this all about?'

Jane grinned mischievously. 'Yes, well, that's the second thing. The senior tutor appears to have an admirer, a young man, handsome, who seems to hang on his every word. It's very touching. Literally, in fact; Adonis keeps holding Knowles's arm and patting his back.'

'If you're right, it's Ganymede not Adonis. But how intriguing. I wonder if it's the same chap I saw Knowles with the other evening. I bet it is – pretty tall, fair hair, blue eyes, well proportioned.'

Jane commented, 'That sounds about right, Hitler jugend sort of guy.'

As she said that, an awful thought struck me; perhaps this young man was in Knowles's sights for appointment as his PA. I expressed this thought to Jane.

'Oh no, surely you don't really think so? Knowles couldn't be so idiotic to fix a favourite into a college post. Could he?'

She answered her own question without waiting for my reply.

'Of course, he could. Well, I'm staggered. We shall have to wait and see. It'd be typical of Morris's set, nepotism. Anyway, apart from all that, little else happened. Blake left immediately after the Principal's wife incident. He couldn't bear to hang around any longer.'

The Reverend Dr Donald Blake was our chaplain, a man of definite views and high moral principles. As well as being the Anglican celebrant and looking after the pastoral side of college life, he taught theology and helped the classicists with a little Greek. His aim, I worked out, was to line himself up for appointment as one of the canons of Christ Church. I was rather surprised that he had been at the Principal's party at all. He was a vocal critic of any rule-bending and always acted as the college conscience.

'OK,' I said, 'but did you enjoy yourself?'

'Oh yes, as usual it was fascinating.'

'Who did you talk to?'

'I spent most of my time with Jacob, his wife, and a journalist from the *Telegraph* who had come with the Master of St Christopher's. He was interesting. He tends to work on big financial stories and also writes leaders. He's obviously important in the *Telegraph* hierarchy. You should have met him. He was good on the present deficit problem.'

We changed the subject and briefly talked about matters to do with our teaching for the politics, philosophy and economics degree. We then went to our rooms.

As it was a Saturday, I did not propose staying long in college. I made a couple of phone calls and went back out through the lodge. I thought I would walk back to my house through the university parks.

The head porter was on duty in the lodge which was unusual for a Saturday. I commented on his presence.

'We've got one man off sick. There was no one else to do it at short notice. The wife's not too happy, but there we go.'

There were some tourists looking in through the lodge at the main quad. A familiar voice sounded out, 'Excuse me. Let's get through.' The three tourists, probably Chinese, stood aside. Knowles hurried in followed by the young man who now always seemed to be in tow.

'Morning, Johnny,' he said to me and rushed on. He did not introduce me to his young friend who followed quickly. The head porter said, 'That young lad's always with him these days. I wouldn't be surprised if we don't find him as Dr Knowles's PA.'

It did not surprise me that the lodge staff, and especially the head porter, knew exactly what was going on in college business. They were notorious for their monitoring of intelligence and knowing confidential matters before they were released to the general community. As often is the case, the lodge was the information control centre of college affairs.

'Do you think so?' I said. 'Do you know anything about the young chap?'

'Not much, yet. Nice enough from what he's said to us. Charming, polite. We'll see, sir.'

I couldn't wait to be introduced. I determined to engineer a meeting with the fair young man.

6

That afternoon when I was back in my bungalow and I was tired of reading, I thought I might follow up on Est. So, I rang her. It was something I had never done before and I wondered what sort of reaction I would get. There was no reply. I had rung her at home. I went out through some open French windows on to a sunny paved area surrounded by herbaceous borders. It took me some time to think and decide what to do next. On the south, shady side, the border beds had the green globes of Annabelle hydrangeas that would gradually develop into a brilliant white which would light up the red brick wall against which they grew. Eventually, after a few minutes, I tried Est's college phone number; it was her personal line and I did not have to speak to the lodge.

I let the phone ring for longer than I usually do; I was just hoping that perhaps Est was coming through the door, or that she was finishing writing a sentence. As I was about to despair and accept her absence and the impossibility of making contact with her, the receiver was picked up. Rather startled because I had already accepted that she was not there, I said, 'Oh, it's me, Johnny. That's you, Est?'

She replied not quite tetchily but certainly wryly, 'Of course it is. Who did you expect it to be?'

'No, of course,' I said. 'Sorry. I suppose I'd given up and was just letting the phone ring.'

'Well, here I am. What do you want?'

Her brisk tone brought me back sharply to reality. I had been living in a world of the imagination where Est was already my lover.

That was not so. I remembered that at our last meeting and farewell we had not even kissed.

'Well, sorry, I just thought, if you weren't doing anything, we might meet up. Perhaps supper this evening.'

'Johnny, don't keep saying sorry. Anyway, tonight's no good. I've other things on. Tomorrow, yes. Why don't you come to my place – say seven o'clock.'

She didn't say what the other things she was going to do that evening were, but she was certainly business-like and decisive. She put me to shame, and clearly she was not suffering the same illusions I was about the possibility of being lovers. Naturally I accepted readily.

'That's wonderful. I'd love to. I'll bring a bottle.'

'Don't bring champagne,' she said satirically. 'We're not celebrating anything.'

I could sense her enjoying mischievously my unease. I stuttered back at her, 'No, no, no, of course not.' She laughed softly. Then she said, 'Come on, Johnny, I'm teasing you. Bring what you like. In fact, champagne would be fine.'

And so, I was left thinking that anything less than a bottle of Bollinger would be inadequate. She was someone I did not know how to handle.

As much as I would have liked to suppress my imagination, I was so excited by the prospect of having supper with her the following day that I could not. She came alive in my thoughts all the time, and for the rest of Saturday and Sunday we lived ecstatically in the fictional world of my fantasy. It was considerably different from the reality to which I nevertheless knew she would bring me back.

I went into college just before lunch on Sunday. None of my colleagues seemed to be about; there was little interest in the college at weekends. The main quad and the cloisters of the chapel had students coming and going. The atmosphere was lethargic; after all, it was a Sunday morning. Most students kept to their beds, either by themselves or with convenient partners of the opposite or same sex, until midday or so. The tower clock struck noon as I entered the cloisters. I walked through to look at the gardens we had been talking about when I had been in the common room the week before. As I was emerging from the cloisters, to my surprise I saw Knowles in the distance walking with the handsome young man. Provided I could work out which way they were going, I decided to ambush them. I stepped back into the little tunnel from which I had just come and observed them from the shadows. They were simply walking round the huge grass lawn in front of what was called the New Building; it had held on to its name ever since it had been built in the middle of the eighteenth century when, of course, it was new. It looked to me as though Knowles was showing the young man around.

When they turned and began to walk up one side of the lawn away from me, I went quickly along towards its opposite side so that if they progressed as I anticipated we would eventually meet. Surely enough they turned twice in their perambulation and we found ourselves walking towards each other in the sunshine. At a distance of about twenty yards or so, I called out, 'All hail, Senior Tutor. Good morning. How are you?'

Frowning slightly he replied, 'Technically, good afternoon; the college clock has just struck. I'm surprised to see you here in college. Our colleagues are not known for their appearances on a Sunday.'

He had not introduced me immediately. The young man stood back from us, watched and listened. I turned to him and said, 'Hi, Johnny James, economics.' He stepped forward. Knowles was thereby forced to step in and say, 'Brendan Naish. A friend. Brendan's recently graduated from Leicester University in law. I'm showing him round.'

Naish held out his hand. I shook it warmly. He moved freely and easily. He had physical flow and balance, which suggested to me that he was a sportsman. He said, 'Very pleased to meet you. Tim here is reluctant to introduce me to people. I think he thinks I might go off with them.' It was said in jest but just a touch coquettishly. He went on, 'I'm not much of a lawyer. I spent most of my time playing tennis and squash.'

Knowles was a bit stand-offish. I could sense that he wished I was not there. I had interrupted his escorting of Naish around the college. There was a certain resentment, almost embarrassment. Brendan Naish said, 'Tim thinks there might be something here for me. I'm looking for a job.'

Knowles quickly interjected. 'Well, I feel I've got a responsibility. I've known Brendan since his second year at university. I feel I should give him help if I can. He's very good. He gets on well with people. I think he'd be good in a PR capacity, human resources, that sort of thing.'

I thought I did not need to know what Knowles was telling me. It was more than he should have been telling me after so short an introduction. It was as though he were panicking, retreating into a defensive position for some reason or other. Naturally I remembered what the head porter had told me. I decided to bait a trap for Knowles.

'It sounds to me that Brendan here should apply for the job as your PA. Or do you know him too well? Nepotism, perhaps? Nevertheless, if he's the best person for the job, he should get it.' I wondered what Knowles's reaction would be to my suggestion. Naish looked directly at him and kept his silence. It was the cue for the senior tutor to speak.

'Yes, well, it had crossed my mind. Of course it would be good. As you can see, Brendan's highly presentable. He could certainly do the job. He'd get on so well with the students.'

'Is that what you want to do?' I addressed Brendan. 'What about your law career?'

Naish shifted his position. He altered his weight to his right leg. He moved easily. He stood like an actor on stage, his left leg slightly forward, his right hand in his jacket pocket, and gestured with his left hand. 'I don't think I want to pursue law as a career. I don't want to do the conversion and the articles; not for the moment anyway. I'd rather do something different, if only for a short time. See how I get on; see what's on offer.'

He was engaging; handsome, attractive and I reckoned maybe even calculating. He seemed to be exploring what was to his advantage. He was on the lookout. He knew he was good-looking. He knew that he could play on his attractiveness; it gave him leeway and an edge on his less charismatic competitors.

Knowles said, 'I'll have a word with the Principal, see what he thinks. If we make a short-term appointment, perhaps we won't have to advertise. Willoughby will know. Brendan's only met him once, very briefly. I'd better do something about that.'

I began to feel that Timothy Knowles considered the matter settled. He had squared me, got my agreement, made me complicit in his plot. Yet, I had lured him into a trap. He was exposed. His intention to place young Brendan Naish as his PA was now obvious.

Knowles did not take long to promote his ambitions for Brendan Naish. I decided to watch what was to happen closely, and to get to know Naish. They walked away; I went towards my room. I noticed that Naish kept close to Knowles and knocked against him, arm to arm, as they proceeded. They were clearly close, familiar; there was something physical about their relationship and Naish was not embarrassed by it, whereas Knowles was.

I made my way through the shady cloisters and as I turned to go through one of the low passages out into the sunshine again, into the large garden quad, I met the chaplain emerging from the chapel choir's practice room. He waved a sort of formal benediction to me and said, 'Good day, Johnny. Nothing on now until six o'clock evensong. Leighton's Responses, Ives's Magdalen Service, and Poulenc's Quatre petite prières de Saint François d'Assise.' In a sepulchral, Episcopal voice he added, 'We hope sincerely that you will join us for the salvation of your soul.'

'Donald, if I can, I will. I'm not sure where I'll be. If I'm in college,

I'll be with you. I'll help to swell the congregation. By the way, I've just been talking to Knowles and his young companion. Have you seen them?'

Donald Blake looked quizzically at me and confided, 'I saw them earlier but avoided them. I spied them at a distance but I didn't feel like getting involved in a chat. What's he like, that young man?'

'Fine – a nice guy. I don't know what their relationship is but I suspect it might lie towards the gay end of the friendship spectrum.'

'Ah, you put it so diplomatically. I think you're right. It's a gay relationship. There's nothing wrong with that; but should we be worried about anything else?'

It was clear to me that somewhere at the back of Blake's mind there lurked a reservation about the Knowles and Naish liaison. He accompanied me on the short walk into the sunshine. We stood looking at one of the famed herbaceous borders that the college was well known for. I commented directly, 'Look, to put it bluntly, but you're probably aware of this already, Knowles wants to place Brendan Naish as his PA. It will be, if he succeeds, an obvious case of nepotism. I think he aims at a short-term, temporary appointment in the first instance, so that the position doesn't have to be advertised. Anyway, that's what he thinks. Do we let him get away with it, or should we snooker him in some way or other? He's talking about lobbying Morris to get his way, which he certainly will, if he does.'

'Is he any good, this Brendan Naish? That's the real point I suppose.'

'Maybe, probably, but if he does the job, he'll owe allegiance to Knowles. He'll hardly be independent in any way. In principle, it's not a good idea.'

At the end of a bed, profuse and overflowing with various plants, there was an old English dog-rose showering its blooms like a fountain. The open, welcoming flowers were alive with feeding bees and fluttering early butterflies. Blake watched the business of the butterflies for some time and then said, 'Let's see what happens. It might yet turn out to be another piece of evidence that will add up to an incontrovertible case of corruption by the executive authorities. Let's wait and see. For the moment, I'm more concerned with the expenses that the executive officers are claiming.'

'Yes,' I agreed, 'a competent strategy.'

Others in college, Est among them, called the Reverend Dr Donald Blake, the crafty chaplain. I saw now that it was not without reason.

That Sunday afternoon I could not settle to anything. The prospect of having supper with Est was disconcerting. I went for a long walk, down through Jericho, across Port Meadow, across the river and went as far as Godstow Priory. All that remained were the ruins of the old nunnery. Everything had been destroyed in the second dissolution of the monasteries. Henry VIII's savage eradication of the vestiges of the old order meant that his predecessor's, Henry II's, refuge for his long-term mistress Rosamund Clifford, the fair Rosamund, had to be rendered into a state of dilapidation. The old stones, a surviving doorway, stood preserved opposite the tourist magnet, the ivy-clad Trout Inn, adorned by its abundant geraniums and cacophonous peacocks.

I looked across the river at the noisy tourists, most of whom had arrived for lunch in their BMWs and SUVs, with their rowdy children, and felt secure with the water between us; I stood alone in the shadow of an old wall. I was sheltered from the mad rush of the modern world by the comforting embrace of history.

The river raced on. I could see beyond some sluices, down towards the meadow and Oxford, some scullers manoeuvring their boats into mid-stream. Beyond them, the campanile tower of St Barnabas church in Jericho still presided over the erratic skyline of incongruous buildings, a lasting symbol of its Oxford Movement founders.

I had seen enough. I strolled back along the river bank, past more rowers, and sailors in single-sailed dinghies from the Medley Sailing Club. On the Oxford side of the river, flocks of geese had settled on the bank and crowds of them stretched back across the water meadow; it was like some awful water birds' Glastonbury festival with a sky full of gulls that had drifted inland circling, squawking and shrieking above the cackling and honking geese.

7

Back in my bungalow I looked through the few bottles of champagne that I kept in a couple of wooden boxes next to my small and inadequate wine rack. There was a bottle of Piper-Heidsieck, a bottle of Moët, four bottles of Veuve Fourny et Fils that I had bought from the grower in Vertus on a trip that I had made to Lyons. I chose one of the Fourny and put it in the fridge.

I have said that I did not know how to handle Est. I knew though that she would be pleased with good champagne. It would start the evening off well. At a quarter to seven I tidied away some papers that I had been reading, took the bottle out of the fridge and walked to Est's apartment. She lived centrally, in a flat that was owned by the college, in the High, at the top of a tall four-storey house. The ground floor was a shop that sold fountain pens; it specialised in them, Lamy, Parker, Waterman, Shaeffer. It stocked a wide range of different quality inks. The woman who owned the business was always complaining that custom was in decline and that the rent rose each year; another year maybe and then the business would fold. She would not be able even to cover her running costs. The ubiquitous ballpoints and felt tips, the hastily written cryptic text messages, and emails, were all bankrupting her business. In my occasional chats with her, I told her, as an economist, that she had to adapt, diversify, change with the times; she should exploit other opportunities and market mobile phones and laptops. I suspected that the greatest obstacle for her was fear; she was afraid of new ways. There was no solution for her. In the end she would close the shop. It would fail.

Est's front door opened directly on to the High immediately next to the pen shop. I rang its bell. The communication speaker gave out Est's voice, 'Is that you, Johnny?' I affirmed to the mike box that I was there. 'OK, just push and come in.'

I did and quickly ascended to the next floor. Est occupied the top three floors.

'Johnny,' she said and proffered her cheek. I kissed her on each cheek and set the cooled bottle of Fourny on the table.

'Johnny, champagne. You shouldn't. We don't need it.'

'Of course we don't. But why not? I picked this up in France. It's authentic – from a small grower. I mean, it's not supermarket stuff.'

'No, I'm sure it's wonderful. I'm flattered.'

She fetched a pair of coupes from a modern, glass-fronted, interior-lit cupboard hung on the wall. As expertly as I could, I released the cork and filled the glasses.

'Here's to the evening,' I toasted.

Est raised her glass and looked me full in the face and was clearly less enthusiastic about the evening's prospect than I. I felt that while my mind raced with ideas of ultimate seduction and a night of lovemaking in her bed, she was thinking of more mundane things and was highly suspicious of my ulterior motives. That state of mind did not augur well for my success.

Est had bought most of the meal ready prepared from a local store's delicatessen. The champagne lasted us through the first course and then we moved on to a 2008 Rhone wine that suited very well our moussaka and green salad. Est had made a dressing herself which was steeped in garlic.

'This dressing is powerful. We'll exude garlic for a fortnight.'

'Stop complaining,' Est replied. 'It's very good for you. It cleanses the blood. Mediaeval literature is full of garlic. They loved it – onions and garlic. Anyway, it's just you and me. We won't notice.'

I could not work out if this was a promise for the future, a statement that any forthcoming intimacy would not be prejudiced by the smell of garlic. The effect would not be off-putting because it would be neutralised; both parties would reek of the root. What she said simply encouraged me to quietly fantasise further about what might happen later in the evening.

'So, what about college politics?' she asked which brought me back down to earth.

I told her about meeting Knowles and Brendan Naish and about Knowles's obvious machinations. I reported what Donald Blake had said. Est commented, 'Things have got to be sorted out. Morris can't go on like this. It's scandalous. He seems to regard the college as his personal piece of turf and he can do what he likes.'

I agreed. 'He's got it all wrong. He's simply *primus inter pares*. That's what he forgets. He sees himself as autonomous, an executive chairman able to initiate without reference to the rest of us. Then, with his placemen about him, he gets away with blue murder.'

'Well, it's all very well, but we need evidence in order to do anything about it. We need hard evidence of abuses. We want to know where and when he has acted without the authority of the governing body.'

'That's exactly what the chaplain is working on. Donald is hot on to expenses claims. He's very good at all that. He's got an accountant's mind; and he's sniffed something fishy and he's determined to find out more.'

Est was silent for a moment. Then she said, 'We must all be vigilant. We must all hold Morris and the bursar to account; and we must not let Timothy Knowles take advantage and indulge in nepotism.'

'True,' I said, 'but if we allow him to exercise his patronage on behalf of Naish, who might be good and worth it anyway, it all might lead on to exposing greater corruption. Let's wait and see.'

'I take your point. I don't like it. But it might be worth the risk.'

'Of course, it won't work anyway. You can't work with your lover. It's bound to fail.' I laid my knife and fork to one side, spooned a little more dressing on to my salad. 'If Knowles wants the relationship to last, he'll need a rest from Naish, his Ganymede.'

Est was in mid-sentence, 'Yes, if he's got him all night, he should have a rest during…' when the telephone rang. Est pushed her chair back, got up from the table and went across to the landline receiver. 'Hello, Estelle here.' There was a pause while Est learned who was at the other end of the line. I heard her say, 'Jane. No, it's fine. I'm just having supper with Johnny. We're between courses. No, go on.'

Their conversation went on for some ten minutes, perhaps a quarter of an hour. Finally Est said, 'Fascinating. There must be more popular feeling than I thought. I'll tell Johnny. Well, things are really hotting up.' She put the phone down. I had finished my salad. She took away my plate, came back from the kitchen and sat down. 'So,' I said, intrigued, 'what's going on? I take it that the Jane you were talking to was Jane Templeton. What morsel, what tit-bit, has my dear colleague got hold of, what relish for my blunted appetite?'

'There's nothing blunted about your appetite. Look at your empty plate. But listen to this. Jane thought I'd like to know immediately; she didn't want to wait until the morning. Apparently, one of her students, one of yours in fact, writes for *Cherwell*, Susie Runciman. She hopes to be editor next year. She's seen papers that concern college expenses and it looks as though there's a story in it all.'

I thought for a moment and then commented, 'Susie's not at Holt. We see her on exchange from All Saints. So, she has no inside track from here, that's to say from Holt. What are the papers?'

'Jane says they are the agenda for the last finance committee meeting and a photocopy of the minutes and some sort of bursarial document to do with claims made by the Principal and the senior tutor. They've either been left lying around or have been deliberately leaked.'

'More like the former,' I said. 'I can't think that anyone leaked them.'

I poured some more wine into Est's glass and topped up my own. Est said, 'Well, brace yourself. Next Friday's *Cherwell* will run a story.

That won't do us any good, certainly not Willoughby. Do you think we could get her to hold off for a bit?'

'Knowing the press, probably not. If they've sniffed at a story, they're going to make the most of it. And, of course, if there's anything in it, which there is, the national press will pick it up, if Susie hasn't sold it to them already. We should probably sit back and wait for the fireworks to begin.'

'What do you think Morris's reaction will be to publicity? How will he take it?'

My retort was abrupt. 'Oh, he'll brazen it out, or try to at least. He'll have an answer ready. These people always do. He'll evade, he'll spin. There'll be some reason, well justified in his view, for whatever excess, whatever misdemeanour, he has been involved in.'

Est sipped her wine and thought. 'Look, I think you should talk to Susie. It's not in our interest at the moment for this to go public. Tactically it's wrong. It's too soon. If we're going to get rid of Willoughby, we want him on toast. You're right; now, he would brazen it out. He'd talk about mistakes in the past and being sure to do better in the future. We need to hold Susie and her machine for the coming assault; but it's not yet. Have a word with her. Tell her there's bound to be more to come. It's worth waiting for.'

Est got up from the table and went to the kitchen. She came back with some cheeses on a small board. She sat down and described the three cheeses to me, a mature Gouda, a crumbly Cheddar and a west country goat's cheese. I took some of the Gouda.

'Well, I'll do my best. I'd better talk to her in the morning, though I doubt she'll be persuaded. From her point of view, it's quite a good story as it is; and it can develop, get better. If she waits, someone else might make capital out of it before she does. I'll have a go.'

In our conversation we passed on to other things. The evening was pleasant enough. Yet in the end I was disappointed. When it came time for me to depart, Est did not encourage me to stay. She was warm and affectionate but somehow wanted to keep me at a distance. At her front door, which let me out on to the pavement, she kissed me with pressure and passion; or at least I felt I detected the passion.

That was it; I walked sadly away not having achieved what I had imagined or expected. I managed to buoy myself up by thinking that these were early days; the joy was in what was to come. Lurking at the back of my mind was the thought that I was deluding myself. Est was a woman of sophistication; she knew what she was doing, and she was not going to get emotionally involved with me. That was my fear that haunted me as I walked back to my tiny house.

8

Trying to persuade Susie to delay any publication of potential scandal at Holt was not easy. She was going to be with me that following afternoon, Monday, for a tutorial. I had teamed her with a Holt student, Howard Ainsworth, at the beginning of the year. They were due to turn up at my rooms at five o'clock. Howard arrived first. He had been playing tennis and was still in his tracksuit trousers and sports kit. He told me that he had seen Susie earlier in the day and that she was extremely busy; she was working on a long article about government funding of education. The government had just published a white paper on educational finance and all commentators were reading the small print and writing their views. It was important that *Cherwell* made an immediate statement and did not fall behind the pack in criticism, creative or otherwise, of government policy. 'I don't suppose she'll have finished her essay. So, I expect she'll want me to read mine again.'

'Maybe,' I commented, 'but it might not be what I want. She has to do her bit on the work front. She'll never become editor of *The Times* if she can't meet her deadlines. We want to hear her essay.'

At that moment there was a knock at the door and in walked Susie.

'Sorry I'm a bit late. A lot going on in the big wide world.'

'So I hear,' I said. 'Besides all that, are you up to date with your work? Have you an essay for us? I hope poor Howard hasn't got to read again this week.'

She shuffled among the sheaf of papers she had been carrying and said, 'No, it's fine. I wrote most of this before the government broke the news, and I've managed to just put the finishing touches to it. It might be a bit ragged round the edges towards the end but here it is.'

So, that was fine. Susie read her essay and we had a constructive discussion. I wondered how I was going to broach the subject of Holt's leaked expenses documents.

Five minutes before the end of our session, I said to Howard that if he would not mind excusing me, I had to see Susie on her own. He was eager to get away, packed up his things and left. Then came the difficult part.

Susie got up from her chair and looked somewhat mystified. 'You want to see me? What about? What's the matter? Are you worried about my work?' She looked arch and said coquettishly, 'You've no need to worry about me. I know what I'm doing. You don't have any complaints, do you?' She made me feel like a client of an escort agency; she was making sure that I was going to report well of her.

'No, no, of course not. But this is a rather delicate matter. It's to do with *Cherwell*, and I don't want to appear as interfering with the freedom of the press. I don't quite know how to put it.'

I explained to her that we knew *Cherwell* had information about possible expenses abuse at Holt. I told her that Jane had heard about it and, in turn, had told Est and me. We were aware of trouble in that particular area but wished to adopt a strategy that would allow us to collect substantial evidence. We needed time and any premature publicity would almost certainly encourage the guilty to cover their tracks. Susie listened carefully. She saw the point of what I was saying. She asked some questions, 'Why wasn't the college more active in keeping the executive in check?'; 'Were there external checks from the university administration?' I explained that the majority of fellows were supine, wanted a quiet life, and simply got on with their own teaching and research. The university itself had little power to interfere with the day-to-day running of the independent, autonomous colleges.

Susie responded quite quickly in a business-like way, 'Fine. I see the point. We'll hold off a bit. We'll print something about rumours in general about extravagant expenses claims but we won't point the finger. But you have to promise us an exclusive story. Otherwise we go our own way. We can help by the way, if we get info, we'll keep you informed.'

I agreed. 'That sounds good. I can guarantee that Jane Templeton, Dr Treisman, the chaplain, and anyone else associated with us will cooperate. I can't speak for others, but I shouldn't think there will be any trouble. There could be some reverse spin if the establishment, as it were, gets wind of any forthcoming publicity.'

Susie accepted that and we parted. My next students were waiting for their six o'clock tutorial. She went away downstairs and I knew as she left that our agreement was shaky; even an undergraduate journalist has to keep in mind the urgency and demands of what is known as public interest, and also the risk that the competition might get to the story beforehand.

Meanwhile, Knowles had been busy. I received a note in my lodge pigeonhole, along with all the other fellows, signed by Willoughby Morris, which informed me that a Mr Brendan Naish had been appointed PA to the senior tutor for a trial period of six months. It was thus a temporary position, paid on the lowest level of the administrative grade, and therefore the Principal deemed that no official endorsement by the governing body was needed. He was confident that all would agree with his decision.

I rang Est that evening and commented on Morris's note. Est was righteously appalled. 'He steamrollers. It's a fait accompli. He knows the majority will sit back and take it. He really is awful. We shouldn't let him get away with this.'

'Well, we do at the moment,' I said. 'It gives us ammunition.'

'Yes, but we mustn't let it blow up in our faces,' she warned.

There was no hope of us meeting that night. Est was busy. Tantalisingly she did not tell me what with. Naturally, I imagined that she had another date. My anxiety unsettled me completely. I very nearly gave into my impulses and walked round to her flat in the High; but I didn't. I held back. Reason prevailed. After all, we were not in any close and reliant relationship, at least, not yet.

9

The Principal bustled in, his gown flowing. He settled into his chair like a great flapping crow landing on the college lawns outside. He was followed in by one or two stragglers, latecomers, one of the modern languages fellows and two scientists. Morris waited, looking around over the top of his glasses, then tapped the table in front of him and said, 'Good afternoon, ladies and gentlemen. May I remind you all that I like to start these meetings on time. We have much to do, both here and elsewhere in our respective studies. I suppose I've always thought it polite to arrive before the chair is taken. Perhaps I'm old-fashioned but that's the way I like things done.'

There was an undercurrent of murmur from the far end of the long table along which all the fellows sat for the governing body meeting. It was Wednesday afternoon and the scheduled fellows' meeting had begun. It was clear to all except, seemingly, Morris that many of the fellows disliked being reprimanded in this way.

'Now, to business. Let's get through things as quickly as possible. Firstly, the minutes of the last meeting – matters arising?'

The chaplain stirred, hitched the left shoulder of his gown and commented, 'Well, I don't think our discussion of expense allowances was properly recorded in detail. The minutes are hardly the work of a stenographer. There should be at least a reference to future work that was resolved to be done on the expenses issue.'

Morris was quick to respond. 'Bursar, please note that. Hardly necessary, of course, but we'll reference it. Any other points? No. Good. Minutes passed then. Let's move on.'

Various following items on the agenda were dealt with. Nobody was inclined to involve themselves in long discussions. The vast majority of items were routine, ones that came round each term and could be settled without discussion. The last item before 'any other business' was about the Development Office and fundraising. Mayhew, the mathematician, felt that the turnover of staff in the office was too frequent and wondered what the reason was for that. The recently appointed director had just announced that she was resigning. No one knew what her real reasons were. The bursar said she had cited an increase in family responsibilities but he said that Brendan Naish, the senior tutor's newly appointed assistant, had heard a rumour that she was off to Ridley College. Naish had reported that she was unhappy with the atmosphere at Holt, the establishment attitude to fundraising and her lack of executive power.

'Right,' the Principal declaimed, 'we had better have a sub-committee look into this. What I'll do is appoint a chair and ask three representative fellows from among you to investigate. I'll let you know who I think suitable.'

I was sitting in between Jane and Jacob Black. Jacob muttered sotte voce, 'I h-hope he doesn't a-ask me. I'll refuse. It will be p-pointless. He'll w-want to run things, d-dominate as usual.'

Morris looked towards us and frowned. He went on, 'This is a suitable juncture to mention another matter to do with fundraising. I have been in touch with our Old Members' groups in Delhi, Bombay and Hyderabad.'

There was an uncomfortable shuffle from Est who sat on the opposite side of the table from me. She had on previous occasions pulled up the Principal about his use of Bombay instead of Mumbai and Peking instead of Beijing, but he was not to be shifted. Est had pointed out that many Indians and Chinese would be surprised, if not offended, by the use of the old-fashioned names, but Morris was not to be moved. He was stubborn. He maintained that Bombay and Peking were names that everyone recognised. Attempts by the media, newspapers and the BBC were perverse and simply political correctness gone mad; look at how Myanmar had reverted to Burma – even the *Guardian* used Burma. He simply was not going to go along with that sort of thing. He noticed Est's unease, paused and rather relished it, then continued.

'I have arranged to visit those three places, Delhi again, and together with Islamabad and Lahore where the college has quite a strong presence. There will be meetings with Old Members of the college and it should all prove fruitful ground for raising cash. Certainly in India, we have one or two very wealthy individuals who ought to be supporting us and so far have not. There's Raji Singh, for instance, who some of you will remember. He now owns one of the country's most successful software companies. He might well contribute. Such a nice fellow; he was an outstanding batsmen, got a cricket Blue. Anyway, I shall see what can be done.

'It's an opportunity that should not be missed, particularly in India, a thriving, emerging powerhouse of a country. We must cultivate our contacts. We should consider setting up a special class of fellowship for them. They need to have something tangible for their support and donations. But another time.

'I just want to stress that, after talking with the bursar, I shall be making the usual call on college funding for travel and hotel expenses.'

I just detected Donald whispering, 'Here we go again.' Morris did not hear.

What I could not work out was why he should wish to go to Pakistan. To my knowledge we had very few Pakistani graduates; I did not know how many expats were working there. India was different. The college had a long and distinguished connection with the country. There were many Old Member graduates and a constantly changing population of expat alumni in India. There, I felt, was fertile ground for funding tillage.

'The bursar assures me that there is no problem with the finance of the trip. It will be in keeping with what has happened before. Usually, he tells me, these trips easily pay for themselves by subsequent benefit for the college. Isn't that so, bursar?'

Jeremy Eedes raised his head from looking at the notes he was making and said, 'Indeed that is so, Principal. I think we should all thank you for your efforts and wish you well on the forthcoming trip.'

Morris nodded. 'Thank you, Bursar. I should add that the Pakistan visit is very opportune. There is a scientific conference to which I have been invited. It takes place in Islamabad. Two birds with one stone, you might say.

'Now before we come to the end of this meeting I should like to say that I am studying a scheme for the improvement of our salaries. This would be to a level above the average of most college fellows in the rest of the university. I shall have more to say about this at a future meeting, maybe even the next one.'

Jacob muttered, 'And s-so shall I.'

Morris heard the remark, turned towards Jacob and said forcefully, 'Don't worry, Professor Black, there will be an opportunity for debate of this matter when I have the scheme clear in my mind. I'm sure we all want to benefit as much as we can from the college's resources.'

With that he stood up, declared, 'Good afternoon, ladies and gentlemen', swirled round and left the room. Eedes picked up his papers and followed swiftly.

Jane touched my arm and said, 'What was all that about? What nasty little scheme has he got up his sleeve?'

Jacob had thrown up his hands as if in despair and left. I said to Jane, 'You can be sure it's not straightforward. He'll see an opportunity for raising his own remuneration or there will be something of bribery and coercion. I simply don't trust the man.'

Donald Blake had come round from the other side of the table. 'We must keep an eye on what he claims for this proposed trip to

India and Pakistan. He's bound to want to make a profit. Personally, I don't like the sound of it. Our alumni in both those countries are limited. He's probably using us.'

The Reverend Dr Donald Blake sighed audibly, smiled at Est who had followed him to where Jane and I were standing, and left the room.

Est stood next to Jane and began to take off her gown. I quickly stepped towards her and helped her. She folded it across her arm and said, 'What a performance. He's impossible. What's he going to get up to next? Look, this is getting serious. He thinks he owns the place. He's behaving like Tony Blair. We have to do something.'

I was excited by her proximity. She looked to me both attractive and seductive. Jane said, 'We shall. Things can't go on like this. It's a dictatorship. There's no transparency. There's just collusion and deception.'

Est cut in, 'I wouldn't trust either Eedes or Knowles. What's the matter with them? Knowles is making it worse by indulging his own desires, wanting his sybarite with him all the time; hence Naish as his PA. We have to do something.'

Est was impassioned. She spoke with resolution and determination. I loved her strength and peculiar display of brio. She turned to me, 'Johnny, what do you think we should do now?'

I was flattered that she should ask me outright. She wanted my view, valued my judgement. 'I think as Donald has said, we should bide our time. Remain vigilant. It's almost as though Willoughby's out of control. Power's gone to his head. It's clouding his reason. If he doesn't pull back, it'll lead to disaster. So, for the moment we wait and watch. Our moment will come.'

The two women agreed. Jane picked up her handbag and papers and left Est and myself standing, gazing out of the windows. I could not resist asking Est to be with me that evening. I had such an aching longing to be with her; but she said she was busy. Once again as always in such situations, my imagination saw her with some other

71

lover. I lapsed into silence. I did not know what to say. Est obviously sensed my disappointment, my unhappiness; she said, 'Come on, Johnny, don't mope. I lead a busy life. Tonight's short notice. Let's say tomorrow. How's that sound? Does that cheer you up?' And of course it did.

'Great. As soon as poss after seven, at my room? Is that OK? We'll think about what to do, where to go.' I reached for her hand and held it briefly. She warmed to my touch and responded, squeezing my hand gently. We walked out into the sunshine, crossed the quad, paused, and parted to go our separate ways.

10

In the meantime something unusual happened. I was at home that evening. I had eaten a light, scratch supper – salad, and some pasta with a little cream and lemon sauce, garnished with a few strips of smoked salmon. It had taken me no more than ten minutes to prepare. I treated myself to a glass of Alsatian wine, Muscat Reserve, Clos des Capucins, Domaine Weinbach, 2007. It was deliciously fragrant and bone dry. I secretly toasted my prospective success with Est the following day.

It seemed a perfect evening. The fading light was roseate. Somewhere beyond the rooftops, the sun was beginning to set and where it sank over the horizon the sky must have been a fiery red. It augured well for the weather of the next day. After I had eaten, I played a CD of Maria Callas singing in *Don Giovanni* and sat sipping the wine.

No more than a minute into 'Non mi dir', the discordant note of the telephone sounded. I moved from my chair, turned down the volume and picked up the receiver. 'Hallo. Johnny James.'

'Ah, is this a good time to ring?' I recognised the voice of Tony Gill. It was unusual. He hardly ever rang me at home; in fact, he hardly ever rang me at all. In addition to his academic duties of research and teaching, Tony was also Vicegerent, deputy to the Principal. His had been a controversial appointment. Tony had been instrumental in finding and putting forward Willoughby's name for the principalship. Once Morris had been elected, it was necessary to elect his deputy. Morris more or less insisted that it had to be Gill. The fellowship went along with that and Tony was duly appointed. Once in place, Tony found himself eclipsed. Morris was dominant, brooked no criticism from Tony, and kept the exercise of power as his own preserve. Tony found himself completely sidelined and tactically ignored. With Morris as Principal and Tony in his deputy's post, the Vicegerent withered in significance and might just as well not have existed; it had no force, no power. With Callas in the background, I expected a lament from Tony Gill, a heart-to-heart complaint about the way he was being treated. It was not the case.

'Yes, it's fine, Tony. I'm on my own. What's the form? What's going on?'

'You might well ask, and I haven't a clue. Anyway, it's just this. I had a call from Lord Crammond. He wonders if one or two of us would like to join him out at Fenmore on Sunday, maybe late afternoon, tea and an early drink. He particularly mentioned you. I have no idea what's going on. Should I leave it at just the two of us if you're free?'

Hugh Crammond had been Principal for five years more than a decade ago. He resigned from the post when he was made leader of the government party in the House of Lords. Fenmore was his family seat in the north Oxfordshire countryside. The house was an accretion of stones and styles. It had been rebuilt in the early seventeenth century, based on the ruins of an ancient fifteenth century manor house, and bits had been added on, renovations taken place, and, of course, the Victorians had embellished it in their view with blocks of Gothic stonework. Hugh Crammond and his wife had decided to move out and lead their daily life from the Dower House a little distant by a quarter of a mile from the dark mansion from which the family's crested banner flew each day. Within the gloomy palace were old furnished bedrooms, a fusty library, a large dining room, and walls hung with Reynolds paintings and a valuable and burglar-alarmed Van Dyck. Hugh Crammond used it mainly for receptions, filling the reception hall and the dining room with his guests and affording them spectacular views of a wide lawn leading to a ha-ha, across a hidden meandering river, to a distant classical folly high up on ploughed land. Either side of the perfect lawn were landscaped gardens designed and originally laid out by William Kent.

Since I knew Crammond slightly and realised that almost anything he did had political motivations, I thought it best to confine the meeting to just the three of us. I replied to Tony's question.

'I think you're right. I'll certainly make sure I'm available Sunday. Let's leave it at just us. Hugh Crammond has certainly got something on his mind. Let's find out what it is. How will we get out there?'

I was hoping that I did not have to drive. Tony answered the prompt.

'I'll give you a lift. Shall I pick you up around half past three? It shouldn't take more than about twenty-five minutes to get there. I must say I'm intrigued to know what's going on in his mind. Why should he want to talk to you especially? He could have made a private arrangement with you. There has to be some college business tied up in this.'

'Well, thanks. I'll expect you at three thirty. You're quite right; but all will be revealed. And whatever else, it's bound to be glorious out at Fenmore – an extremely agreeable Sunday afternoon outing.'

Tony Gill was not so sure. 'Yes, from the aesthetic point of view, but I have a wife and children to deal with. They are not going to be best pleased – an incursion into family life, an invasion of leisure time.'

'No. I understand. It's difficult. Look, if I have any further thoughts before Sunday afternoon, I'll talk to you, either in college, or I'll give you a ring.'

'Yes. Good idea; and likewise.'

Tony rang off. I turned up the volume of the Callas CD. The incomparable music raised my spirits, entered my soul, and I stood listening until the performance played itself out.

11

When Est arrived at my rooms the following evening, just after seven, I wondered if I should mention Crammond's invitation. I decided not to talk about it; it would be better to wait and see what his concerns were. Est was in a very good mood, vivacious and provocative.

The first thing she did was to kiss me on both cheeks, which she rarely did. We operated usually on a daily, professional basis; we nodded at each other's presence, accepted that we were there, wherever it was, to do our work, and, you might say, took each other for granted. It was the ordinary working environment relationship. That evening it was different; she was warm, flirtatious, intimate.

'Right, we're dining in. I booked us in this afternoon. I thought it better. No problems about where to dine. And afterwards we go back to my place. We don't have to hang about and make boring conversation.'

I was quite taken aback. I had noticed that she was carrying her gown but I supposed she had been to a lecture or some official meeting.

'OK. That's fine by me. I haven't actually dined in since first week of term – about time I did. Do you know who's in tonight?'

'Well, of course, it's a guest night. So, Morris will be there and he's bound to have a guest, or two, or three. I expect his lovely lady wife will be there too. Otherwise, I know Knowles and Naish will be there.'

I was not all that pleased by the prospect of the company so far. 'No doubt Mrs Morris will arrive slightly over the top with drink and will leave totally drunk. She usually does.'

Est put on her gown and commented, 'Yes, she'll provide the cabaret; not very good but better than nothing.'

I took my gown from a hook on the back of the door and hitched it up and on. 'We'd better go. We can just about make the common room for a quick sherry before we're shuffled into hall.'

And that is what we did. At ten past seven we were sipping our Tio Pepe sherries. On the stroke of seven fifteen Willoughby Morris swept in, trailed by his wife and a solitary female guest and, without stopping, proceeded into hall. There was no question of shuffling. Est put down her glass still containing most of her sherry. I gulped down what remained of mine. Jacob Black followed Morris at a deliberately leisurely pace so that there was a considerable gap between them. Then went Est as the next most senior fellow, followed by me; then the chaplain, Knowles and Naish who was there as Knowles's guest, and then the rest who were lecturers of the college. It was a small gathering, no more than twelve people.

By the time we arrived at high table in the grand and beautiful hall, Morris was fidgeting with the gavel and looking impatient and displeased. Jacob looked mischievously unconcerned. He had positioned himself three places away from Morris, down the table and with his back to the undergraduates. At Morris's right hand stood his guest and next to her, Willoughby's wife Elizabeth. Morris waved Est to be next to him on his left. I kept her company, as was our intention, and stood on her left side. The rest arranged themselves along the table.

Morris banged the gavel on its wooden block. The hall went quiet; the hubbub of student voices stilled. At the near end of one of the long tables set out in the body of the hall, a student in a scholar's gown started reciting grace in Latin. 'Nos miseri et egeni, pro cibis quos nobis ad corporis subsidium benigne es largitus, tibi Deus omnipotens...' So, we the unhappy and unworthy men were called upon to give thanks to almighty God for the sustaining victuals provided. We were exhorted to pray for the food of angels and the true bread of heaven and, in the words of the Book of Common Prayer we were invited to feed on the flesh and blood of Christ so that we might be sustained, nourished and strengthened in our daily lives.

The grace came to an end. There was a chorus of relieved 'amens'. The abated noise rose again to the ancient rafters, and the waiters and waitresses started serving dinner. At our high table, the head butler who had been standing at Morris's elbow signalled to the wine waiter who began to pour a white wine, first to the Principal, then to his guest and so on anti-clockwise to Elizabeth and the rest of the table. I noticed the label as the wine was being served to me; it was a Côtes de Bourg Blanc, Château de La Grave Grains Fins, 2008. It was delicious, fragrant and lemon fresh. Morris was making sure that no expense was spared.

I was intrigued by Willoughby Morris's guest. He had not announced who she was beforehand to my knowledge. Usually he was proud and insistent when entertaining guests. Without any subtlety he would let as many people know as possible who he was having to dinner, or who was staying at college for a day or two. He picked up his glass and took a sip.

'Elizabeth, this is Dr Estelle Treisman and Dr James.'

At first I could not understand why he should have been introducing us to his wife. Then I realised that the two women had the same Christian name.

He announced, 'Dame Elizabeth Wright.' He leant towards his wife and said, 'Liz, introduce Elizabeth to the senior tutor.'

'Willoughby, please don't call me Liz. My name is Elizabeth. You know I can't stand that familiarity.' She was clearly put out and certainly a little drunk. She was obviously in a prickly mood and was not prepared to be upstaged by Dame Elizabeth.

'Sorry, my darling – just to avoid confusion.'

'There's no confusion between me and Dame Elizabeth.' She turned to Timothy Knowles. 'Timothy, this is Dame Elizabeth

Wright.' She leant back in her chair to allow the two to acknowledge each other. 'Dame Elizabeth runs MI5.'

Est and I listened to this exchange. I had known that the name was familiar but I had forgotten that Dame Elizabeth now occupied that very sensitive seat of power, one of the few women ever to have held the position.

We settled back in our chairs. The waiters brought some Dover sole, rolled and stuffed with white grapes. Morris sat beneath the founder's portrait; the old Archbishop, Walter Grimmond, looked down benignly on the assembled college members; the artist had caught a look of self-satisfied approval on his face. Above Elizabeth Wright on the oak-panelled wall hung a more severe looking portrait of William, Earl of Chester, depicted as a younger man and looking considerably more critical and censorious. In the centre of the back wall, over the head, as it happened, of Brendan Naish, sat incongruously a portrait of George II; he had endowed some fellowships and graced the college with several visitations.

The Principal's wife said rather more loudly than she intended, 'Well, Dame Elizabeth, I don't know how you find the time to come and join in our frivolities. You must be awfully busy. Aren't there hundreds of extremists you're supposed to be rounding up?'

'Elizabeth dear,' Willoughby cut in, and I was at first not sure whether he was addressing the Dame or his wife, 'Dame Elizabeth must be allowed some time off from her demanding duties. What could be nicer than a leisurely evening at an Oxford college? She will enjoy good wines and excellent food. She will be reinforced for the struggle ahead.' He looked round for acceptance of what he said. Jacob stifled a snort of derision and tucked into his fish. Est and I concentrated on our sole. Knowles took a deep gulp of wine followed by a swig of water. I sensed a difficult evening ahead for Morris.

By this time, Elizabeth had finished her glass of wine and was tapping her glass for a refill. Dame Elizabeth had hardly touched hers. Est engaged Dame Elizabeth in conversation. Morris occasionally burst in and pontificated about the current political situation; he had strong and trenchant views. Dame Elizabeth, who was in her late fifties, smartly dressed in an ordinary sort of way as though she had just stepped out of Peter Jones rather than Marni, was reserved in her opinions and gave an immediate impression that she was shrewdly summing up the Principal. Her glasses hung down and balanced on her bosom, suspended from a black and gold cord.

I said, to break a pause in the conversation, 'There must be a degree of dark romance in your work – agents and operatives, deception and intrigue, surprise and disguise.'

She almost snapped back, 'On the contrary. My work is routine, deeply unromantic. I am an office worker, an administrator and, if anything, a thinker and researcher.' She was clearly used to dispelling the views that I had put across. 'I am presented, more often than not, with problems that require moral and ethical decisions that are extremely difficult to make. That, I think, makes my particular work just as arduous and demanding as any operative, or agent as you would call it, working in the field.'

Est cut in, 'I've always wondered how people like you who have to make momentous decisions which affect deeply people's lives, indeed who make life and death decisions, are accountable. You can't be to the public in general. By its very nature your work has to be secret and you and your employees have to be experts in deception.'

'You're quite right, my dear,' Dame Elizabeth responded, 'but I answer to the Home Secretary and the Prime Minister; and there is one committee that keeps a very watchful eye on what I do. Sometimes it's frustrating and the scrutiny slows things down.'

While his wife moved her food around her plate without actually eating much, and continued a constant sipping of her wine, Morris raised his voice in order to be heard and said loudly so that most at the table heard, 'I know what you mean, Elizabeth.' His wife abruptly turned to him but immediately discovered that she was the wrong Elizabeth. He continued, 'In a minor way it's just the same here in college. I am continually frustrated by interfering commit-tees. Someone is always watching out for me. My dear, I feel I'm not trusted.'

Some absorbed his remark in a subdued silence, but the other Elizabeth saw an opportunity. She said, before anyone else could add to the discussion, 'Quite right. You shouldn't be trusted.' Then with a slight slur to her speech, she added, 'Let me tell you, dear Dame, the more people who keep tabs on him, the better.'

I could see that Dame Elizabeth was embarrassed. Willoughby flushed a little. 'Now then, my dear, let's not exceed the bounds of polite conversation. We shall bore our guests.'

He was rattled by his wife's indiscretion and like me could see the discussion descending into something other than what the majority of us intended.

I volunteered, 'Fortunately college affairs do not involve matters of life and death. By comparison they're trivial. I don't envy you those terrible decisions that have to be made. I suppose you have to be something of a High Court judge.'

Morris took that up. 'Yes, of course, that was not what I was getting at. Within our context, matters seem just as important. I would like the head of house, the college Principal, to have more directly effective power.'

Jacob, who on and off had been quietly sniggering, scoffed audibly at this remark. He managed to get out, 'That's p-precisely w-what we wouldn't l-like. W-we are a collegiate b-body. The f-fellows are equal in p-p-power and responsibility. We are not a b-business r-run by a CEO.'

Jacob leant back and visibly relaxed after what had been for him a great effort. Jacob spoke little in public; all his lectures were read verbatim when most of his stammering was lost.

'Oh yes,' Morris pronounced, 'I know what you think, and your arguments, but you've got to move with the times. We have to run these places efficiently. Speed of decision-making is crucial. Don't you agree, Elizabeth?' He was clearly addressing the Dame but his wife looked up sharply and said, 'I don't know what you're talking about. Don't you have to do what the college wants?' She tapped her empty wine glass with her pudding spoon. The wine waiter hurried to her side and refilled her glass. Dame Elizabeth's wine had hardly been touched.

By the end of the meal, Est and I had managed to engage Dame Elizabeth about current politics and learned about her experience as a cross-bencher in the House of Lords. We successfully kept the peace between Willoughby and his wife. There was certainly a tangible feeling of hostility between them that evening. There was not always, but something must have happened before they appeared for dinner. Perhaps they had indulged in some mean domestic argument, or perhaps she believed he was commencing an affair with the Dame. The reasons for her provocative remarks were not clear but whatever problem it was, she was trying to take the edge off it by drinking.

It was entertaining. Needless to say, Morris was irrepressible. Nothing ever diminished his appetite for the public forum, an aspect of which High Table presented to him. As his wife became more and more drunk, so he increasingly ignored her. He became expansive and engaged everybody in his conversational embrace. It had to be allowed him, that as the evening progressed, he developed as the occasion's dominant social creature.

Est and I had decided beforehand that we would not stay for dessert. After dinner and the *post cibum* grace, 'Confiteantur tibi, Domine, omnia opera tua et sancti tui benedicant tibi', on a guest night with all the works of the Lord acknowledging Him and all his saints blessing Him, everyone would retire to a separate room close by, shedding their academic gowns, like snakes their skins, on the way. Again it was oak-panelled and hung with portraits of bishops and lawyers, poets and academic divines important in the history of the college. The room, known as the parlour, would be candle-lit;

those taking dessert would be seated next to people different from those they had been sitting next to at dinner. The table was provisioned with grapes, pears, kiwi fruit, preserved ginger, and various sorts of chocolates. A bowl of walnuts would be in the centre of the table. Whoever was at the head of the table, usually the chairman of the common room, would circulate dessert drinks, decanters of port, Madeira, Sauternes, and the claret or red Burgundy that had been served at dinner. A box of snuff circulated as well. The decanters made their way round the table at a leisurely pace, passed on each time to the person's left; they were sent round twice. Then formalities came to an end and anyone who wanted to would retire to the common room for coffee and a further nightcap if desired. Est and I were sure that Elizabeth Morris would be partaking fully of any drinking opportunity that evening. We were glad that we had opted out of the dessert proceedings on that particular evening.

We looked into the common room, walked through the college grounds to the lodge and out on to the High. One of the assistant porters was on duty and we waved goodbye to her. For just over a year we had decided to employ women in the lodge as well as men. We were a college in the forefront of reform; we had been one of the first group to open up hitherto all-male colleges to women applicants for student places and to appoint women to the governing fellowship. So far as I was concerned, Est was the benefit for me of this innovation.

Across the High, Est and I entered her flat. At the top of the stairs I could feel the warmth emanating from her rooms. She had kept her central heating system running so that a low background temperature was maintained in her apartment against the low chill of that summer evening. She liked to keep warm.

'Thank goodness we didn't go to dessert. I don't think I could have stood it. That was quite enough of Willoughby for one evening. As for his wife…' Est started to sort through half a dozen or so of bottles that were on a sideboard. 'Look, I hardly ever use these. In fact, I'm not even sure what's here. Why don't you just help yourself.'

I went to the sideboard. There was a bottle of dry Vermouth unbroached, a two thirds empty bottle of Jura malt whisky, a bottle of gin reduced by about an inch, an unopened bottle of Sainsbury's claret, and an old bottle of white wine that had a glass or two left in it which would have changed to vinegar from longstanding. Est was obviously not a lone drinker.

'What will you have?' I asked. Est was in the kitchen.

'Thanks. I'll have a small white wine. This will be our dessert.' She laughed.

'Not this white wine,' I said. 'It's way off its sell-by date. Have you any other.'

'Yes, I think so. I'll have a look.' I could see her bending down, crouching and searching the low shelf of a larder cupboard. What struck me was that she had a beautiful figure. In another context she might have been a model. She rose elegantly and stood resting her weight on one leg, leaning against the kitchen worktop.

'I've got this. Somebody gave me this when they came round for supper. Is it any good? I know nothing about wine.'

I took the bottle she had found and looked at the label. It was respectable enough, a Wine Society white Burgundy 2009, but nothing outstanding.

'This is fine,' I said. 'It won't be cold but never mind. It'll do.'

With a glass in her hand she went to the CD player and we enjoyed our drinks to the muted background virtuoso singing of Pavarotti. She sipped her Burgundy: I sipped a malt whisky. We sat and relaxed. We imagined the scene back in college; Morris would be intent on dominating the conversation, his wife would be continuing her advance into alcoholic stupor, Dame Elizabeth, no doubt, would be finding the evening growing more and more tedious. We were happy to be out of it.

'Let's leave the college behind. Let's talk of other things,' she said. And so we did. She talked of her parents who lived on the border between Essex and Suffolk; she described it as Constable country.

She said she phoned her mother virtually every day; if she failed to do so, her mother would send her a worried text. I marvelled that such a sophisticated woman as Est could be so in thrall to her mother's demands and anxieties; but she was kind, caring and considerate. I gently ridiculed her for her attentiveness but she obviously regarded the daily contact as a moral duty that, in any case, she wanted to carry out.

I admired her enormously. I wanted to be part of her life, her existence, her world. I wanted to share responsibility for her parents. I could not express that. It would have been gauche and intrusive. I found myself becoming more and more in love with her; or that is what I thought it was. I felt I was growing intoxicated by her. She was mesmerising me.

As the evening wore on and we both grew pleasantly mellow with the drink we consumed, I confessed in an awkward way my feelings.

'I know, Johnny. I can see what's happening. You don't have to say anything. Sit back, relax. Let's see what happens. I think you're super, but I don't want to push things. Let's wait and see.'

'But I don't want to wait,' I confessed. 'We should make the most of time.'

'You sound like Andrew Marvell and I'm your coy mistress, "If we had world enough and time, This coyness, lady, were no crime". Don't fret; there's no hurry.'

'That's not what it feels like to me. I feel oppressed by "time's winged chariot".'

Yet I suppose what was important that evening was that we established our positions. So far as I was concerned Cupid had blindly shot his arrow and it had landed in my heart. Est, it seemed to me, had avoided his next shaft but somehow she was affected by the effects of the balmy boy on me. I reckoned if she kept close to me, she might in the end be struck as well. In the meantime there was nothing I could do but wait. Est was not going to jump into bed with me that night. I resolved, though, not to give up. We were compatible. I was convinced of that. Our minds could be one; they would coincide.

Around half past eleven Est said she was tired. Rather unsubtly I said to her holding her hands, 'Wouldn't it be a good idea if I just stayed the night?'

Mockingly she replied, 'But where would you sleep? I've only one bed made up. Surely you weren't thinking of sharing my bed? That would not be proper. What are you thinking of?'

That depressed me. 'Oh, come on, Est. Of course I'll share your bed. I want to look after you. We're grown-ups. I want to stay.' I suddenly felt entirely miserable.

'Sorry, Johnny. I'm not going to make fun of this or you. I don't feel quite the same way as you, and I'm not ready for this just yet. Go slowly. It'll be better.'

And that was that. The evening terminated. We kissed and I hugged her. I walked disconsolately back home.

12

Tony Gill turned up on time. That Sunday afternoon the weather was fine, the sky clear, just a slight coolness in the air. I was ready for him. I had spent the day until that point wondering where my relationship with Est would go after the evening before, and trying to predict what the purpose of Hugh Crammond's summons was. I had no satisfactory resolution to either mystery.

Tony and I rattled off in his rather wretched Ford Focus estate. It had been converted completely and totally irretrievably to a family car. It was full of debris created and cast off by his children. There was a baby seat fastened on to one of the rear seats. It was stained by overflows of baby milk and what appeared to be dried yoghurt. Fine crumbs of some kind sat in the angle of the seat like a small heap of sand. Children's books were strewn over the passenger seats and the rear ledge that separated the car interior from the boot space. On the floor were plastic wrappings from takeaway fast food, more books, a couple of model cars, a model unicorn, and three water bottles, two empty and one three quarters full. As we had got into the car Tony had thrown a child's coat from the front passenger seat into the back and said, 'Sorry about the mess. Haven't had time to sort it out. Still, I don't think you'll catch a disease. It's simply the problem of trying to manage three children.'

We reached Fenmore within half an hour. During the last part of the journey we had followed a long low wall overhung by ancient yew trees until we finally arrived at the entrance. A small lodge stood to one side, its tiny garden immaculately kept and manicured, trimmed bushes of box and lavender, a scattering of standard roses and two feature beds of hybrid roses. I had been told that one of the gardeners for the estate now lived there. The one-bar swing barrier that guarded the entrance was open. We drove through.

On either side of the long drive were fields full of cattle. On the right side there was a herd of black Friesians with a considerable number of very young calves. Each had a registration tag clipped firmly into its right ear and the tag had a name in broad black inked letters clearly written. Thus there was Lucy, Laetitia, Lettuce, Lady, Lilac; but there were too many for the creative writer and in the end some were just numbered 1, 17 and so on.

In the field to the left hand, a herd of longhorns were grazing. One or two had the most extraordinarily bent horns, crooked and rather horrifyingly vicious-looking. In the distance were two magnificent and mighty bulls. Tony said that he had been told by one of the herdsmen on a previous visit, that one was called Redemption and the other Moonraker. We drove slowly in order not to frighten the cattle, and after about half a mile arrived in front of the great house. It was at its best in the strong afternoon light. An avenue of old oak trees stretched away across now cultivated fields into the distance; farm buildings were just visible lying off to the left. It was one of a few afternoons in the year when the house was open to the public. As we passed the stable yard, converted by necessity into a car park, we saw about half a dozen cars. Such was the secrecy of the place that it was never crowded. Hugh Crammond did not court the crowd; he was gradually breaking the place into a tourist attraction. As we drove on past the manor house, past a line of cottages, to the Dower House where Hugh and his wife had retreated, we were greeted by two peacocks and a peahen. They were closely followed by a group of busy feather-legged chickens. Hugh had once told me that it was a difficulty keeping their numbers up because of predatory foxes. The peacocks could look after themselves. It was necessary to coop up the chickens at night and a great nuisance rounding them up each evening.

We drove off the lane into the Dower House's gravel circular

apron with a flower bed in the middle. There was an old and dilapi-
dated dog kennel to one side of the house's imposing door. The brass
door knob and its companion knocker in the shape of a human face,
reminiscent of the knocker that Brasenose College is named after,
shone in the sunlight burnished by much rubbing. Having parked
the car, Tony knocked a couple of times, a solid sound on the oak
door. Eventually, after a pause, Hugh opened the door.

'Ah, very good to see you both. Come on in.'

'A wonderful door-knocker. It must be old,' I commented.

'Yes, the original. It goes with the house. Anthea's pet project is
to keep the thing brightly polished all the time. You might see her at
the break of day or in the evening at the elbow work.'

Anthea was his wife, a rather well-bred daughter of the gentry
who had attended art school in her twenties and had a remarkable
flair for painting and garden design. It was her inspiration and dedicated effort that had been behind the restoration of the gardens after
seventy or more years of neglect. The Fenmore gardens, originally
laid out by William Kent, now revived by Anthea, stood as arguably
the most beautiful gardens in the country. Hugh told us that she
and the head gardener, the wife of their tenant farmer, directed and
looked after the upkeep of the grounds.

As we went through the house's entrance into a hall, a small cloak-
room lay off to the left. Neither of us had coats, but I could see
walking boots and wellingtons, and, hanging up, an assortment of
country coats.

'Now,' said Hugh, 'where shall we go? We could use the drawing
room, or my apology for a library. I know, let's start in the library.'
He ushered us into the room. It was crowded with books. The shelves
were crammed. In one corner, away from the windows that gave out
on to a lawn and herbaceous flower beds, there were piles of books.
In the bay of the windows was a large table used quite obviously as a
working desk. It, too, had untidy piles of books on it and a typescript
that was clearly being checked or revised.

'Excuse the mess. I'm trying to perfect a speech I've written for a Lords debate next week. Once a working life peer, always a working peer. Perhaps I should disappear into the background and leave the battle to others. I do seem to waste my breath upon the midnight air. Still, it keeps me out of mischief. Anyway, come with me. I'll brew a pot of tea.'

He took us out of the library, along a corridor, and into a well-equipped modern kitchen. He made the tea, strolled over to a window, turned and said, 'Why don't we grab our mugs and wander in the gardens? We can get into the main gardens through that door in the wall. It's such a lovely afternoon.' He pointed to a white-painted door in the Cotswold stone wall.

Tony nodded approval and I said, 'Great idea. I'd love to walk around.'

'Good. Grab a mug and off we go. We can discuss matters as we wander.'

Going through the white-painted door in the wall was an Alice in Wonderland experience. Hugh lifted the latch, gave the bottom of the door a shove with his foot, and through we went. It gave on to a lawn, in the middle of which stood a tall dovecot; pigeons flurried to and fro. At one end there was a box maze. At the other end there was an ancient mulberry tree and four inset beds of hybrid roses. The walls of the dovecot were covered with climbing roses. Along the eastern side was a brick wall whose long bed afforded in the early autumn one of Fenmore's best displays, a crowded bed of brilliantly coloured dahlias. We continued down half a dozen steps into a huge walled vegetable garden. Then, turning left, we proceeded into an expansive arboured garden which led through a topiaried yew hedge to the lawn that led away from the manor house down to the river and the view beyond. In the distance, up towards the top of some rising fields, and roughly in the centre of one of them, was a pictur-esque classical folly, Fenmore's landscape eyecatcher. We sauntered along towards the other side of the lawn, sipping our tea.

'Now to the point, and to business. I think it's time to come clean. I'm sorry to drag you out here but I thought it important to be discreet and away from the noise and chatter of university life.

'I have to tell you that I am worried, deeply concerned. Certain pieces of intelligence have come to me. I'm told that the college is not a happy place. There are rumblings of discontent. Via a dear friend who sits in the House with me and who has a son at Magdalen, rumour, so far, has it that Willoughby is taking advantage of his position and is pushing through business by diktat. He grows more and more unpopular.

'Now I don't know how true these rumours are; but I want to find out.'

He paused. There was a silence. Neither Tony nor I quite knew what to say. At last, Hugh went on. 'The college is close to my heart. I can tell you, once you've been Principal, you can't rid yourself of its welfare. At least, you can't if you're someone like me.'

I thought to myself, but not if you are like Willoughby Morris; that is, self-serving, ambitious, autocratic, and without any visible feelings for place or people except a few cronies.

Tony said, 'But what is it your friend's son says?'

'You have to understand that the only reason I take any of this stuff seriously is because the boy works on the undergraduate newspaper *Cherwell*. Apparently they are sitting on a story about Willoughby that could be scandalous; which, of course, would not be good for the college's reputation if it's true. It might have to do with the college's finances.'

I thought back to my conversation with Susie, and, of course, it became immediately clear to me that if she knew something about Morris, then others at the newspaper would know too. I was calculating all the time how much I was prepared to tell Hugh Crammond. I decided, for the moment, to let Tony do the talking and so reveal his hand.

'Well, I think everyone's in agreement about that,' Tony

commented. 'If there is a scandal about finance, it could have a very damaging effect. Admissions might suffer. The college's status and reputation within the university would certainly suffer, and most importantly, it would be sure to affect funding. Donors would be none too keen to give to a corrupt institution.

'But this is all rumour. We don't know what the facts are. I've known Willoughby a long time. I've never known him to be corrupt. I can see he has a side to him that is irritating. He's too autocratic, pushy; he likes to get his own way. Yet you can't say he fails to get things done. His force and dynamism are dramatic.'

We left the lawn with its lengthy vista to the distant folly and passed into a small wood where a fast-flowing rill led to a long and leafy corridor of trees that, at its end, afforded a view of a statue of the winged Mercury on a stone plinth. It stood majestic, Mercury's pointed forefinger of his right hand raised above his head. In his left he held the caduceus, the sign of his herald's role, the wand with its two entwined serpents. The Fenmore sculptor had followed the design of the most famous of all Mercury sculptors, Giovanni di Bologna. In the shade of the over-arching trees we made our way towards the flying messenger of the gods.

Hugh said, 'We must establish the facts. What about the finance committee? Has anything got to them? Newspaper people, even if only students, are not going to sit on a scoop story forever. We have to know the facts; and we should do everything to play down any rumours that start circulating. We don't want any of this reaching either the national press or the mags like *Private Eye*. Johnny, what's your view?'

I was silent for a moment. 'Yes. We should keep things under wraps so far as is possible. But if there is anything in this, it'll come out anyway. We have to establish the basis of these rumours and see if they are true. Nothing has come to the notice of the finance committee. Maybe the bursar, Jeremy Eedes, knows something we don't. I suppose we'd better do some ferreting around.'

Hugh said, 'Yes, and we'd better do it quickly. If there is a story here, it will only hold for a couple of days. But we'd better keep this to ourselves, away from as many people as possible. Otherwise there is more likelihood of a leak, the more people who know … If we can establish that there are no grounds for any sort of allegations concerning corruption, then we can immediately rebuff any newspaper gossip. Perhaps you both could regard this as a priority and we could meet in Oxford Tuesday. What do you think?'

It was really a request that you could not turn down. Hugh Crammond was being his patrician best. You felt that you had to go along with his suggestions; otherwise you would appear churlish and uncooperative. You would be judged as not having the best interests of the college at heart.

We both nodded assent.

'A quarter to one in Quod. We can have an express lunch. It'll be on me. Is that OK?'

Again, Tony and I nodded agreement.

We reached Mercury and turned up into the wood on higher ground and made our way back to the house and the lawn. We passed in front of a colonnaded stone retreat where you could sit and look down on an ornamental pool full of goldfish. The path led upwards and we passed by a huge plinth with a mighty statue of a dying Gaul set on it. The depiction of this anguished warrior with downcast look, resting on one arm and struggling to rise was deeply moving. Hugh remarked, 'One of our best pieces here, don't you think. The folly of war; this is what it leads to, death in battle, a terrible waste of talent and life. That poor man is doomed, and he knows it.'

On the way back to Dower House, Tony said, 'This is going to be tricky. I reckon Eedes is a key man in all this. Do you think he knows anything we don't?'

'True,' Hugh commented, 'but you should know, Tony. After all, you're Vicegerent. You're supposed to be close to the Principal. You're supposed to have his ear.'

'As maybe, but you know what it's like. Willoughby never confides in me. He regards appointing me as his deputy as sufficient in itself as reward for promoting his cause to become Principal. He sees my position as convenient and ceremonial. The bursarship and the senior tutorship are positions of real power. So, he's in cahoots with them and ignores me. So far as he's concerned, I've served my purpose.'

'Yes,' I commented, 'it comes down to a troika. Eedes and Knowles will be loyal to the bitter end.'

Anthea revived the pot of tea and refilled our mugs. We talked pleasantly for ten minutes or so. Tony was eager to get back to his family and we left soon after.

Tony dropped me off a short distance from Holt. I felt like a walk and gave myself about three quarters of a mile of exercise as I made my way from the boulevard of St Giles to the High and so into college. I thought I would attend choral evensong in chapel. I often took recourse to the evening chapel services. The choir was world class. It was always in demand for broadcasts; its commercial CDs were extremely popular and their revenue added considerably to chapel and college funds. For me the chapel offered respite and a chance to meditate. I took my seat in one of the high seats reserved for fellows. I sank back into the space protected on each side by high wooden arm rests against which you could lean when standing up. In the dim light of the chapel lamps I felt completely private, free to empty my mind of worrying thoughts, or just able to contemplate against the background sound of fine organ and choral music my own personal problems. Each time I went to the chapel services I received a calming experience which I considered an enjoyable, valuable therapy.

That Sunday evening Donald Blake led the service. To the students he was known as the Reverend Doctor, or the singing chaplain because of his perfect pitch when intoning the services. There were two hymns for everyone to sing, one at the beginning and one at the end of the service. The Responses were by Radcliffe, the rest of the service by Howells, his *Collegium Regale* with the anthem by Tomkins, *My Beloved Spake*.

At the end, the choir, in pairs, descended from their pews, bowed towards the altar, and followed by Donald processed slowly out of the chapel. It was customary for the fellows to rise and leave before the rest of the congregation. I was the only one there and that I did, following close on Donald's heels. In the ante chapel Donald always stopped in order to talk with any of his congregation, or simply to bid them goodnight. I paused on my way out and remarked how beautiful the music had been and how refreshing for the soul the whole of the past three quarters of an hour had been. It was true; those of us who were leaving that old noble building had been privileged to take part in an ancient formulary of the Book of Common Prayer and to listen to a world-class performance of English cathedral music. Donald praised the choirmaster, the *Informatur Choristarum* who was also the fellow in music but who was always so busy with the chapel music that he was rarely seen about the college. He was not often seen at college meetings. Morris indulged his absences on account of the fame that the choir's reputation brought to the college. I knew that Morris, far from being in any way devout, simply regarded the choir as a marketing tool. Donald said, 'No, he's just wonderful, inspirational. He composes as well. He will soon belong to the long tradition of composers of the morning and evening offices, and, of course, anthems.'

He paused and broke off from what we were saying and turned to talk briefly to an old lady who regularly attended the services.

'By the way, Johnny, we must talk. Some news, or rather a rumour, has come to me about expense claims. An undergraduate mentioned it to me. If I may I'll give you a ring later this evening. Will you be in?'

I told him I would be at home and I would expect a call about nine. His remark intrigued me; it seemed that rumours were spreading.

I reached home at around a quarter past seven. In the middle of the evening my phone rang; it was Susie. 'Sorry,' she said, 'I don't usually ring my tutors at home but I thought I should. There's some urgency about what we were discussing.'

'Why? What's going on?' I asked. My doorbell rang. 'Hold on. The door. I'll just see who's there.'

The receiver was cordless and with it in my left hand I went to the door, opened it to find Est standing there. I could not suppress a shiver of delight. I could hardly be bothered with Susie.

'Come in. How lovely to see you.' I kissed her on both cheeks. I gestured at the phone in my left hand and said to Susie, 'Sorry. Yes, go on.'

'Well, I just wanted to say, to tell you, that there must have been a leak from somewhere, perhaps even from our office, and that there is a lot of talk about corruption in high places. We'll have to go with this story or lose it. And the nationals will be on to it in no time at all.'

'No, of course, I understand. Thanks for phoning. You'll have to print. But be careful. There will be a battle, obstinate and long. I'll think on these things and get in touch tomorrow. This is all going to be very difficult. Look, I've now got someone with me. I'd better ring off.'

I replaced the phone and turned to Est. She stood in front of me, tall, elegant, refreshed by walking in the open air.

'I got tired of writing,' she said. 'So, I decided to go for a walk. Thus I end up here. I've always wondered what your pad was like and on the off-chance came this way and rang your doorbell. I find you in. How lovely.'

13

I felt the breath taken from me. There was Est standing on my doorstep, come by her own volition. I could scarcely believe it. My sleeping fantasies reawakened. I saw our relationship becoming more and more intimate. She had never been to my house before. I was amazed, pleased and in a strange way frightened. It seemed to me that it could not be true and that this piece of natural good fortune would crash to ruin. Yet, she stepped towards me, kissed my cheeks and nuzzled her face against mine. She turned her face to mine and murmured, 'Johnny, I'm so glad to be here.' If anything her remark scared me even more.

'Come, have a drink,' I said. 'What will it be? I'm going to have a Scotch.'

'Just fizzy water, or a tonic, if you've got it.'

'Are you sure; a little stronger?'

'No, I'm sure. Today I abstain. I'll feel so much better, physically and morally. A bit of discipline; a little Buddhist, perhaps, but very good for me.'

I gave her a glass of tonic water and I poured myself a Scotch and soda, the Famous Grouse.

'I'm not as virtuous as you. I'll sin and take the consequences.'

Thus the conversation took a flirtatious turn. I felt I could have developed its direction into highly erotic territory. I gave into caution and resisted. Est would have to lead the way.

I told her about Susie's call and about Donald's promise to phone me later.

'A leak. That's more like it,' she said. 'Things are heating up. I like it. I sniff scandal in the air.'

We decided not to discuss the subject any more until we had heard what Donald had to report. It was necessary to stay put in my house until he rang, and so I ferreted around for something to eat. Est continued her abstemious mode towards eating as well as drinking. I found some anchovy fillets, black olives and sun-dried tomatoes in my fridge. I oven-toasted some thin slices of wholemeal bread, opened a small triangle packet of Brie cheese and we settled for those small offerings as something to eat that evening. In the event, they were all we needed. We became so engrossed in the emerging scandal that we needed no more. We fed on conjecture and gossip.

Donald kept his word. It was about half past nine when the phone rang. It was him as we had expected and what he had to report was significant.

'So, I had this long chat with one of my chapel clerks, Lindsay Croft; he reads French and Russian. He said that he had to photocopy some music sheets. The chapel office's copier wasn't working. He went to the college office and asked one of the secretaries if he could use their machine. He started his copying and noticed two or three sheets of A4 lying on the floor, half hidden under the copier. He picked them up and couldn't help reading what was printed on the reverse sides. At first, after the first few lines, he thought he shouldn't go on, but it was so intriguing that he couldn't resist.'

Donald at that point paused and coughed. I said into the mouthpiece, 'Are you OK, Donald? You sound as if you're choking. Is it as bad as that? Have you breathed in too much incense?'

'No, it's all right. Just a tickle in my chest. I'll be fine. I'll survive.'

He went on and described the A4 sheets as part of the minutes of the finance committee meeting. They had negligently been dropped and not noticed. The word *confidential* was clearly typed on the right-hand top of the page. Even so Croft had read on. After all, he had said, anything lying around on the floor for anyone to see ceases to be confidential. What it said and made very clear was that someone on the committee was extremely worried because he or she was convinced that the Principal was claiming far too much in expenses. The sum so far in the current financial year when there was virtually another six months to go, exceeded any previous year's total by approximately 50 per cent. There were listed the usual entitled expenses, entertainment, travel mostly within the UK, but there were unspecified claims under general, catch-all headings. The minutes stated that all expenses should be itemised. They also pointed out that when the committee member had brought up the issue with the Principal, he had blustered and told off the committee member for not taking the larger view. The sum showing so far in the accounts was insignificant compared with the amount of work he was doing, and, so far as fundraising was concerned, peanuts. The broader view should be taken. The promise of things to come made such complaint and scrutiny seem meagre and mean. He quoted Shakespeare about the 'expectation of plenty'.

The final paragraph which was interrupted mid-sentence made it clear that the committee's deputy chairman had formally asked the bursar, Jeremy Eedes, who was also *ex officio* of the committee, to produce a detailed and itemised account of the Principal's expenses; 'The analysis should run up to the last day of July and should take into account all…' and there the minutes broke off because a fresh page had been reached.

'So, Croft showed this to you? Where are the pages now? Have you got them?'

'No, he didn't bring them with him. I assume they're in his room. I should think he's bound to have shown them to friends. Wouldn't you if you were in his place? It's a marvellous piece of gossip and scandal. You'd hardly be able to keep it to yourself.'

'Thus the contagion spreads,' I commented.

We decided that, first thing in the morning, the bursar, Eedes, should be informed of this breach of confidentiality, this leak of information into, at that moment, a semi-public forum. Donald wished me a good night and commended me to the angels' safekeeping.

I turned to Est who had been listening, trying to follow what had been said. I explained the details of Donald's news.

'Now, what will Willoughby do? Eedes is bound to tell him. He'll know very quickly. Can't wait to see what happens.'

14

Donald's call provided the main conversational topic for the rest of the evening. We made progress; but Est and I grew more and more intimate, more and more engrossed in each other. We explored our family histories and reminisced about our earlier years. She even went so far as to describe her last boyfriend, a chemist from UCL in London who had been far too sexually aggressive. She sloughed him off. He had been persistent but finally she rounded on him and they had a stand-up row in the middle of Marks and Spencer at Marble Arch. She had humiliated him beyond any redemption for the relationship, and blazing with fury she had marched out of the shop to a small ripple of applause. In hindsight, it was more than faintly amusing; at the time it was blisteringly painful.

We parted at about eleven thirty. She would not allow me to accompany her. We embraced and kissed. She stepped back and then came forward again. That time our kissing was passionate. She whispered, 'No, Johnny, not tonight. That's enough. I'm not ready.' She kissed me again, turned and left.

Naturally I was disappointed. I put *Die Zauberflöte* in the CD player and in doing so I remembered that there was going to be a concert at the weekend in the great Tom Quad of Christ Church. I would ask her to go with me to it.

The following morning I was busy with tutorials. I met Est at lunch. As usual, the SCR was crowded. Everyone came to lunch; few attended dinner. Est, too, had been teaching all morning. I told her about my idea for the Christ Church concert.

'So, it's in the open air. What's the forecast like? I bet it will rain.'

'I had a look. It's not too bad, unsettled, but with any luck…'

Est said, 'OK. What's it all for?'

'It's a big concert in aid of setting up scholarships for New Zealand students from Christchurch, New Zealand. The city's been devastated by earthquakes over the last year. The college here thought it a good idea to give some help. Kiri Te Kanawa will sing. She's really retired but she's going to sing some Mozart for this concert. Should be good.'

'OK. I'd love to. Let's keep our fingers crossed.'

'Right. Saturday. We can have a late supper. We'll think about that later.'

Donald came in late for lunch. He helped himself at the buffet and sat down next to Est and opposite me.

'I suppose you know what's happened this morning,' Donald said. 'Everyone seems to be talking about it.'

Est looked surprised. I commented that I did not know what he meant. He then revealed that there was an article about the college in the undergraduate newspaper, *Cherwell*. Donald said that it stated generally that there were problems in the college to do with governance, that changes in the executive structure had taken place and that the Principal had either been given powers to act decisively or unilaterally, or he had assumed those powers without meeting any opposition. The reporter wrote that there was an ongoing investigation on the part of the newspaper to find out what the position really was. It mentioned that there had been a leak, a breach of confidentiality that showed that the college was worried by excessive claims for expenses. The article did not specify that any particular individual was responsible. It did describe the incident of the discovered minute sheets of the finance committee.

As Donald finished telling us what had happened that morning, Morris came in. He was very late for lunch but the steward sat him down at the end of one of the long tables, poured him a glass of water, and the two whispered obviously about what Willoughby wanted for lunch. It was a long-held custom that the Principal was not a member of the SCR by right but was a guest. That is why the steward or one of the waiters always greeted him.

'Morris doesn't look too happy,' Donald commented.

'No, he can't be too best pleased. Things must appear to be catching up with him,' I said.

Est warned, 'Whatever you do, don't feel sorry for him.'

Most of our colleagues were finishing lunch or had already gone. Jeremy Eedes was still there. He got up and went to sit with Morris. Willoughby looked flushed and furious. Eedes leant towards him and they spoke in low tones. At one point Morris threw down his napkin in exasperation and banged his fist on the table. The bursar leant back and remained silent. It was clear that the Principal was not enjoying himself.

As we left Est said, 'He's really cross – beginning to look like the stag at bay. We must see how this develops.'

'Yes,' said Donald. 'It looks as though the slow fuse has been lit. There might well be some minor explosions before the big one. Who knows?' He went towards the chapel.

I turned to Est. 'I'll get some tickets for the concert on Saturday. I'll do that right now. It should be good.'

As we said goodbye and went towards our rooms, Morris came out of the SCR with Eedes. Morris was red-faced and talking emphatically. The bursar walked with him, listening. I would have liked to be privy to that conversation.

Later that afternoon Susie rang me in my college room. I was in the middle of a session with one of my doctoral students.

'We had to publish something or we would have missed the scoop. Now everyone's on to it. The nationals have been ringing us all day. You wouldn't have thought that the promise of some minor financial scandal in an obscure Oxford college would elicit such interest; but it's the times. Here we have something symptomatic of the state of the nation, after all the MP expenses excesses. Anyway, sorry, but that's the way the cards fell. There will of course be more. I'll keep you informed.'

'Thanks, Susie, I'd appreciate that.'

'Got to rush. See you soon.'

15

Morris called an extraordinary governing body meeting the following day. It was scheduled for 5 p.m. A good number of the fellows were there. Jacob Black came in and sat next to me. He muttered to me about the inconvenience. What was all the fuss about? Why was Morris so exercised? Perhaps he had a guilty conscience. Est was there, and Tony Gill, Bennet, Mayhew, both the bursar and senior tutor. I was surprised to see Naish sitting next to Knowles; after all he was not a member of the governing body. Only the college secretary, outside the membership of the fellowship, attended to take minutes. There were one or two notable absentees, mostly scientists who did not usually have much interest in college politics.

The Principal blustered in, his gown flying, falling off one shoulder. He hitched it irritably up to a more comfortable position and sat heavily down in his chair. Eedes, who was secretary to the governing body, stood and announced the purpose of the extraordinary meeting. The reputation of the college was under attack, the integrity of its members and its committees were being maligned in the press, and therefore the Principal considered it best to hold a meeting to decide what measures should be taken to avoid such negative publicity in future and combat the present malign charges.

Jacob Black stood up. 'M-mister S-secretary, P-principal, I s-spy a st-stranger in our midst.' He looked directly at Brendan Naish. 'Mr N-naish should not be here.'

Timothy Knowles spoke up. 'Mr Naish is here as my personal assistant. His role is confidential.' Brendan Naish looked embarrassed.

He looked around and then kept his eyes focused firmly on the floor in front of him.

Jacob responded. 'Nevertheless, h-he is not a m-member of this body.'

Morris stood up; Eedes sat down. Ill temper showed itself clearly on his brow. He almost shouted. 'Professor Black is quite right. This is a governing body meeting, for goodness' sake. Nobody should be here except official fellows. Mr Naish, you will have to leave.' Morris was annoyed; and he was questioning the judgement of his close ally, Knowles. To my mind, that showed how bad things were. I calculated that we were in for a pretty bad time.

The Principal sat down and Eedes stood up again. 'The Principal will speak of his concerns for the college's reputation. Principal.'

It was all rather farcical. The two of them were up and down like yo-yos. There was no need for the Principal to have sat down; he should have carried straight on. He was obviously agitated. He stood up again and addressed the meeting.

'Firstly I should say that I'm disappointed that many are not here who should be here. This is an extraordinary meeting called because of extraordinary circumstances. It's important. People should turn up.' He did not seem to realise that those he was admonishing were not there. His indignation was wasted. 'The main point is that there has been a serious breach of confidentiality. Some pieces of A4 copying paper that had been accidently left in the office have been circularised, given to the public eye. This will not do. All college papers are confidential. Whoever is responsible has behaved reprehensibly. It exposes us. Our linen is not dirty but nevertheless even our clean linen should not be given a public airing. Our reputation is paramount. We must not let ourselves down. Reputation is everything. I suppose it's useless asking for the person who has passed on the information printed on that piece of paper to own up. It's too much to ask.' A note of sarcasm sounded in his voice. I could hear JOB muttering, 'Anything left lying on a floor, for all to see, is not confidential by definition.'

Morris detected the undertone of muttering and stared at Jacob, but thought better of referring directly to JOB and reprimanding him. What he went on to say was entirely predictable. We should deny any suspicion of scandal. The college operated in a well-regulated way. Everything to do with expenses was overseen by the bursar. We were vigilant over any irregularities. What suspicions there were, what needling charges were being made about abuses, were not founded on facts. All college members should do what-ever was in their power to stop rumour. He had heard that besides certain national newspapers reporting the gossip, *Private Eye* was going to run an in-depth article on the college's finances. If we were approached, we should make no comment.

At that point, Jane interrupted and said that in her experience to offer statically no comment as an answer to a journalist's questions, simply made matters worse. Morris, who was visibly getting more and more irritated, insisted on no comment.

Willoughby was quite a big man who inclined to corpulence. Agitation made him sweat. His top lip, I could see, was covered in perspiration. He threw back his head to emphasise a point and I saw the glisten. I could see, too, his collar was damp. Donald raised his hand and signalled that he wanted to speak. Morris waved the gesture aside.

'I don't want any discussion at this point. I simply want to make sure the rules are clear and lines are drawn. No one should confer with those outside the college about this. The less said the better even inside the college. It's important to close ranks. The press and the public must get nothing from us but silence.'

He turned abruptly away from the table just as Jacob said loudly enough for him to hear, 'The M-Mafia. Omerta, the c-code of silence.'

Morris chose to ignore his remark and strode out. Jeremy Eedes followed immediately in his trail.

Outside Naish was waiting for Knowles. I heard him say, 'I didn't think you'd be long. The Principal was in no mood for a long debate.'

Est and I stepped into the quad. I shrugged off my gown, wrapped it into a bundle and put it under my arm. Est kept hers on. We walked towards the chapel. Donald was briefly held in conversation with Timothy Knowles and Naish.

'Why on earth should that awful Naish ever think that he could sit in on a governing body meeting. He must be really stupid; at least totally insensitive. Do you think Timothy encouraged him, or even sanctioned him?'

'I've no idea. It's just bizarre.'

'Anyway, the main question has been begged. What's all the fuss about? If there's no scandal, why should the Principal be at all agitated? He should just come out in the open and say the leak and rumour are both nonsense. Everything is as it should be and show the evidence. Why hasn't he done that?'

'Presumably because there is something to hide.'

Donald joined us at that moment and heard my remark. 'Precisely. Of course there is. Otherwise Willoughby wouldn't be so rattled. The terriers of the press are on to him. He's got to run and hide in his hole.'

Est smiled and said, 'I like your image, the old fox on the run. Still, you're not giving one of your sermons now. To use another cliché, there's no smoke without fire.'

'Yes, you'll have to forgive me, Est. I like to practise my rhetorical tropes and use them later. You've just been a victim of my rehearsal.' He laughed and then followed up seriously, 'The wretched Naish was saying that Holt's embarrassment is now all over the university. Willoughby has little hope of closing everything down. And Knowles said that someone on the finance committee must be blowing the embers into fire. Oops, sorry, Est. I'm doing it again.'

I said, 'Well let's keep each other informed. Someone should keep Hugh Crammond in the picture. I'll get Tony Gill to give him a ring.'

Donald went on and into the chapel. The organ scholar had been waiting for him at the door.

'I have a seminar at five. It's bound to go on until six thirty, a quarter to seven. Are you dining in this evening?'

'Well I thought I would since I was teaching most of the day today. I put my name down.'

Est said, 'In that case I'll talk to the steward and see if I can squeeze in late. I'm sure he'll do it.'

'For you, anything. He has a soft spot for you.'

Est waved a hand at me and laughed. 'It's only a dull old college dinner I'm asking for. Nothing else. I'll see you later then.'

16

I rang Tony. He did not answer his landline, but I raised him on his mobile phone; he was on his way to the High Street shops on some domestic errand.

'Yes, I agree,' he said. 'I have the same thoughts as you. I was going to phone Hugh the moment I get back. So, don't worry, it will be done. What transpires reflects more or less exactly what he told us.'

'Good. Ask him what, if anything, we should do.'

'Thy will be done,' Tony intoned in a passable imitation of Donald. He liked to mimic Donald's priestly delivery. He was not a believer but he did attend chapel occasionally as an admirer of church cathedral music and he was always amused by the pious tone and accents that Donald used in the recital of the church offices.

Later I took dinner in hall with Est. Disappointingly she had to meet the train due in at Oxford station at twenty past nine; her parents were coming for the weekend to stay at the Old Bank Hotel in the High. On Saturday evening they had been invited to dine in All Souls by an old colleague of her father. So, it was not until Saturday evening that I saw her again. The Christ Church concert started at seven thirty. We met at a quarter to seven in Quod; she had a martini, I had a medicinal Laphroaig. The spirits seemed precisely right for a chilly evening.

The weather was in fact awful for an open-air concert. There had been heavy showers, one torrential, and the temperature had dropped. What had been anticipated as a warm summer evening turned out to be a decidedly cool, blustery, inclement one. We went into Christ Church through the Oriel Square entrance. The bowler-hatted porter inspected our tickets, touched the brim of his bowler and passed us through the wrought-iron gates. As we walked through Peckwater Quad, a great gust of wind whirled round us. Est stopped and shivered. 'I'm going to put on my coat. I don't care about convention. I'm going to keep warm.'

'Likewise,' I said. I wrestled myself into my Aigle waterproof anorak. The published information for the concert instructed that dress was formal, evening attire, no umbrellas. It was obvious that few people were taking notice of that stipulation and were wrapped up in winter defences against rain and wind. The brave minority kept to the rules, men wearing dinner jackets, women in long evening dresses. Rashest of all were some who even brought umbrellas; but they were unusable. Even the largest and strongest would have been blown inside out by the force of the unpredictable wind.

In Tom Quad, the largest, most expansive quad of any Oxford or Cambridge college, seats had been laid out facing the east side. There at the end of the huge sunken quad, next to the entrance of the cathedral above, a covered, domed pavilion opened out to the audience, reminiscent of the covered stages at pop concerts where you might hear Radiohead or Foals. On either side rose banks of loudspeakers that formed the sound system to broadcast the music and Dame Kiri's voice to the widely dispersed open-air audience. Fortunately the rain had stopped a couple of hours before and the wind had helped dry the seats, but here and there people were wiping down the chairs with tissues or the sleeves of their coats.

Est and I found our seats, in the middle of the quad almost next to the statue of Mercury in his central lily pond. There were about five minutes to go before the concert began. We sat and watched the audience assemble. I said to Est, 'The naked Mercury, winged helmet and heels, holding his caduceus, ready to fly off to warm Aegean or Mediterranean seas. I don't blame him; the sooner the better.'

Clouds moved swiftly from the south-west. The wind descended in great bursts of feverish, chaotic activity into the quad. It whirled round what had been transformed into a vast wind bowl. Est and I hunched up in our coats. 'Feel my hands,' she said. They were, like mine, freezing cold.

Seated in the row in front of us was an old Classics don I recognised. He was tall and aquiline with a long bridge to his nose. He was dressed in black tie, his wife in a long evening dress. His two daughters, both students at one of the colleges of the university, who I knew were twins, were also dressed formally. They wore light chiffon dresses and had silk shawls around and over their shoulders. No concessions had been made to the appalling weather. The girls possessed a slender, elegant youthful beauty, clear complexions, soft and shining shoulder-length hair, a minimum of make-up cleverly judged, and each showed a version of their father's nose shape. The long bridge gave them a formal elegance that Italian renaissance painters depicted in their portraits of noble ladies. As the concert proceeded, they both shivered visibly and their necks turned blue. Their old parents seemed impervious to the cold.

Ahead of us I saw Willoughby Morris. He was standing up, looking round, surveying the crowd as though searching for some latecomer who was just about to make it before the performance began. I recognised, though, a particular trait of his, which was to make sure that he showed himself off in public. It annoyed me. He always had to be seen.

I huddled towards Est as a particularly fierce blast of wind racketed up and down in Christ Church's great quad. 'Look at Willoughby. Is he here with his wife?'

Est responded to my body's contact and warmth. She whispered, 'I can't see. Isn't that just typical of the man? He simply has to be seen.'

He walked a few paces round the central pond. He was in black tie but at least had the good sense to wear an overcoat on top of his suit. The wind tousled his hair and he looked red-faced as though his blood pressure had risen because he had had too many Scotches. He did not see us. His gaze went over our heads. He was like one of those annoying people at a drinks party who look over your shoulder to see if there is someone else more interesting, more important, more fashionable to talk to. You could sense his detection powers trying to find the Vice-Chancellor or some minister of state, someone who might say, 'Oh, there's Willoughby Morris, Principal of Holt. We must invite him to dinner.'

The orchestra assembled. Kiri was to be accompanied by the BBC concert orchestra who would additionally play some Brahms, Mozart and Beethoven. As they took their seats, Willoughby sat down. I could see that he was with his wife, Timothy Knowles and Brendan Naish.

'That's a little party to be avoided during the interval,' I said to Est. She agreed. The orchestra fixed their musical scores to the stands and started to tune up.

The concert began with a couple of orchestral pieces by Strauss and Holst. There was a break in the clouds and the westering sun shone briefly but gloriously on the sandy walls at the east end of the quad. The stone seemed suddenly to radiate a glowing, beautiful warmth in the sunlight but it did not reach the audience; too soon it was gone and greyness returned. Then Kiri Te Kanawa appeared from the back of the stage. The conductor took her hand and led her to the front where she stood and smiled to the audience.

The house was not full. The seats to the sides were sparsely populated. Yet on such a night as that, it was no surprise. The wind continued to rush sporadically into the bowl of Tom Quad. Kiri was superb. The programme notes told that she was sixty-eight, emerging from retirement for the good deed that she was performing. Tall, immaculate in a long white gown, fortunately long-sleeved in the chilly air, she raised one hand to the heavens and smiled with a gesture of resignation towards the elements. The conductor introduced her. She spoke about her beloved New Zealand and of the devastation caused by the Christchurch earthquakes. She then embarked on her recital of a selection of famous opera arias. Her voice had lost none of its pitch and power. She began with 'Vado, ma dove?' from *Die Zauberflöte*. As she finished and turned away from the audience to confer with the orchestra's leader, a gale of wind hurled itself round the quad. Sheet music from the music stands was blown away; musicians chased their scores as the white sheets soared like seagulls into the air. The conductor and Dame Kiri stood powerless to help. Some minutes later order was restored. The sheet music had mostly been put back in its proper place and the players composed themselves. Two more arias followed and then Kiri embarked on 'Un bel di vedremo' from *Madame Butterfly*. She was no more than a few phrases in when she moved to stand sideways to the audience, and then again after a few moments she signalled to the conductor to stop.

She apologised for the pause and spoke closely into the microphones. There were two standing upright and parallel but they had blown apart and had twisted in the wind. 'Apologies and please excuse me. Bill, is it all right if I reposition the mikes. Otherwise I stand crab-wise.' Bill, who was obviously the sound engineer, was monitoring the performance from a spot just in front of Mercury. He watched the recital through a camera that projected the concert on to two enormous screens either side of the main platform. At the same time he wore earphones, and checked and controlled sound quality.

'Yes, yes. Do. That's OK,' he shouted back. Kiri jerked the slender mike stands back into position. She tested them with a professional touch, tapping them and speaking carefully at them. Bill shouted, his voice getting lost in the wind, 'OK, that's fine. On we go.'

By the interval, we were miserably cold. Est had endured enough and as Kiri left the stage, it was clear that she would not be singing in the second half.

Est said, 'Let's go. The weather's too bad. I'm frozen.' I eagerly agreed. We made our way towards the ancient, massive gates of Christ Church's main entrance. They had been locked and bolted shut on the assumption that no one would leave until the end. Two stewards and one bowler-hatted porter were explaining that the gates would not be opened until the end. Various people expostulated with them. I saw one irate old fellow of Magdalen gesticulating with his umbrella and shouting that they had no right to lock us in. Suddenly someone began to chant, 'Out, out, out,' which was taken up by the rest of the growing crowd. About seventy or eighty people were chanting. The staff capitulated; the bolts were shifted, the huge key wielded and the lock turned, the great gates pushed open and with a cheer and a chorus of hand-clapping, the disaffected crowd spilled out into St Aldate's. It was a mediaeval post-siege scene. The poor BBC Symphony orchestra was left to play out the rest of the concert to a faithful few who were game enough to stay. I noticed that the aquiline don, his wife and two frostbitten daughters were still hovering around their seats, unsure of whether they should stay or go. I had lost sight of Willoughby.

I remarked to Est as we walked quickly away in order to restore some circulation to our chilled bodies: 'Well, I wonder what Morris and his little party are doing. I didn't see them.'

Est replied, 'Oh, I saw them making straight for the bar. They'll probably stay there until they're thrown out.'

The programme notes had shown that the interval was a ludicrously long three quarters of an hour. Canapés and drinks were to be served in a marquee set up in Peckwater Quad. That would have been fine for a sultry summer's evening, but utter madness for conditions on that day.

'He'll warm himself with a few more whiskies,' I said. 'Elizabeth will get more and more drunk and they'll escape through the back gate into Oriel Square. He won't go back to the music for sure. Basically he's a philistine anyway.'

Est agreed. 'Yes, he's not here for the music or the Christchurch fund. He's just here for self-publicity. But if I were him, I'd be trying to keep a low profile at this particular time. I reckon he has no judgement; or he just thinks he can brazen it out.'

'It's more like the latter. Why has he embraced Naish? That's too strong a word; it brings up awful images. But he seems to have accepted Naish. He doesn't question his role as Timothy's adviser. I would if I were him. Naish is a pushy little manipulator who doesn't know his place. He's going to get away with anything Knowles and Morris allow him. He's got to be watched.'

We made our way up St Aldate's, through Cornmarket Street, to the Randolph Hotel. The usual Saturday night crowd was in town. Noisy youths roamed the city centre. The fashion shops had left stacks of cardboard packing boxes on the pavement outside their shops. One small gang of yobs ran along kicking the boxes into the middle of the street. There was no one to stop them.

'You would have thought there would be community officers around on a Saturday evening. None in sight,' Est complained.

We arrived at the shabby hotel. It was as if it were preserved in aspic; it had moved so slowly with the times that it had only reached the 1960s. It was drab and gloomy. At least it was warm. We went to the Star Bar. Once again that evening I ordered a whisky for myself and a dry martini for Est. The young barmaid poured my Scotch; I added my own water. She then poured a wine glass full of dry vermouth. 'That'll be thirteen pounds seventy-five.'

I pushed the vermouth back across the counter towards her. 'No, I ordered a dry martini.'

'That's it – a dry martini vermouth. Look, it says so on the bottle.'

'Look, I don't want to tell you your job, but a dry martini is one part gin, two parts dry vermouth, a green olive and in this case, since you're not mixing it in a shaker, a cube of ice.'

'Oh, I've never made one of them before.'

'Have you had any training? Are you new to this job?'

'S'right. They're short-staffed. Asked me to do it. I usually help the rooms manager.'

At last, after my tuition, Est was given her cocktail. When I reached for my wallet to pay, I noticed that the bill charged me for a glass of vermouth, a whisky and a glass of gin. That way it came to considerably more than a Scotch and a dry martini. I complained to my trainee behind the bar. I think she understood and consequently called for the duty manager, who, full of apologies and appeals for me to bear with her, adjusted the bill. We made our way home to my house.

That was the first night Est and I slept together. There was no awkwardness about her staying. It just happened. It seemed quite natural. There was no discussion. The situation evolved. Late on towards midnight, Est simply said, 'It's very late. I want to stay with you. It's time. I'm ready.' Of the two of us, the one who was not ready was me. It came as a small but significant shock because I had not expected her initiative. I soon adjusted because, of course, it was what I wanted as well. As Samuel Pepys so often said, 'And so to bed.' The plots and devices that I had long harboured in my mind, the strategies for seducing Est into my bed came to nothing. They were simply not needed; and they probably would not have worked anyway. She, with superb confidence and assurance, led the way; I followed.

17

The next morning, Sunday, we rose late. I made some coffee and we decided to stroll down to Jericho where there were one or two fashionable cafés. The weather had changed and suited our mood well. The sun shone and the temperature quickly soared. Neither of us mentioned the suddenness of our liaison in bed that night. It stood as a simple fact. On the way to Manos's, a splendidly casual café, run by a young Greek who gave his name to the house, I bought a newspaper, the *Sunday Telegraph*. We both ordered cappuccinos and croissants and sat at a window table that looked out on to the street. I laid the paper out on the table, took in the front-page headlines, and turned to the inside pages. There, on page seven of the home news was a short article on Holt College, Oxford. 'Oxford college expenses scandal,' ran the headline. Briefly it mentioned unrest and resentment in the college over the executive dictatorship of the Principal and referred to alleged but unspecified expenses abuse. It quoted the bursar of Holt College, Dr Jeremy Eedes, as saying, 'There is no truth in the charges levelled at the Principal. Government of this institution is collegiate, by a number of committees if you like. The Principal is simply chairman of most of those committees. Expense claims are legitimate and fall into line with the practice of all the other colleges of the university.' The Principal was unavailable for comment.

Est, holding my arm, leant over and read the piece. 'The seed is sown,' she said. 'Now it's in the newspaper everything will ratchet up. So much for Willoughby's wish.'

I commented, 'If there is a serious leak, then it'll get bigger.'

'What do you mean, if. Of course there's a leak. How else would this story have started? I wonder where it comes from – who it is. We must watch and listen, try to work it out. Have you got any ideas?'

'Well, what about Donald, the crafty chaplain? Or Brendan Naish?'

'No, I don't think it's Donald. He's not all that crafty and it's not his style. Naish? He really hasn't been around long enough to be worked up about everything and, what's more, it wouldn't be in his interests; he's of the other party. We'll have to think again.'

I remarked to Est that I was beginning to feel as if I were a bit-part actor in a Shakespeare play. Rumour and speculation were rife; reputation and honour were being weighed in the scales. Patiently we had to wait for the resolution.

Both of us had to prepare for the week ahead but we were in no hurry. Eventually we walked leisurely back to my house. We then walked into college.

That night we slept apart. Monday was the first day of the seventh week of the Oxford eight-week term. It was going to be busy. Monday and Tuesday were teaching days for me; I had a full schedule of tutorials and seminar groups. On Wednesday there was the usual governing body meeting; and then on Thursday in the social calendar I had been invited, with a guest if I liked, to a short Mozart opera, *Il Re Pastore*, not often performed, in the garden of the Warden of New College. Naturally I was going to ask Est to join me. Thursday and Friday I would spend writing. The opera was going to be an excellent break, an interval on Thursday, from my desk.

When I arrived in college first thing on Monday morning, I found a note waiting in my pigeonhole in the lodge. The assistant porter on duty drew my attention to it; he said that the Principal's secretary had put a note in one or two pigeonholes and had asked him to make sure the recipients picked them up as they came in.

I wandered into the main quad and opened the envelope. It was a note from Willoughby Morris that summoned me to an urgent meeting with him at midday; could I make sure I was there because it was very important. It was a nuisance. I had to go to my room and phone a graduate student who was due to come at noon and rearrange a time for her. I wondered who else had been told to attend but I thought it would be inappropriate to ask the porter who the other people were who had received the note.

At just after twelve o'clock I knocked on the Principal's study door. Morris called out, 'Come in.' As I turned the door knob, Knowles and Naish appeared. They followed me in. Morris was seated behind his desk and in the room already were Eedes, Donald and Frank Bradshaw. It was an inner core of the body politic of the college. I worked out that it was obvious why Eedes and Knowles were there; it was by virtue of their positions. Donald was there because he was chaplain; and I supposed that Frank represented the scientists and I the humanities. Notable by his absence was Tony Gill. Why Naish was present was beyond me.

We all sat down in a jumbled half-circle in front of Willoughby at his desk, and then he pronounced, 'I'm sorry to bring you all together like this but it is very important and crucial for the college's reputation. Brendan here, in a secretarial capacity, will take notes of this meeting; not official minutes. I would rather that this was seen as off the record. But I shall value your views.

'I must tell you that last evening Hugh Crammond telephoned me and asked me what was going on. His phone had not stopped ringing since the middle of yesterday morning. The majority of calls were from Old Members wondering about the report in the *Telegraph*, but one was from the Minister for Higher Education. Naturally he didn't like that. The Old Members were trying enough but to have to explain matters to the Minister of State was really difficult. He said he didn't know much of what was going on although he had heard rumours, mainly from students.'

Willoughby stressed that we should all emphasise the college's integrity if we were called upon to comment at all on the rumours.

It was deeply necessary to underline that individuals, whether it was the bursar or indeed even himself as chairman of the finance committee, were people of the highest integrity, all doing their respective jobs for the benefit of the college as a whole and society in the wider context. I detected that he was beginning a campaign to strengthen his position and defend himself from further attack.

'I have to remind you,' he continued, 'of what I warned about the other day. The issue of *Private Eye*. Since the story has reached the national press, I know from a journalistic source in London that one of their investigative writers is here in Oxford digging up information about the college. The question is, what should we do? You, gathered here, might have some useful ideas. Personally, I think we should lock down as much as possible. Anyone who leaks college information to the press should be asked to resign. This is for the good of the college.'

Donald was the first to respond. 'Firstly, might I say, with all due respect to Brendan, that what you are talking about is essentially a college affair and therefore should be a matter just for the fellows. Brendan, in his own interest, should not be party to discussions of this nature. It puts him in a difficult and vulnerable position.

'Secondly, I'm not sure what all the fuss is about. If the college has nothing to hide, as I'm sure you would protest, then who cares what gossip there is. We can be utterly transparent and justify our position. If the contrary is true, then we deserve to be publicly admonished because we are publicly accountable.'

Morris did not like this. 'I know we can rely on Brendan's good judgement. I don't want to discuss it. That is my decision, an executive one, which I am entitled to make. As for transparency, all institutions must be allowed to conduct some of their business confidentially. I think everyone would agree to that.'

I felt obliged to follow that up. 'Maybe there are one or two areas where that is true, but not to do with finance. Accounts must be clear, transparent and, of course, audited. We should not be afraid to have scrutiny of our accounts and therefore of our system of allowances and expenses. We know that the public at the present time is very sensitive over expenses to do with public institutions.'

Willoughby was not happy.

'I don't want the press prying into our business. You never know where it all might end. They have no discretion, no judgement based on years of practice within the college. They can't hope to get it right.'

There was a pause, a brief, rather awkward silence. Frank broke it. 'Actually, the finances should be very simple. I don't know what you're worried about. Publish. Let them see. We've nothing to hide.'

'No,' Willoughby said firmly and defiantly, 'that's not the way to do it. It would be a surrender to their impertinence. We must maintain our integrity and not have them prying into our private business.'

Frank was not going to be put down. 'But in a sense, it's not private. We are very much a public institution. We have autonomy to order and organise our affairs based on centuries of precedence but all that does not obscure the fact that we receive funding from the government both directly and indirectly. I think we'll make matters far worse for ourselves if we fail to be completely open. People will think we have something to hide.'

'Preposterous,' Willoughby virtually shouted. 'They cannot impugn our honesty. We must not give into pressure from journalists. They are cheapskate opportunists.'

I thought that was amusingly outrageous. Willoughby Morris in the past had courted the press and had entertained several editors of national newspapers to dinner in college. He fawned upon them for favours. He was behaving like some pop star that has encouraged journalists in the past to write eulogies and then complains when justifiable stories are printed about misconduct. I was becoming more and more convinced that we were listening to protestations that were supposed to be hiding some personal malfeasance.

The debate then proceeded to limp along, no one apart from the Principal himself really knowing what to say. It was clear that in his present state of mind, Morris was not going to cooperate with any press investigation.

In the end he said, 'Well, thank you, gentlemen. So long as I am Principal we shall not be giving into the blackmail of the press. I shall keep them at arm's length. As I said at the extraordinary meeting, I require everyone else to do the same.'

That was conclusive; it signalled the end of the meeting. Outside in the quad, Frank, Donald and I agreed that he seemed not to be living in the real world.

'We are talking here of a bunch of academics who above all else value academic freedom, freedom of speech, individualism, conscience and goodness knows what. Can't he see that it's totally unrealistic to dictate to a collegiate fellowship? He's got to be losing his grip.' Frank made to walk off, but Donald made him hesitate. 'Well, he's obviously got something to hide. He's guilty of something.' I added, 'At this rate it will soon be revealed. With *Private Eye*'s private eye snooping around, it will be quick.'

Neither Donald nor Frank were going into lunch. I went to the SCR. Timothy Knowles had gone straight in and next to him Brendan Naish was sitting. I sat on the other side of Knowles. I had just settled when Est appeared. I stood up and waited until she had sat down. Est acknowledged Knowles and said rather forthrightly and in a way that slightly embarrassed me, 'Brendan, I didn't know you were a member of common room.' Knowles immediately said, 'He isn't. He's here as my guest. We've been at a short-notice meeting with the Principal.'

I commented straight-facedly but I hoped with a trace of sarcasm, 'Perhaps Willoughby could organise Brendan's membership if it's important for the good running of the college.'

Timothy Knowles was unfazed. 'That's a good idea, Johnny. I'll have a word with him and maybe I'll propose him.'

I thought to myself, 'That won't get through.' Yet it would be typical of Morris if he tried to accomplish Brendan's membership.

As soon as Knowles and Naish left, I told Est about the meeting with Morris.

'Where were the women then? Was this the Principal's kitchen cabinet? I thought this college had gone mixed. Aren't we co-residential, co-ed? Aren't our interests equal? Jane should have been there, or I should've. Mind you I would have walked out. I'm not going to be party to that sort of manipulation. I'm surprised you stayed.'

I explained that it was better to know what was going on, to stay in the picture, than be in ignorance of Willoughby's manoeuvrings, but essentially, of course, I agreed with her. Est said, 'He's obviously worried, even scared. I think he's panicking. He should play the whole thing differently. He should affect calm and indifference. He's simply making it worse for himself. Anyway, I'm going to have a word with Jane. I think we'll haul him over the coals about the lack of women in his consultations.'

I could see she was determined. 'I think he sees that meeting as private and off the record, but you're quite right. If he asks, tell him you heard about it from me. This is beginning to sound like a police state and we're becoming neurotic about permissions.'

The rest of the day was spent in teaching. We devoted our time to our proper business and ignored the distractions of petty college politics. That night we had dinner together, and again slept together at my house.

Back in college the next morning, I looked quickly through the papers. The *Daily Mail* had picked up the story. 'Holt College expenses scandal: investigation continues.' The article mentioned that Hugh Crammond, ex-Principal, was now involved in trying to discover the truth behind various rumours. It noted that the present Principal was being uncooperative with the press. Their reporter had been refused an interview with anyone. I remarked to Est: 'They didn't ask me. Still, I suppose it would be premature and perhaps undiplomatic to talk with journalists at the moment.'

'You're probably right. Let's see what Hugh Crammond comes up with.'

Est and I met again that afternoon when we went to the SCR for a cup of tea. She said that she and Jane Templeman were going to see Morris at six; the female voice of the college had to be heard. 'I'll come to your room afterwards, around seven,' she said.

We looked together at the *Oxford Mail*. It built on the *Daily Mail* story and intimated that there was something extremely suspect in the way Holt College was being run, particularly its finances. Again it reported that there was no clear college statement. Their inquiries had been met by the parrying 'no comment'. Morris was sticking to his policy of silence. No doubt he hoped that the whole affair would die down, the more time passed. The papers would lose interest and find other topics more immediate. I thought he did not recognise the true nature of journalists. If they thought they had the whiff of scandal, they would follow it, and dig and dig, and like terriers they would finally unearth the truth.

So later that day, I was waiting in my room for Est. She turned up on the dot of seven. 'We finished with Morris ages ago; or rather he thinks he's finished with us. I thought you might be teaching. It was a short interview.'

'OK, tell me what happened.' I could see that she was still pretty cross.

'Well, we were there at six. We went to see him – like girls presenting at the head's study – and he was pacing the room. He didn't look very comfortable with himself, a bit annoyed. He asked immediately what it was about; why did we want to see him. I explained that we had heard that a meeting had taken place with which he had called to discuss current problems in the college but that no women were there. Jane said that wouldn't do; it was quite inappropriate that women's voices should not be heard. He protested that what we had heard about was an informal private meeting and that he could ask to it whoever he liked. He began to ride his high horse. He demanded to know the source of our information. And since you said it would be OK to mention you, I told him you had told me. He looked painfully indignant and almost started shouting. No wonder there were leaks. He had made it quite clear this morning that he did not want anything discussed to go beyond his study's walls. He even said, to my astonishment, "And remember this, young lady, I'm the Principal and I can call whatever meetings I like. I am not answerable to you or your colleague here." Young lady, indeed; and Jane, my colleague! What do you think of that? He clearly has a severe attack of *folie de grandeur* and, of course, he is in the end answerable to me and everyone else on the governing body. I think he's lost his wits.'

'What an appalling display, lack of judgement and lack of manners. I can see I'm now in the firing line.'

'You said you didn't mind.'

'No, I don't, but I shall have to prepare my defences and prime my guns. If he's done something wrong, then why doesn't he come clean, take advice, and solve the problem?'

18

That Tuesday night we spent together in Est's flat. Our relationship had suddenly transformed itself without any discussion into the closest intimacy when we were in private beyond the reach of anyone else. It had all been unspoken. There had been no need for long debate. It was a natural evolution that we both accepted and welcomed. There was no awkwardness, no embarrassment, no reservation. We each knew what the other wanted in every respect, in bed and during the daily round.

The next morning we both went into college. I went back home first. I shaved and smartened myself up and then was in my college rooms for an eleven o'clock postponed tutorial.

At midday, as the undergraduate I had been teaching left, Susie appeared.

'Have you got someone coming now?' she asked. I replied that I did not. We went back into the room and she sat. I stood by the window and looked down on the quad below. Various people came and went, some I knew and some I did not. I turned to face Susie but as I did so I saw Morris hasten across the quad, document case in hand. Jane Templeman appeared from a staircase exit and as she walked towards him she obviously greeted him. Morris totally ignored her. He made no sign of recognition and kept his eyes straight ahead of him. After they had passed each other, Jane stopped and turned round. She looked at him as he disappeared, shrugged her shoulders and proceeded to the library where, at its entrance, Jacob Black waved to her. They paused and conversed and I could imagine what they were talking about; Willoughby Morris's odd behaviour, uncivil and blatantly rude.

'Sorry, Susie. I was just studying some of my colleagues. Not very edifying. This business is not good for the ease of personal relations within the working body.'

Susie nodded. She told me why she had called. 'I was walking past the college and I just thought I'd call in to see if you were free. We've had another anonymous leak. Somewhere there is a whistle-blower. I should think it must be one of the fellows. The information is exact in that it refers us to expenses claims over the last year and it says that we should inquire into the Principal's claims in particular. There we shall find, as the note says, examples of malfeasance. This time there was another sheet of paper enclosed and seems to be a bursarial account of your Principal's travel and subsistence claim for a trip to India. He claims for two business class seats on return flights to Delhi and hotel expenses. The writer asks the question, who went with him? But you can answer that.'

'Yes, I suppose it was his wife. She often goes with him on trips abroad; but I can check on that. It's hardly likely to have been his mistress, if he's got one. Still, he is attractive to certain sorts of women, so I'm told. I'll find out.'

'It might be a good idea.'

'Malfeasance. Hmm, misconduct, crime in public office. I wonder if he is guilty of that. He might be, I suppose. We shall see. Anyway, thanks for keeping me informed. There's nothing you can print now except rumour.'

Susie thought for a moment. 'No, that's right. It's in our interest to keep the story simmering. What we need is another scoop. If we could pinpoint the source of any leak, especially if it were a fellow, or if we could be sure the Principal was misrepresenting his expenses claims, then we could really make a headline story of it. So, I'll keep you informed, and you keep me informed so far as you can.'

I admired her professionalism. There she was, an apprentice journalist, someone who was learning the arts, some of them dark, of journalism, and she was already adept at nursing a story to its full fruition. She would go a long way. I expected to see her in a few years to come as an editor of some prominent daily newspaper. She was good at the job.

At two fifteen there was the weekly governing body meeting. There were quite a number of items on the agenda in this penultimate week of term. Most of them were to do with domestic matters. Donald wanted to retain an assistant chaplain for three years; but she would require a small salary to maintain herself. The Reverend Ms Harriet Smith was an American who had just completed her doctorate on the doctrine of reserve as interpreted and practised by the founders of the nineteenth century Oxford Movement, John Keble prominent among them. There was not much opposition to this proposal. She was well liked in college, helped with the welfare of women students, and was well known as someone who could lend a sympathetic ear to anyone who was in mental or spiritual trouble. She originated in Brooklyn. She knew the rough side of city life. Her theological studies were carried out firstly at Columbia University and then at Oxford.

Our senior chemistry fellow did raise a small but qualified objection and said that he thought she should be supported financially by Keble College since her research interests lay with the Oxford Movement. He had been one of the leaders, mostly scientists, who had earlier proposed that the office of chaplain should not be obligatory by statute and that the chapel building should be open to use for other purposes besides celebrating the services of the Church of England. On that he had been defeated, largely because of a threat by a powerful group of Old Members to withhold future donations and legacies for the college if the proposal were to be passed by the fellowship.

Once again he was defeated, although he had not been altogether serious over pressing the point. Everyone agreed that for such a small outlay as her stipend would demand, Harriet, her research, and her services to the college were worth it.

Morris was fairly muted when it came to discussion of such things. He did not seem to be in a very good mood. He was abrupt and business-like. One of the items was the termly report of the finance committee. The minutes of its last meeting had been circulated. They were short and to the point; they referred in two sentences to the possible leak of information to the press and noted that an ongoing investigation into the leak was taking place. The last paragraph censured severely the careless lack of security over committee papers. That clearly referred to the negligence of leaving photocopied sheets lying around in the college office. Morris steamrollered the minutes' acceptance, not wanting discussion. He emphasised that there was not much point in long debate when the most important point to do with leaks was being looked into. He did not look embarrassed as I expected him to do.

When it came to any other business at the end of the meeting, Jane Templeman, who, I felt, had been waiting for an opportunity to needle Morris, posed a question about the proper nature of the position of Brendan Naish.

She addressed the long table around which sat the college fellows. She did not look at the Principal who was seated at one end, on his right the Bursar Eedes and on his left, the senior tutor, Knowles. Rather she ignored Willoughby Morris and talked directly to the rest of her colleagues.

She started by saying that she regarded the matter as one of significant importance. She did not want to see any erosion of the fellows' position. It was not a question of prejudice, pride or pique. It was to do with the college's constitution and practice over the years; a matter of order and degree. What had to be realised and properly understood was that Brendan Naish was only an assistant, and in particular assistant to the senior tutor, no more than that. He should not be allowed, or regard himself as being allowed, to impinge on or intrude into the functioning of college business that was the affair of the fellowship. 'He is not an elected fellow; he is an appointed assistant.' She quoted T.S. Eliot, rather cruelly, I thought: 'He is not Prince Hamlet. He is, if you like, "an attendant lord, one that will do/To swell a progress, start a scene or two." To continue the poem, he should be perhaps, "deferential, glad to be of use". He should not sit in on meetings between fellows that are, even if not official, then semi-official. Our business is our affair; it is not that of Brendan Naish or any other secretary, assistant or PA. We should all remind ourselves of that.'

There was a general murmur of assent around the table. Both the Principal and Timothy Knowles looked discomfited. Morris said, rather too loudly, 'Senior Tutor, perhaps you should answer that.' He added tetchily, 'And may I remind you that everything should be addressed to and through the chair.' He glared at Jane who continued to ignore him with a calm dignity.

The Principal showed no embarrassment; but he did show his impatient annoyance. On the other hand, Timothy Knowles was made to look uncomfortable. I detected that he resented Morris's referral of the problem to him; after all, the Principal had been party to the inclusion of Naish in fellows' discussions, he had raised no objections and, I felt, regarded him as an extra ally. Knowles was apologetic but, again, I thought he was forced to be by the circumstances. I was not sure how genuinely sorry he was. At least, for his comfort, Brendan Naish was not there.

'I'm truly sorry that you feel like that, Jane, and I register that most of you feel the same way. I can assure you that Brendan is a person of complete discretion and loyalty. I know him to be totally reliable. You should not worry that there has been, or will be, any breach of privacy. It just seemed to me that it was helpful, certainly for me, and, I hope, for the Principal, to have him present on some occasions.

'Obviously, judging from the general reaction here, his presence is not popular and I shall make sure that he doesn't attend any meeting at which he is regarded as supernumerary.'

I thought that was a curious way of putting it. What was clear to me and to virtually everyone else present was that Knowles, probably because he was so infatuated with Naish, wanted him around him all the time. Knowles liked to exercise a powerful kind of patronage over Naish, and it was one that Naish appreciated.

Before Morris had a chance to speak, Jane, ignoring his strictures about addressing all remarks through the chair, reinforced her complaint. 'Good. It's important, and surely the fellowship agrees with me, to maintain the sovereignty and identity of this body. If we dilute it, the independence of the college will gradually disappear. We must guard our position as a democratic collegiate body, our meetings watched over by an ever vigilant chair.'

Again, there was a murmur of assent. I interpreted her speech as an underlining of the Principal's role. He was not a chief executive officer. He should be a benign chairman.

Sure enough Morris did not like what he heard. He did not like one of his chief allies, Knowles, being reprimanded, and he did not like being reminded of his constitutional position. He had made it abundantly clear on so many occasions that he saw himself as exercising executive powers. Now, someone was questioning his decisions and entire mode of operation.

As Jane paused, Morris cut in. 'Thank you, Dr Templeman. I still have to remind you to speak always to the chair. This is not a political meeting on the hustings that you seem to think it is. It is a college meeting. You seem to like referring us to the rules of procedures. You might abide by the conventions of debate.

'Let me remind everyone of the fundamentally important issue that we have brought up here today. We must resist bad publicity. We must defend our interests. Do not speak to the press. We must try to keep our affairs private.'

With that, he picked up his papers, stood up, said something to Eedes and left the room. Eedes followed him out.

The meeting dispersed. I stood with Est and Jane in the quad. I could not help smirking and I said to Jane, 'Well done. It's about time someone made it clear to Willoughby that he's been acting out of order. The Naish case gave you the perfect opportunity. You killed, or at least wounded, two birds with one stone. Old Morris is such a crook. He wants to keep things quiet to avoid a scandal; a scandal that I'm sure is there. I just feel there is an inevitability about his eventual exposure. I'm convinced there is something dreadfully wrong.' Est and Jane both agreed.

Est commented, 'And anyway, Brendan Naish has had his nasty little wings clipped.'

That evening, before Est and I went home to my house, we had a drink in Quod. Around seven thirty Timothy Knowles and Naish came in. Est and I were sitting at the bar and a shoulder-high plinth that had a huge display of flowers on it, ferns, lilies and some unidentifiable large orchid-like blooms, obscured us from the vision of people entering the restaurant. On the other hand, we could easily see who passed. No one bothered to look beyond the magnificent flowers. Knowles was still in his lightweight summer work suit. He had taken off his tie and was looking relaxed. Brendan Naish was dressed in a tight, black, cotton polo-necked T-shirt. His trousers too were black as were his loafers. He wore dark glasses and it all contrasted vividly with his blond hair.

'That's a bit much,' I said to Est. 'Naish looks decidedly camp. He belongs in Old Compton Street in that rig. He'd be sure to pull in the punters.'

She took a sip from her martini and leant forward to peer round the flowers and through the bar area to see where they were going to sit. 'He sure likes to dress the part. Do you think he looks a bit like Andy Warhol?'

'I suppose he does. But he hasn't the gifts. Distinctly a minor version. Poor old Knowles. He's almost cast in the role of sugar daddy. Could he be twice his age? Still he's happy. He ought to keep his intimate relationships apart from his work though.'

Est laughed. 'How terribly old-fashioned you are. Acceptable in the workplace, acceptable at home; it doesn't matter. Let them get on with it.'

'Yes, but that's not the point. You've just seen what happens. Knowles's easy infatuation makes him get Naish into trouble. It's not Naish's fault that there is now controversy about his place in the administration. It's Timothy's. He should not have let it happen. He should've known better.'

'Yes, of course you're right. Let's leave them to their tryst. What do you think is going to happen to the college now?'

'Well, the end of the week looms. The press will have been to work. *Private Eye* comes out this week. It'll be interesting. I reckon Willoughby's surely in the firing line.'

We discussed Willoughby's predicament. We assumed that he was guilty of some sort of financial misdemeanour. Maybe it was fairly minor. Perhaps he had managed to claim more than he was entitled to for travel expenses or he had done what many people do, claim for first class travel, use economy and pocket the difference; or claim for a five star hotel but use a three star.

'It has to be more than that,' Est protested. 'I can't imagine Morris being bothered with that sort of trivial scam. What has he been up to?'

'Well, that's what's going to be revealed and I reckon it'll be this weekend; or at least it will begin to become clear and by the end of next week I'd say that we'll know all.'

'What would you do if you were in Morris's position? It's fascinating to put yourself in his place.'

'It's simple really. If I had been fiddling expenses in some way, now that the heat is on, I'd confide in my colleagues and crave their indulgence and forgiveness. And I would make myself more agreeable to the fellowship in general. Indeed, that's the main point. I'd give up my seigniorial role and try to accommodate myself better with my colleagues.'

We wondered how he was getting on with Elizabeth, his wife. No wonder she took to drink. He must have been wretched to live with. No doubt he was as domineering in his private life as he was in his public, working life. Est said that if she were him, she would make an announcement to the press that the college was carrying out a full investigation of the rumours and that the college believed in full transparency. A comprehensive press release would be made when the investigation was complete.

Est said, 'Poor old Willoughby. He's got himself into such a mess.'

That was not my view. 'I have no sympathy. He's a power player, a control freak. He's no idea of how to handle people and he certainly doesn't understand how a college should be run. It's Eedes and Knowles who are unforgiveable too; they are compliant and support him because they think it's to their advantage. They're dangerous toadies.'

We concluded that whatever we might think, Morris was not going to change and that he was inevitably heading for disaster. No doubt the fruit would ripen and fall within the space of the next ten days.

19

Thursday was one of the days, during term time, I dedicated to writing. In the evening Est and I were going to New College, to the performance of *Il Re Pastore* in the Warden's garden. All day the weather was changeable, what forecasters describe as 'showery with sunny periods'. As it turned out, it was mostly showery but in the late afternoon, early evening, the sun broke through the clouds.

We went with a friend, who was a fellow of New College, and his wife. The idea was to provide a picnic dinner that you laid out on reserved tables in the college cloisters. The opera was to start at a quarter to seven, the picnic dinner would take place from eight until nine, followed by the second half. Richard and Rachel were to provide a first course and the main; we took along a pudding and the wine. In the end, for lack of time, Est had bought a blackcurrant cheesecake from Waitrose and I organised a couple of bottles of Italian white wine, a 2009 Verdicchio Monte Schiavo and a 2009 red, Vino Nobile di Montepulciano.

Yet things did not turn out quite as planned. We had met in the cloisters, established our table and had a glass of the Verdicchio. We took our time and strolled to the Warden's garden. We went out of the rear college gate next to the chapel into New College Lane. It was like entering a mediaeval street; it wound its way down to the High from underneath the Hertford College bridge of sighs at the Catte Street end. It was cobbled and enclosed by high stone walls. Across from the entrance in the wall opposite, two huge ancient wooden doors had been opened into a secret world never seen by the general public. The Warden's private garden, a lawn surrounded by herbaceous borders, a few trees here and there, fig, walnut, apricot; delphiniums blossoming triumphantly, and what pervaded the air was the scent of lilies and lavender. On one side the majestic high windows of All Souls's Codrington Library looked down on us. It was an idyllic setting hidden away by high walls.

We found our seats and as we sat down a bank of dark cloud obscured the last of the day's sun. I noticed Morris and his wife in a group of six with the Warden and his wife. It looked as though Willoughby was being extraordinarily demonstrative. At exactly a quarter to seven the New College music fellow stepped to the front of the stage. Behind him was a small orchestra under a canopy. He told us a little about the unfamiliar opera and outlined the plot. The orchestra tuned up. From behind the stage a singer appeared and the performance began. Within a minute a light drizzle of rain began to fall. After three or four minutes, it was raining sufficiently for everyone to feel extremely uncomfortable; and the rain was drifting under the canopy. The player of the virginal looked distinctly worried about the state of his instrument. The music fellow stepped forward, signalled the conductor to halt, clapped his hands and announced that the weather forced us into the Ante-chapel where the opera would recommence. The opera was short enough to run the two acts together, perhaps with a very short interval. It would be a good idea to go back to the cloisters, have our picnic suppers while the orchestra moved to the Ante-chapel which would take a little time. We should reconvene at eight o'clock. The singers who were barely into their first duet ran quickly round to the back of the tented canopy. The rest of us made our way, with coats over heads and umbrellas raised, to the chapel and cloisters.

The Warden's little party put up three garishly striped golfing umbrellas and went through a door in one of the rose-covered walls to the Warden's private lodgings. I heard Willoughby saying loudly from under his umbrella that sported the colours of Holt: 'Well, never mind. We shall have to have another drink or two. Every cloud has a silver lining.' The Warden's wife responded with a strained smile.

When we arrived at our table in the cloisters, Est and I found to our delight that Richard and Rachel had provided a magnificent dinner. First we each had a small salade niçoise and then Rachel produced a chunk of fillet steak wrapped in tin foil. She laid it out on a plate and Richard carved it into slices. We ate it with some cold minted potatoes and broad beans in olive oil. Our pudding was a poor companion to such cooking. Naturally, most of our dinner conversation concerned New College and the opera but, of course, about halfway through the meal they wanted to know what was going on at Holt. Such was the publicity that they reasonably thought we would be able to give them the inside story. We were both circumspect but made it plain that there was something wrong at the core of the administration and pretty soon all would undoubtedly be revealed.

At other tables we could see people we knew or, at least, recognised. The Lord Lieutenant was there with a group of about eight people. His appointment had always amused me. He had been junior to me by two years at university and when I was researching and spending time in the research institutions of America, he graduated and went into the Ford Motor Company. After a couple of years he gave that up and trained as a lawyer. He was called to the bar and then went back into business. With remarkable speed he had become chairman of a City insurance company and somehow had succeeded to the lieutenancy at a young age. At another table were a local solicitor who had become a Bow Street magistrate and his wife, a local circuit judge; they were accompanied by a prominent GP. There was a scattering of dames and knights, theologians and demographers. It was a gathering of the great and the good. I made that remark to Est. She replied tartly: 'Some of them might look it but we know stories about some of these folk that makes them neither great nor good. What about our own member of the glorious club, Morris? He, for example, is neither great nor good, even though he would like to think he's fabulously important.'

At five to eight we were summoned by the music fellow to take our places in the Ante-chapel. No sooner were we seated than there was a loud babble of voices and the Warden's party entered. The Warden and his wife, who came in first, immediately stopped talking but Morris, who was in debate with another guest, did not drop his voice at all. He was clearly spurred on by what he had drunk. I heard him saying, 'The trouble with my college is that I don't get support from all my fellows. It's important to present a united front. My wretched colleagues won't do this. I'll have to insist they fall into line.'

Many people heard him. The Ante-chapel had fallen silent. Richard caught my eye and winked. Est whispered, 'What an idiot. How did we ever choose him? What a disaster.'

The performance went ahead splendidly. The opera was sung, presided over by Epstein's dramatic statue of the risen Lazarus. For a short time the late evening light was filtered through the tall stained-glass windows designed by Joshua Reynolds. During the short interval we spoke with a theologian and his botanist wife. He had a long, broad beard, and looked like a major prophet, or like Edward Lear; there might have been birds nesting in his beard. We all agreed that the acoustics were much better in the chapel than they would have been outside in the Warden's garden.

At the end many people went back to their cloistered tables for a final glass of wine; some finished off with a little cheese. We heard Willoughby once more propounding the virtues of New College as compared with Holt. A minor judgement was about to befall him. The Warden was just ushering his guests past the entrance to the cloisters, when Willoughby, in full spate, appeared to trip. He let out a mighty bellow and fell awkwardly forward. He lay for a moment or two groaning, and was then helped to his feet. He held his right wrist in obvious agony. The GP who had returned to his table hurried to his assistance. There was a subdued murmur of consultation with the GP holding Morris's hand and wrist. Willoughby endured some manipulation and then took a sharp breath and exclaimed loudly: 'Stop. That's extremely painful.' The GP advised something to be done and went back to his group. After that Morris was led away. Subsequently we learned that he was taken by taxi to the Radcliffe hospital where it was found that he had broken a bone in his wrist and it had to be set in plaster. That, we knew, would not please Willoughby. He was by nature an impatient man and his injury would add to his frustration and bad temper. We could not hope for an untroubled time during the following final week of term, which was always fraught and busy. At least there was the prospect of the weekend; but we knew that the journalists would be active around the university and beyond, investigating the Holt College rumours.

20

What we did not know up to that weekend was that there was even another side to Willoughby Morris that we were ignorant of. It was the journalists who discovered it and it came to us via Donald. Our crafty chaplain took me to one side after chapel on Saturday evening.

I often went to evensong on Saturdays because it was not well attended. I enjoyed the lack of a crowd, much enjoyed the music and thought, in any case, that the chapel tradition needed support. The line had to be held against the assault of those fellows infected with what Donald called 'the Richard Dawkins virus'; that is those who wanted the chapel and all its trappings of religion to be shifted into the secular arena.

At the end of the service, according to custom and practice, the choir processed out followed by Donald and then the attendant fellows. I was the only one as usual for a Saturday and Donald who was standing saying goodbye to various members of the congregation said, 'Hold on a minute, Johnny; a word in your ear.' I stood to one side and tried to retreat into the gloom of the antechapel. A couple of undergraduates stopped and chatted for a moment and then hurried off. By the time that Donald had finished his duties, five minutes had passed and I thought I was going to be late for meeting Est. Donald and I stepped through the doors of the chapel into the cloister. Donald was still robed in his cassock and surplice. He lifted his doctoral hood over his head and put it over his arm. Then, likewise, he took off his stole and folded it on top of his hood. 'Look,' he said, 'something important and rather disagreeable has come up.

There's a *Times* journalist here in Oxford, along as we would expect with many other journos. He's an old friend, once a student I taught, and he's done some work for us on the security side.' Donald, who was a Russianist of some considerable accomplishment, was a recruiter for the security services, and particularly MI6. I suppose officially people were not meant to know about this role of his, and if you did you were not expected to talk about it. Yet it was very much common knowledge even though Donald himself was discreet. Donald went on, 'He called to see me briefly and what he had to say was fairly shocking. It adds another aspect to Morris's predicament. Apparently he and his colleagues from other newspapers have discovered that Willoughby is seeing a young girl student from St Cecilia's. They are very careful and never meet in Oxford, always outside. Often it's in London, but otherwise somewhere in the country near here. So, that's a surprise.'

I was astonished by this intelligence. I had never thought of Willoughby as a philanderer; and it certainly complicated the issue. It added another dimension to his character and, maybe, called into question his integrity. In one respect I was not surprised and I said to Donald, 'Well, Elizabeth is a great deal to put up with. I suppose he needs to look for light relief elsewhere. If you've a difficult harridan of a wife, what do you expect?'

Donald sniffed. 'I wouldn't put it as strongly as that. I don't think you can call her a harridan. Think of it like this; she's an awful lot to endure with a husband like Morris. I should think he's pretty unbearable. I have quite a great deal of sympathy for Elizabeth. Maybe he'd drive anyone who lives in close proximity to him to drink.'

'Well, what next? Will there be any more revelations?'

'Who knows? Most of this story came from my man and the *Private Eye* sleuth who has good contacts among the undergraduates. It does call Morris's judgement into question. Another thing the *Times* man mentioned was that some students think he's taken a shine to the senior tutor's catamite as well. But I don't give that much credence.'

'No, that seems bizarre. I suspect his interest in Naish is entirely to keep Knowles on board. He sees himself, Eedes and Knowles as the ruling troika. Still, who knows? It's all most intriguing.'

Donald hurried off to the disrobing and rehearsal room. Already the choirboys were coming out and running through the cloisters to join their parents and friends.

Donald called out like a schoolmaster, 'No running in the cloisters, boys. Due decorum and all that.' They slowed down and laughed. Donald got on well with them and had he not been an academic cleric and a proficient linguist, he would have made a very good school teacher.'

That evening with Est I reported what Donald had told me. Her reaction was one of surprise and resignation. 'What's it going to be like when this hits the press, when it's printed, there for us to read in the clear light of day? Oh well, it's a nemesis about to happen. What has Willoughby been doing?'

While Willoughby Morris's fate was being decided by the gods over that weekend, we had been offered a diversion. Hugh Crammond had invited everyone to a summer party he was hosting out at Fenmore. All the locals of his district had been invited as had his old college friends. He had told me, too, that some friends were coming down from London. It was going to be quite a gathering. Fortunately the weather had turned for the better. We were called for at around four o'clock when there would be tea served. Then there would be a drinks reception on the great lawn in front of the house followed by a supper in a marquee that had been erected in a side field. The evening would be rounded off by a bonfire and fireworks. Hugh loved these occasions. He enjoyed being host and revelled in his seigniorial role.

Early on Sunday morning, Donald rang me. Est and I had stayed overnight in my house. We were late up and were sitting at breakfast. Donald asked if I was going to Fenmore and, if so, could he have a lift. Of course I said it would be a pleasure. He told me that Harriet

Smith, his nice American assistant, would be taking evensong for him.

So, that afternoon we three drove out to Fenmore. It was looking glorious. Its surrounding fields had Hugh's herd of long-horned cattle in them. In one, in the late eighteenth century, the cattle's own house had been built, a sort of neo-classical folly solely for their shelter. There the two bulls were isolated; they sported ear tags with their names inscribed: Moonraker and Redemption. I had asked Hugh on a previous occasion, why Redemption? He had told me that when the calf was born he had just seen a film of that title; he gave it to the bull calf.

Lord and Lady Crammond were strolling around welcoming people as they arrived. Hugh kissed Est on both cheeks, shook my hand and patted Donald on the shoulder. He and Donald were great collaborators in all sorts of affairs that I knew little about. I realised that they were mostly to do with government business and most probably security. 'We must all have a private word a little later on,' Hugh said, 'if we can find the right moment. I'm sure we'll be able to. I think what I have to say is of growing urgency. So, delay won't do.'

'Ah,' Donald immediately responded quoting Shakespeare, '"Dull not device by coldness and delay."'

'Precisely,' Hugh confirmed.

I wondered what was afoot. I suspected that Hugh and Donald had already been talking together about Morris's troubles. They both moved off in different directions. Est and I walked into the gardens. The roses were in full bloom. The borders fabulously lush with summer flowers.

'Willoughby is going to find himself isolated, and very quickly too,' I said. I could not quite place the Shakespeare quotation Donald had used but another one came to my mind as I thought about Willoughby's setting himself apart from most of his colleagues. Why should one remain loyal to a man who was, seemingly, so dedicated to his own downfall? Rather we should leave him to his own destruction. 'The loyalty well held to fools does make / Our faith mere folly', thus Enobarbus in *Antony and Cleopatra*.

We walked into the walled kitchen garden. Ordered rows of carrots, onions, broad beans, beetroot, peas had been set out by the gardener and her part-time assistants. A space of a couple of yards separated them from ridges of potatoes of differing varieties. Then again there was a space and next there were more exotic plants, artichokes, asparagus, courgettes, tall lines of raspberries and loganberries. The brick walls that surrounded the garden not only reflected sunlight but partially absorbed it and consequently warmed the large enclosure. Against those walls were espaliered fruit trees, apples, pears and plums. All the tree fruits were still forming, growing to ripeness, to be harvested in a month or two's time. A door in the northern wall opened to a lawn intersected by trellised, bordered walks. Along the trellises were more espaliered trees, all exclusively apples. Some of the old, gnarled trunks showed them to be maybe seventy to eighty years old.

Est and I walked in the grounds and talked. We sat by the side of the river Cherwell on an ancient stone seat, reputed to have been a favourite resting place of Alexander Pope, and watched a pair of herons delicately dipping and fishing. At six we wandered slowly up to the great house. There Hugh Crammond was giving champagne to his guests. There were many familiar faces from the university and from political circles in London. I noticed the local vicar, a retired chaplain of Brasenose College. The Bishop of Oxford was there. A notable absence was that of Willoughby Morris, Principal of Holt. He would have been an expected guest as head of Hugh's own college and his successor as Principal. It was a sure sign of Morris's diminishing esteem among his peers.

Est and I were introduced to various people, most of whom we had not met before, by Lady Crammond, a brilliant hostess, who moved people effortlessly and easily between groups. She was immensely capable and sociable. The maintenance of the gardens was her inspiration and her self-imposed duty. We met the Conservative chief whip in the House of Lords and the cabinet secretary. The company, I began to think, would be as intoxicating as the champagne, but in effect those people were without pretension and had ordinary concerns that we all suffer. Talking with them was so different from talking with Willoughby Morris, who was invariably bombastic and always seeking to impress his listeners.

Dinner in the marquee followed. Two long tables had been arranged, each seating about sixty guests. Each place was elaborately set out with cutlery and glasses. The centres of the tables were decorated with small vases of roses fresh from the gardens. The sides of the marquee had been scrolled up because of the warmth of the evening and a slight breeze fanned through the tent.

It was at the end of the dinner, after Hugh had stood and proposed the loyal toast, 'Let us raise our glasses and propose the good health and long life of Her Majesty the Queen and the Prince of Wales; may God bless them', that he managed to bring Donald, Tony Gill who was present, Est and myself, together. Most of the guests were still seated. Some had moved around, had exchanged seats, and were sitting with different friends. Others strolled back and forth between the house, the gardens and the marquee. Hugh took us to stand a little apart from the marquee and there, after a little discussion, he suggested we walked down the lane to his house. 'We have about half an hour before the bonfire is lit and about three quarters before the sun goes down. That should just give me time to discuss with you what is on my mind.' We went with him down the lane to his house. There in his main reception room he offered us claret, whiskies or brandy. Donald took the claret, Est a brandy, and the rest of us took drams of Glen Grant 15 year old.

'As you might have noticed, I did not invite the Principal. In the circumstances I thought it best to leave him out of these proceedings. We all know the difficulties he's facing. It is all becoming more and more embarrassing daily. The matter is being discussed openly in London. One, the Secretary of State doesn't like what's happening and is wondering why we can't sort it out. Two, Holt's Old Members don't like it either. They held a committee meeting a couple of days ago. The president rang me and said how disturbed everybody was because of the disrepute the college seemed to be bringing on itself. His suggestion, and really mine is the same, that now, no matter whether the rumours are true or not, Willoughby ought to retreat.'

Tony Gill, who after all was Vicegerent, said, 'Retreat! What do you mean, resign? He's not going to do that. It's not his nature.'

'Well,' Crammond said, 'that's what I do mean. It could be done both tactically and tactfully. The Old Members think the same. In my day, when I was Principal, there were one or two other heads of houses who were moved on and out of office in a political way that passed as triumphs of diplomacy. In fact, they were given an ultimatum but their departures were eased. What I'm saying is the governing body should think seriously about implementing this sort of agreement. It will have the backing of London and I'm sure some compensatory post could be found for him. You people have to make the initial moves.'

Donald had been nodding in assent throughout and it rather confirmed to me that he might have had previous talks with Hugh about the idea.

Tony Gill said, 'It's going to be tough; and I suppose it means I shall have to stand in for a bit if it happens.'

Hugh Crammond agreed. 'That's the constitution. Yes. Then the process for finding a successor to Willoughby will start.'

'Well, I'd better tell you all that I am seriously considering applying for the headship of two other colleges, Hereford and Villiers. But those are long-drawn-out procedures and don't start until the second half of next term.'

'OK, if you have to stand in, it will help your chances, I'm sure,' Hugh commented.

Est patted Tony on the back. 'That's good news, Tony. Good luck. I hope you make it.'

I brought our meeting back to the main business. 'With regard to Willoughby, he has to see that his position is hopeless. Otherwise he'll never agree. He has to be presented with evidence that he can't refute. Rumour he will deny. There has to be fact. In a sense the press has to get a move on, to the point where he can no longer hold out.'

I paused and Donald quickly interjected: 'We can't stop the journalists anyway. They'll inevitably find out what's going on, and nothing's going to stop them printing a good story. They especially relish corruption.'

We discussed the impact that all this would have on Holt. Hugh said, 'Well, we are one of the greatest of the Oxford and Cambridge colleges with a hugely distinguished tradition. We are one of the oldest foundations and we have to show that we, the present guardians of the college's welfare, are worthy to safeguard the college's continued interests.'

Of course, I agreed wholeheartedly but he was beginning to sound as though he was speaking in the House of Lords. All of us there, Est, Donald, Tony Gill, me, and Hugh himself did not need to be reminded of our responsibilities. What Hugh was underlining was explicit in the oath we had to swear when we were admitted to our fellowships, 'to the good health and long continuance of the collegiate body'. It was Willoughby who had forgotten his oath.

Hugh commented, 'I wonder if this business will come to a head this coming week. In a way I think it would be good if it could. The boil would be lanced and the patient would have time to recover over the long vacation.'

I knew that both Est and I thought that it was highly likely that something dire would happen in the final week of term, and Donald made the case for a swift crisis. 'I know the *Private Eye* spook is close to a coup, she claims to have a source inside the college. The *Telegraph* reporter, too, I am told, is about to write a definitive charge against Willoughby; the *Telegraph* is very active, as we know, in hunting down cases of public corruption. So, I think we'll see serious developments this coming week. If the charges prove irrefutable, then Willoughby will not want to hang around. Like the beleaguered dictator of some rogue state, he'll want a quick way out.'

Again I agreed; but I thought the evidence had to be unarguable, or, like Gaddafi, Morris would cling to power.

Hugh summed up. 'That's good. We see things the same way. I shall hear tomorrow if various people in London can come up with some offer to Willoughby that will ease the transition and the pain for him, although I don't really see why it should be made entirely easy for him. But it will be better for the college. We must remember that Principals are here today and gone tomorrow. It's the college as an ancient institution founded in 1286 that's important. Let's keep closely in touch. I'll liaise with Donald and in college he can be the conduit from me to you and vice versa. Is that OK?'

We all agreed. Donald, the crafty chaplain, could live up to his nickname. I was pretty sure that there was little he would enjoy more than playing out that role in the conspiracy and intrigue.

We returned towards the marquee. There was a large tent next to it that had been set up as a bar. Other guests were standing around in groups, most of them with a drink in hand. As we arrived back and mingled with various people we knew, Hugh's tenant farmer who was acting as master of ceremonies gave a shout and called for quiet. 'We're just about ready to light the bonfire, everybody. I'll hand over to Lord Crammond to do the honours.'

Hugh stepped forwards, took a burning brand from the MC, and said to those assembled, 'So pleased to see everyone here. We do hope you're enjoying yourselves.' He embraced Lady Crammond with the flourish of his left hand, approached the great stack of wood and set it alight. It burned slowly at first and then the flames gathered pace and intensity. When the conflagration was at its zenith the farmer and an assistant set off the beginning of the firework display. It lasted some twenty minutes or so, extravagant bursts and showers of colour, great blitzes of crackles and bangs, ferocious rushes of rockets that burned out just when it seemed they might reach the moon. The children present were mesmerised and when the last of the fireworks had finished, they danced round the dying flames of the bonfire and attended its glowing embers, their parents watchful of their safety. The darkening evening as the fire died down was filled with calls and shouts, 'Mind out', 'Keep back', 'Don't go too near', 'Oh, do come away, dear'. We decided to return to Oxford. Est and I sought out and found the farmer and thanked him for the organisation of the party; we thanked warmly Hugh and Lady Crammond.

Donald we found deep in conversation with Tony Gill. Tony's back was to us. I signalled to Donald that we wanted to leave. He looked at me and understood the message. He brought his conversation to a close and patting Tony on the arm left him to join us. We walked away from the party and went to where the car was parked. By that time most of the children were sitting on straw bales simply watching the guttering fire. When we were well out of earshot of Tony and anyone else, Donald said, 'The trouble with Tony is that not only is he ambitious but he lets his ambition show. That's a serious fault. He was asking me if I thought he had a chance of taking over on a permanent basis from Morris when the inevitable happens. I was trying to tell him, as tactfully as possible, that he would do better to concentrate his efforts on applying for headships elsewhere. I explained that mostly colleagues you've worked with for a long time think they're just as good as you and if you want to be Principal then why not them. So, in the end you get voted down. If, on the other hand, you get invited by your colleagues, then that's another thing. But that's not going to happen to Tony. If either of you gets the chance, reinforce my view; I'm sure it's right. It'll be much better for everyone if he doesn't put himself forward.'

Est and I agreed with him. There was no doubt that Tony was able and for some colleges might make a good principal, but perhaps he would not do for Holt. I drove Est and Donald back to Oxford. I dropped Donald off at college and Est and I returned to my house.

The next week was going to be busy, both academically and politically. We saw Willoughby as the beleaguered president of some autocratic state, vulnerable and under siege because of his own weaknesses, blindness to reality, and sheer obstinacy. We wondered if anything significant in the development of the Willoughby Morris affair would materialise that next Monday morning.

22

It did. Est and I had to get up early. It was going to be a busy teaching day for both of us. At half past seven I walked the short distance around the corner to our local shop, a newsagent and small general store. I usually bought the *Guardian* but on that occasion I thought I should buy the *Telegraph*. Sure enough on one of the inside pages of the Home News section, there was an article on Holt College and its Principal. That article was written, so the byline stated, by Nick Wright, a *Telegraph* staff reporter, and Susie Runciman. The Susie in question was, of course, *Cherwell*'s reporter.

The burden of the piece was that *Cherwell* had received a leaked, supposedly confidential, document from Holt that showed expenses claimed by its Principal for trips abroad made during the financial year up to April. There were apparent irregularities. His wife's expenses, for example, had been claimed for and paid by the college whereas the college's policy document stated clearly that 'reimbursement of travel expenses explicitly refers to "members of the college" or "employees of the college obliged to travel during their duties".' Expenses had been claimed for four trips, two to North America, one to Japan, and one to India. The document showed that a business class upgrade had been claimed for the India visit, a cost to the college of £1,900.

The *Telegraph* article questioned the legitimacy of the claims and said that the college needed to explain further how the claims were waved through the bursarial and accounting processes. Although the colleges of Oxford and Cambridge were autonomous institutions, their finances should be open and transparent in view of the fact that they were partly supported by government funding.

The final paragraph hinted that there was a rumour, substantiated in various Oxford quarters, that the Principal might have an involvement with a female undergraduate from a different college. Over the weekend, Dr Willoughby Morris, Principal of Holt College, had been unavailable for comment.

Est and I, at the same time as trying to digest our breakfast, tried to digest that news.

'I must have a cup of very strong coffee. Everything is accelerating out of control,' I said. 'It looks as though Susie is benefiting from this revelation. She's reserving a post on the *Telegraph* for when she graduates. Whoever leaked from Holt has certainly done her a favour. I'm supposed to be seeing her at eleven thirty. I'll see what she's got to say.'

Est sat there reading over the piece. 'The last paragraph is the final dagger thrust here. There must be something in it otherwise they wouldn't print it. It would be too libellous. Morris is in for a hammering. What's his response going to be? Will he defend himself and protest? What's going to happen?'

'Your guess is as good as mine, Est. I should think he'll say as little as possible and fight on. That's the sort of person he is. He'll find some way of justifying his behaviour. He'll try to find a loophole in the regulations. I know him. That's the way he works.'

'He'll find it difficult to justify the last paragraph. There's not much wriggle room there. I suppose some time today he'll issue a statement.'

We decided to hurry and go into college as soon as possible.

When we arrived, the head porter greeted us. 'Morning, sir. Morning, Dr Treisman. Come to join the throng? There are so many newspaper people around this morning, I'm having difficulty holding the fort and keeping them out. They all want to speak to the Principal, or his secretary, or the bursar.' As he spoke one of the paparazzi, his camera at the ready slung round in front of him, strolled into the lodge and asked Est if she could direct him to the Principal's lodgings. She referred him to the porter who firmly but diplomatically told him that the college was closed to the public until 2 p.m. and even then parts of the college were out of bounds to the general public including the Principal's lodgings. He advised ringing the Principal's secretary and asking for an appointment. I admired his calmness and control. I could see that there would be trouble at 2 p.m. when a little table was set up in the lodge and the public were charged two pounds to enter. The journos would pay their due and enter the college if they had not managed to infiltrate the grounds in some way beforehand. It would be impossible for the porters to keep them out. No doubt Jeremy Eedes would solve the problem; college entry and security were part of his brief. Nevertheless, I wondered how he would deal with it.

The last week of term was always extremely busy. The culmination was a long round of what are called termly collections, when each undergraduate is interviewed by his or her tutor together with the senior tutor and the Principal. A brief report on the term's work would be presented followed by the Principal's comments and any remarks in reply from the student. It meant that each tutor had to find time to write the report, which would eventually be archived.

At eleven thirty Susie presented herself with her tutorial partner, Howard Ainsworth, as usual. Fortunately for Susie it was not her turn to read out her essay. She explained, 'I'm very sorry. I haven't been able to finish my essay. Would it be OK for me to hand it to you before the end of the week? I've been so occupied with other things this week.' There was no other response but to say that it was all right. I recognised that she would have been busy with her journalism and particularly the *Telegraph* article.

At the end Howard Ainsworth left, Susie delayed and made a show of packing up her trappings, notebook, essay, handbag and sports bag in which she carried everything. 'I wanted to say that there has been a fresh leak about the Principal and a female student. Are you aware of that?'

I told her I had read about it in the *Telegraph* under her byline and congratulated her on her breakthrough into proper journalism. 'Well, you see, I have the right training. *Cherwell* is a wonderful apprenticeship. Anyway, obviously we wouldn't have printed that part of the story unless it could be backed up. We have witnesses and the girl herself will quite possibly spill the beans. She can see that her brief and superficial affair with her sugar daddy will not last. The *Telegraph* reporter says that they can make it worth her while if she's in any way reluctant to cooperate.'

'I see. What's the next move? What do you think will happen next? It's important to know for the sake of the college. Naturally we have the college's reputation to think of. That is what most of us are concerned with, not the Principal's.'

'Well, all I can tell you is that the journalists will chase this to the end. They'll dig around now until they get some version of the truth. *Private Eye* has a good underground presence here with many informants. I reckon it won't be long before the Principal will be forced to make a statement on every aspect of this business.'

At lunch I made sure that I sat next to Tony Gill. I told him as much as I knew about what the press was doing. I asked him what he thought we should do about protecting the college's reputation. After some discussion, we thought a meeting of the finance committee should be called and a special sub-committee formed to investigate in detail all the allegations that were being aired. Tony, in his capacity of Vicegerent, would have to broach the matter with Willoughby, who of course would resist the establishment of such a sub-committee; he would have to think of some way of presenting the move so that he would have no choice. In the first place he would have to persuade Morris to call the extraordinary meeting.

Later, Tony told me that he said to Morris that even if he refused to call the finance committee meeting, some other measure would be taken to investigate the charges that were being made against him; it would be far better for him to call it and have some control rather than none at all. That is what happened. That afternoon, Tony approached Morris, who was by turns irate and moody, but in the end agreed. So, the finance committee convened at 2.30 p.m. the following afternoon, on the Tuesday of that week.

Morris was outraged. He was red-faced. He slapped the table with his good hand. He was like a bad-tempered child. 'Why do I have to have my integrity questioned? Why should I be impugned in this way?' Thus his protestations were heard. At this point he was still in the chair. 'And, Tony, I don't see why you're here. You're not a member of this committee. The constitution of the college is being ignored. In fact this meeting is totally unconstitutional.'

While Willoughby paused for breath, Tony Gill interjected, 'I'm here as Vicegerent. I think you'll find that in circumstances such as we find ourselves in, it is entirely proper that I attend. It would probably be wise too that I take the chair. All of this can be regularised tomorrow at the governing body meeting.'

The final governing body meeting of term was to happen the next day, on the Wednesday. Tony Gill continued, 'If the fellowship doesn't like what we're doing, then I will stand back. Obviously the whole college must have the last say.'

Morris was belligerent. 'Yes, well, until then, I'm still in the chair and your presence is not necessary.'

Tony looked straight at Morris and with an unaccustomed edge to his voice, he said, 'Principal. I intend to stay. It's part of my responsibility as Vicegerent. As I have explained, this is an extraordinary situation. Perhaps the others here will support this view.'

There was a general murmur of agreement, Eedes alone remained silent. Even Knowles thought it should happen. So, Tony stayed.

'Let it be noted that I resent this undermining of my authority. Now, what is the purpose of this meeting? I must say that I find it completely unnecessary. I am by no means convinced by the Vicegerent's explanations to me prior to this meeting. I have only come here to defend my position against slanderous accusations. I wish to remind you all, and emphasise, that you are acting illegally.'

At this point, Jane Templeman stood up and said, 'I wish to propose formally that we set up here and now, very quickly, a sub-committee that will look into all allegations of financial malpractice, malfeasance, and corruption, mainly to do with expenses claims but also concerning any other financial affairs of the college.'

Morris nearly exploded. He sniffed and snorted. 'Why on earth should we want to do that? We can handle all such matters within the confines of this committee here and now.'

Jacob Black responded. 'T-that is d-demonstrably n-not s-so. A f-few p-people concentrating on th-this will b-be good.'

'Will anyone second me?' Jane asked.

Frank Bradshaw, Jacob and I all raised our hands. Jacob spoke. 'I'll s-second.' And that was that. The sub-committee was established. The Vicegerent was chair; and the members were the bursar, Jane, and Frank Bradshaw. It was agreed that it should meet as soon as possible after the next day's governing body meeting, once Willoughby Morris's objections had been dealt with. Morris marched out. He spoke to no one, not even Eedes or Knowles.

21

I spent the evening with Est and brought her up-to-date with what was happening. I told her that after the finance meeting, Frank, Jane, JOB and I went into brief conference. We thought it best to lobby as many members of the governing body as possible. Anyone we met, we would talk to and underline the seriousness of the imminent crisis for the college; everyone had to be made aware of the bad publicity. Everything turned back on to the college. The *Telegraph* article had said that a university spokeswoman had stated that it was not directly the concern of the university but that it was all a private matter for the college. Frank said he would concentrate on the scientists and Jane would cover as many of the arts fellows as possible. Jacob and I would do some personal lobbying. We considered the prospect of Willoughby in self-denial and making declarations of innocence and outrage simply appalling. It was essential that, for the moment, Tony should stand in as Principal so far as chairing meetings and making public statements were concerned. It would be true to say that generally the prospect of Tony assuming the principalship was becoming more acceptable; he had shown himself as firm and decisive. Naturally that was not to stop Willoughby making personal statements but he should not be speaking on behalf of the college.

The second half of Tuesday and then Wednesday morning were busy: my teaching was interrupted by the phone ringing many times and my having to ask undergraduates to step outside my room for a short time while I explained the case that we had worked out.

Eventually the time arrived for the final governing body meeting of term. It was two o'clock and everyone, with the exception of two or three members whose absence was unavoidable, had met in the long room of the senior common room where sometimes on guest nights dessert was served. A really bad portrait of Elias de Holt, one of several but by far the worst, looked down on the Principal's empty chair. In that particular picture, Elias de Holt wore a wickedly impish expression; but somehow, by contrast to the other two portraits of him that the college owned, the contours of the face were wrong and altered mistakes in the painting's execution were obvious.

We waited. Fellows chatted among themselves. At getting on for two fifteen, Tony Gill tapped the tabletop where he was sitting. There was a gradual silence and Tony said, 'I think that by two fifteen we should ask the bursar to go and find out where Principal Morris is. Is that a good suggestion? Shall we do that?' There was general subdued comment of agreement. Jeremy Eedes went out, his gown flowing behind him. Around ten minutes later he returned and reported that Morris would be with us by half past two. He had told Eedes that he had understood the meeting to be called for at two thirty. So, at two thirty Morris appeared. Far from being apologetic or dejected, he was again belligerent and confrontational.

'It's a pity someone did not make the time of this meeting clear to me. Neither I nor my secretary knew that it was called for at two.' He said this in spite of the fact that all governing body meetings began at two. Either he was being obstructive and it was his tactic to keep everyone waiting, or he was so preoccupied with the meeting of the finance committee the day before, that he had genuinely mixed up the start time. I knew what I believed: he was pursuing a tactical battle with his colleagues. Yet he ought to have known that it was one he was bound to lose.

'Now, I have to say first that I regard several events over the last few days, the holding of meetings, private manoeuvrings, and I really don't know what else, as abuses against my executive power, which you have given me by electing me as Principal. I have said before, and I'll say it again, I think we should do and say as little as possible during the present crisis and let it die down. The press will soon lose interest. I am very sorry, not to say surprised, that some fellows have ignored what I said. When we know the details I might have to call for suspensions or resignations. It's impossible to run an institution like this and, at the same time, be constantly undermined by gainsayers. I don't want to waste time. I'll come back to this most unsatisfactory business a little later. Let us look at the agenda.'

Morris seemed completely oblivious to the fact that he was publicly under suspicion of having an affair with a female undergraduate. He was ignoring what was staring him in the face. It appeared that some form of paranoia had gripped him, a sense that he was being accused unjustifiably, and that he was blanking it all out.

'You have all had a copy of the last meeting's minutes. I don't propose to have them read out. Are there any objections?'

One of the history fellows spoke up, 'Well, I do on principle; but if my fellow fellows want to speed things up since we have much to discuss, I'm happy on this one occasion to let my objection pass.' Again, everyone agreed.

Willoughby gruffly muttered, 'I don't accept that there's much to talk about. It's the usual end of term business. And, looking at the agenda, I've disallowed one item that directly relates to me – the proposal that I should stand aside and let the Vicegerent preside over college affairs until things settle down. I certainly don't agree to that and I've struck it off the agenda.'

Jacob Black shuffled in his seat and looked severely agitated. Others glanced around and there was a visible feeling of unease.

JOB pushed back his chair and rose to his feet. He started to say, 'Th-there are n-no g-grounds for d-disallowing the motion as p-presented. I sh-shall not be p-party to this ab-buse of d-democracy.' Morris tried to speak over him. I think he was trying to say that Jacob had no right to speak at that point, but JOB was so concentrated on getting his words out, that he drove on and won the battle to be heard. Jacob turned away in order to walk out of the meeting.

At that point, Tony Gill who kept his seat, tapped his pen fiercely on the table, waved down an attempted interruption from Morris, and said firmly, 'In this present predicament that the college finds itself in, many of our colleagues and I myself think that I, in my office as Vicegerent, should chair meetings for the present. This is regrettable but necessary. The Principal should stand aside temporarily until various issues have been resolved. But before I go any further, do I have the confidence of the fellowship? Perhaps a show of hands would be the best and quickest way to signify agreement.' There were two objections, one from the Principal, the other from Eedes. I noticed that Knowles abstained. Every other member of the governing body raised a hand. There was silence and then Tony Gill declared, 'Thank you; in which case I shall assume the chair.'

He stayed sitting where he was and there followed a short silence. It was as though Morris could not believe his ears. Suddenly he registered the fact of his deposition and he exploded. He shouted, 'I do not accept this. I am Principal. You elected me. You should now do as I say. This action is against the college's constitution and I shall immediately talk to the Visitor.' I thought to myself, and a lot of good that will do you. The college's Visitor was the Bishop of Winchester, a divine noted for his scholastic theology, and not someone like the founding benefactor, Walter Grimmond, who had been an astute, wily politician.

'Note, I leave under protest. I'm not staying at this illegal meeting.' He stormed out, followed in a more dignified way by the bursar. Tony Gill then moved to the head of the table and took the Principal's vacant chair. He took up the Principal's gavel and knocked once. 'I shall proceed through the business agenda as quickly as possible and then we must discuss the present situation. Something has to be done, some gesture made, which will give the public some sort of view of our concerns; otherwise the press will have more of a field day than they are having already.'

Tony was a brisk, efficient, shrewd chairman. When he practised his office he became a different person from what he was in private. In his family situation and with friends he was diffident, deferential, almost subservient; but when invested with office he was confident, clear, and decisive. He did not allow speakers to stray from the topic under discussion and he was firm with those who tended to monopolise discussion. He was meticulous in allowing all to give their views. It was all so different from Willoughby's style of autocratic control.

When it came time for debate about Willoughby Morris and his position in the college, if it had not been for the presence of Jeremy Knowles, opinion would have been unanimous. Knowles kept to his policy of abstention. It was decided that the college under the office of the Vicegerent should issue a press release stating that the Principal was standing aside for the time being until matters were clarified and resolved. The Vicegerent would be acting head of house, and the college was committed to thorough investigation of irregularities. A report would be published by the college authorities as soon as possible.

Donald proposed, after that motion was passed, that the Principal, for his own good and so that he could defend himself, should make a press statement. Knowles said that it would be impossible to make Willoughby issue a statement but he did see that it might help his cause. Tony asked Jeremy Knowles if he would be prepared to suggest such a move to him, and Jeremy Knowles agreed.

Tony stressed that everyone should be especially conscious of security and confidentiality. The leak of information should be stopped. We had to handle our own affairs from now on. Negative publicity was bad in many ways, but perhaps the worst was that it gave the government, which was hostile to the autonomy of the colleges of Oxford and Cambridge, a means of persuading people that the government itself should take over complete control of the colleges. Jacob Black agreed. 'The g-government is like H-henry the Eighth d-despoiling the monast-steries. It w-wants our m-monies and our l-lands.'

So, it was agreed that Tony should draw up the text of a statement very much along the lines of what he had already said and it should be published as coming from the college authorities. Knowles was obviously going to recount to Willoughby what had passed at the meeting and presumably he would publish his own statement. If he were wise, it should not be too much in conflict with the college's statement, but as Jane said, who knew how Morris would take it; it was possible that he would do himself more harm than good.

On Thursday morning Est met Brendan Naish who told her that Willoughby was none too pleased with our statement, which followed almost exactly what Tony had said about the Vicegerent taking over until everything had been investigated and clarified; but Knowles had been able, with Timothy Eedes, to persuade Morris to make a diplomatic statement. Our statement had been sent over-night to the press in general and all the broadsheets carried it. The *Mail*, *Express* and *Mirror* referred to it and hinted at a developing story. Morris's statement appeared in the local press in the afternoon and in the *London Evening Standard*. It simply said, 'The Principal of Holt College, Oxford, in a press release denies rumours of the misuse of college funds. He states that he has always adhered to the rules set down by the college's finance committee. He has thought it in the best interests of the college for the Vicegerent to stand in for him temporarily.'

The sub-committee lost no time in starting its investigation. It met at midday. I heard about their deliberations primarily from Jane, but both Frank and Tony kept me well in the picture. I simply did not have time to listen to JOB; his stuttering made him long-winded and he tended anyway to ramble off into philosophical byways. Bursar Eedes was required to provide all expenses claims and correspond-ence associated with the Principal's travels and accommodation over the past three years. Frank had been sent to the bursar's office to fetch them. Only the last two years' claims were there; all earlier ones had already been destroyed contrary to college policy and, more importantly, contrary to the instructions of both the Inland Revenue and the college accountants. The removal of that particular year's evidence, the first of the three years, had happened recently, within the last fortnight, just when adverse publicity for the Principal was beginning to appear.

Yet by Friday evening the sub-committee had assembled a comprehensive damning report which indicted the Principal on several accounts. On Thursday evening the four of them had sat late into the night. Tony told me that he and Jacob had finished their scrutiny at one o'clock in the morning; his wife was not pleased. They went about their other duties on Friday morning and during the afternoon they met and drafted their report. Tony sent me an email attachment of the draft. Nothing had been seen of Morris.

After some formal preliminaries, the report hit home; it raised concerns about claims made by Principal Morris over the past three years. It noted that the first year's records had been for some unexplained reason destroyed. It questioned claims made for a number of international trips and claims made by the Principal's wife who routinely travelled with the Principal on college business. There were issues to do with those expenses. 'These instances make it impossible for us to have confidence that on all occasions neither college nor university-advised rules were adhered to.'

The claims called into question were half a dozen trips made over the past two years. Three were to the States, one to Greece, one to South Africa, and one to India. On each of the trips, Elizabeth had accompanied Morris and there were claims for her expenses that had been paid. The trip that caused the sub-committee most concern was the one to India. It transpired that Willoughby had travelled to Delhi to attend an international scientific conference at which he gave a paper. His airfare and hotel expenses, and those of his wife, had been paid for by the organisers of the conference; Tony had verified that by telephone to the conference secretary who had confirmed it by email. Apparently what had then happened was that

Willoughby had tried to arrange two alumni events, one cocktail reception, and one dinner, for fundraising. The dinner had taken place; the reception had been cancelled for lack of support. He had claimed for flight upgrades to business class at the college's expense, incurring around £2,000. In effect, by enhancing to business class, he was claiming twice for the trip from two different sources. In the case of his wife, college policy had always been that expenses were paid only for members of the college on college business. According to college rules, his wife was not, no more than his children, an official member of the college. The report noted that there was a case for that rule to be changed. I learned that Jane, quite rightly, had taken the view that a college head's wife was usually so intimately involved in the running of the college that she ought to be at least an honorary member.

Tony sent an email attachment of the report to Morris; it was only fair that he should see what was being charged against him. In addition to the members of the sub-committee, and besides me, a copy was sent to Senior Tutor Knowles, Jacob Black, and Donald. Tony invited comments. He planned to release the report to the rest of the fellowship, by email, on Sunday evening. In the event, the only person with reservations was the bursar but he had been out-voted on the sub-committee. It was understandable because Eedes's competence was being questioned in two respects; why did he sign off claims that were not in line with college policy, and why had records been destroyed?

In the interests of security, in order to guard against any leaks, Tony decided to delay circulating the report to fellows until nine o'clock on Monday morning. He did that from home. It was to his dismay, and everybody else's, that a summary of the report appeared in the *Telegraph* and the *Daily Mail*. The *Telegraph* published a short article and the *Mail* ran three paragraphs in its gossip column, which largely concentrated on Willoughby's ill-judged exercise of office.

Needless to say there was a flurry of telephone calls and email correspondence between fellows. There had been a leak when only the sub-committee members, Morris himself, Knowles, Jacob Black, Jane, Donald and I had seen and read the report. Not even Est knew about it, which she might have done had we been together Sunday night. We had not. She had been in London. How then had the newspapers managed to obtain a copy of the report?

That was the question being asked. We were all trying to work out where the leak sprang from. By lunchtime, and after many conversations, most people were reconciled to the fact that it did not matter anyway. We were used to leaks, and although in itself it was reprehensible, the sub-committee and most others seemed to think that, on the whole, it was quite a good thing. It meant that the college's problems were out in the open and a resolution would come more quickly that otherwise.

Naturally we all tried to assess who could have been the source. My feeling was that somehow Brendan Naish had access to Knowles's email and had used it to tip off the press. What exactly his motive was, I could not define; but other possible culprits seemed more remote than him. I reckoned that none of the sub-committee members were likely to have done it. My second choice of suspect was Donald. He might have seen it as a political opportunity and that the leak would speed Willoughby on his way. Among those of us who spoke together, Naish was considered the prime suspect. It hardly mattered because it was then that everything accelerated.

Willoughby was furious. He fumed. Tony said that Willoughby rang him and spluttered in indignation. He blamed Tony for the leak and accused him of indescribable incompetence. Tony kept calm and advised Morris to maintain a cautious silence. Apparently Willoughby exploded: 'What do you mean. Don't you realise, this is extremely damaging for me? I shall instruct my solicitors immediately.' Tony's response was: 'Willoughby, it's extremely damaging for the college. If you call in your lawyers and fight the college, it will take a long time, be very dirty, and certainly won't be good for you in the long run whichever way the verdict goes.' Willoughby's reply to that was that Tony should mind his own business, stop giving him advice, and just find out who the culprit was. Willoughby finally said that he was no longer going to stand aside but he was taking back executive power. Tony said he himself remained imperturbable and simply told Willoughby that no one, apart from perhaps Eedes and Knowles, would take any notice of him. He should realise that all the college clerical and administrative staff were now answerable to him, Tony. Had Willoughby contacted the Visitor yet, perhaps that would be the best thing to do? Willoughby did not answer that question and Tony felt that he had not.

In the middle of the afternoon, the porter on duty told me, Willoughby left the college by taxi; it was to take him to the railway station. Elizabeth did not accompany him. She remained in the lodgings.

That left only Eedes of the old dispensation. Knowles blew neither hot nor cold. He was probably trying to work out which party it was better to ally himself with. Dinner was provided in college during ninth week, or first week of the vacation. Those who wanted it signalled the SCR butler at any time up to 1 p.m. Est and I had so much to do that we decided to dine in.

The time of dinner was still seven fifteen in vacations. Est and I met at about five past the hour and we both had a glass of Tio Pepe sherry; until the arrival of Jacob Black, the steward always served an amontillado before dinner, but JOB persuaded us of the superiority of the driest of dry sherries before dinner. There was no doubt in our minds that it sharpened the appetite.

I could tell that there was something unsettled about Est. She looked particularly lively; her eyes shone and she laughingly glanced around and was reluctant to meet my usual besotted gaze. I said, 'What's going on, Est? You've either had some extraordinary news or you're holding something back that I'm interested in. I can tell. Come on, what is it? What's it all about?'

'Damn,' she exclaimed, 'you see, I can't hide anything. Have you read the evening paper? I assume you haven't or you would be talking about it.'

'No, I haven't seen the *Mail*. Why? What's happened?'

'I'll tell you when we're sitting down. Things really are going from bad to worse.'

The butler appeared and announced that dinner was served. We followed him into hall. There was apparently no one else dining on high table. One or two undergraduates were at one of the long tables in the body of the hall; most had fled at the first opportunity, on the Saturday and Sunday of the weekend. Est took the seat at the head of the table. She had slight seniority over me since she had been appointed a term before I arrived. I sat at her right. The butler waited at table that night and he poured us each a young Muscadet, which accompanied well the plaice that was our first course.

With my first sip I said to Est, 'Now, come on. Tell all.'

'OK. Well, the *Mail*'s gossip columnist – you know its Spectator column – says that a head of house is pursuing an affair with a girl student at St Cecilia's. It's supposed on the parts of the two participants to be clandestine but every day it's becoming more and more of an open secret.'

'Does it identify the head of college? Could it,' I asked ironically, 'by any chance be Willoughby?'

'No. They're very careful not to name anyone, although obviously they must know who they are talking about. Spectator goes on to say that they never meet in Oxford but they have been seen dining at L'Escargot in London. The final sentence says that there is a connection with a college principal already in the news about expenses irregularities. So, if that doesn't pin the label on poor old Willoughby, nothing will.'

By the time we were being served the main course and a glass of the college Burgundy had been poured, we were trying to analyse what it must have been like to be in the Principal's lodgings that night.

We pictured Elizabeth reading the paper, absorbing the column, and yelling at Willoughby. She would drink excessive quantities of gin and become extremely belligerent. Then we remembered that Willoughby had been seen blustering off to London. She was going to be a lone drinker that night which would make it acutely worse for her.

We debated the purpose and effectiveness of gossip columns. Newspapers needed stories; gossip columns cultivated and nurtured them. Truth and facts were not their major concerns. Est remarked on an old student she had taught who at the last recent general election had been elected Member of Parliament; she had at once become the target of the columnists. She was fashionable, pretty, intelligent, and a prime prospect for a limelight romance. Every week or so, she was mentioned in the columns. She had written a book about the conflict in the Middle East between the Israelis and the Palestinians. The gossip columns kept repeating a myth that she had once been a prisoner of Hezbollah; she had not. Yet it was repeated time and time again. It was inserted into her Wikipedia entry. She edited it out and the next day it would reappear.

Nevertheless, Est and I felt that Spectator's story was so close to the truth as we knew it, the paper must have procured some evidence that it was not at that point revealing.

I finally commented, 'Willoughby had better enjoy himself in London this evening in sublime ignorance of what's being reported in Oxford. He's soon going to know about it, from Elizabeth if not from some other source, hostile or friendly.'

'Yes. The trouble is that what with the nationals and the Spectator column, it's so easy for those interested to put a name to the head of college. Morris has to keep out of the way. He can't face this down.'

I was not so sure. It was Willoughby Morris's nature to fight against the odds, admirable in some ways, but not in this case.

After dinner we met Donald in the main quad. He, like me, had not read the local paper. We told him of our discussion. His comment was that bits and pieces of information were coming from everywhere. People were starting to give intelligence to the reporters that hitherto had been kept secret or merely retained as rumour and suspicion. Everyone was now speaking freely of what they knew; and above all, he said, the college was leaking like the hull of a torpedoed ship. Later, Est and I wondered if, by mentioning the leaky college, he was trying to convince people that he was not the source of the leak, the hole in the old hull. On the other hand, he was right and he might just have been commenting on fact. We were all being influenced, and in a way tainted, by the increasing atmosphere of suspicion.

23

After that Est and I went our own ways. We both had various things to do for the next day, the Tuesday of ninth week. Est was preparing for an appearance on a television culture show when she was to discuss a just-published novel and a new play at the Royal Court theatre in London. I had to meet a deadline for an article I had been commissioned to write for the *Financial Times*. Having struggled to keep my concentration going, I finally stopped thinking and writing and left my house round about 11 p.m. and walked to the High and Est's flat. There we listened to Beethoven's sixth symphony and, not able to part from her company, we spent the night together.

Early the following morning, I went downstairs, crossed the road to a newsagent's, bought the *Telegraph* and the *Guardian*, walked a short distance to a delicatessen and bought a couple of croissants. I took my shopping back to the flat and Est and I took our breakfast together. Est made some strong coffee and we each started searching the two papers for any mention of Willoughby. I ransacked the *Guardian*, she the *Telegraph*. There was not a word printed about him or Holt. The story had disappeared.

'Well, there's respite for Morris,' Est commented. 'He should make the most of it. I don't think it will be for long.'

'Yes, I totally agree. It's in abeyance. It's simmering on a back burner.'

In fact, it was not until the weekend that the story surfaced again. In the meantime, I had to go up to London to meet a famous Nobel Prize winner, an economist, who was going to be awarded an honorary degree at Encaenia on the next Wednesday. Encaenia was the annual summer celebration that the university holds, a festival of renewal, a commemoration. At the ceremony that takes place in the Sheldonian Theatre, benefactors are thanked and distinguished people honoured. About half a dozen world-famous academics, writers, artists, politicians, or contributors in general to the common weal are awarded honorary degrees. The Chancellor of the university presents the degrees and the Public Orator makes a speech in Latin that describes in witty terms the achievements of each individual. The speech is called the Creweian Oration after Lord Crewe who in the eighteenth century bestowed a gift on the university that finances the whole proceeding. The great and the good of the university, together with the honorands, walk in procession in their academic robes after the ceremony to one of the colleges for peaches, strawberries and cream, all part of Crewe's benefaction.

Est was to appear on her television show that Friday. I went up to London on the Thursday afternoon. I met Bevan Clayton at the East India and Sports Club in St James's Square. Clayton was an American, a professor of economics from Boston University. His Boston club had reciprocal rights with the St James's club. He had made many contributions to the practical application of economic theories over the years and had influenced the emergence of Brazil as a powerful commercial and industrial force in the world. He had been made a Nobel laureate for three decades of important work and he now spoke out for a Keynesian approach towards the solution of failing economies; create money and spend out of stagnation and recession.

It was a glorious afternoon. I met him in the library. The porter had directed me there following his instruction. From there we went out into the sunshine and sat amidst the trees and the summer flower borders in the shade of the square's central garden. It was difficult to realise that we were in the centre of the giant metropolis. I talked to him about Wednesday's ceremony back in Oxford and explained about arrangements for him to stay overnight in the guest rooms at

Holt. At six we returned to the club and took a drink in the bar; he drank a gin and tonic and I had my usual Laphroaig whisky with just a small amount of water which I always added after the first sip or two.

Since Monday, I had the reluctant feeling that the Willoughby Morris crisis was gradually going off the boil. There had been no follow-up in the press. I should not have worried. Away from the public eye, matters were taking their own course that would ensure the re-emergence of Willoughby's downfall.

The inevitability of Morris's fate, by pure chance, became clear that very evening. At seven we left the club to walk a short distance into Mayfair to have dinner at one of London's top-rated restaurants. Bevan Clayton had insisted on taking me there. We found The Glasshouse by strolling along the length of a fashionable mews and turning right, and then, by the side of a tall apartment block, there was a downwards ramp covered in what was clearly artificial grass to enter the restaurant under a glass awning. The sides of the ramp were decorated with *pots de fleurs,* of the kind that Henry Miller so detested in northern French towns. I had never agreed with him. These pots showed off white and pink geraniums and more than made up for the rather too verdant reality of the plastic turf.

Once through the two plate-glass doors, Bevan mentioned his name and that he had reserved that morning a table for two, and we were ushered to a table on the far side of the restaurant's dining room, behind a substantial square support pillar that was one of about six that obviously helped support the apartment block. When we were settled at our table, it was clear to me that the restaurant had been created in its semi-basement state from an underground car park; an ingenious conversion.

Bevan thought he would sharpen his appetite with a dry sherry. I thought that a good idea. He signalled a waiter who said that he would send the sherry waiter to us. On glancing round there seemed, at that point in the evening, more waiters and various attendants than patrons. The sherry waiter duly arrived at our table and offered a list of sherries of at least twenty-five different varieties. Bevan made his choice and I followed his suit.

After the brightness of the evening light outside, by contrast, the interior of the restaurant was dim. Two tables had been occupied when we entered and gradually it filled up. Where we sat, we were obscured by the massive pillar from the general view; it was private, a secure table, separated from most of the other clients.

Suddenly I froze. I paused in conversation and Bevan asked me if I was feeling all right. I apologised and said that I was fine; but I had seen someone come in whom I had not expected to see and did not particularly want to meet. With great consideration he asked me if we should move elsewhere; he knew of another intimate restaurant, smaller but probably just as fine in its offer of a menu. I declined and replied that we almost certainly would not be noticed and if we were then it was too bad and I would put up with any possible embarrassment.

The fact was that of all people Willoughby Morris had just come in with a young woman. They made such an odd pair, a late middle-aged corpulent man with thinning hair and glasses and a young, very attractive woman, with short jet-black hair and extremely well made up. She was taller than Willoughby and I estimated that she was probably about nineteen or twenty. I indicated the couple to Bevan and commented quietly that she was maybe a relation, a niece perhaps; I added that the man in question was the Principal, for the moment, of Holt College where he would be staying for Encaenia. It was only when they were both seated and when I saw Willoughby lean across their table, take her hand and look lovingly into her eyes that I realised she was almost certainly the girl student from St Cecilia's.

As the evening progressed, it became clear from our vantage point that indeed Willoughby was in an amorous tryst. It was inconceivable from his behaviour that Elizabeth knew anything about that assignation. Although I was somewhat preoccupied and distracted by Willoughby's presence, I managed to continue an intelligent discourse with Bevan. He, though, understood my position, my curiosity, my astonishment of the chance meeting, and ended up as fascinated as I was with their relationship. Unfortunately Willoughby and the girl were just too far away for us to hear what they were saying.

Towards the end of the evening, as Bevan and I were finishing our coffee and he was sipping a cognac – I had reverted to a malt whisky – Willoughby and his companion left. He had called for the bill, paid with his credit card, and pushed back his chair. He moved her chair as she stood up and as she turned he kissed her on the cheek. They left The Glasshouse arm in arm.

Bevan and I finished our drinks and coffee. We had been discussing the plight of the eurozone countries and what some of the UK's leading economists advised for stabilising the currency. The *Financial Times* had published a long article by one of the members of the monetary policy committee that sat with the Governor of the Bank of England, and it had published a short, pithy leader on the subject. Bevan paid the bill. The crowd of diners had thinned out and once again it looked as though the attendant staff outnumbered the remaining customers. As we walked towards the glass doors, they suddenly opened and Willoughby came back in. He looked flustered and caught sight of me. He pushed sideways past without acknowledging me and went straight up to the major domo. It appeared that he had left a small notebook lying on his table. A waiter must have retrieved it and taken it behind an order desk. The major domo found it for him and handed it over.

Meanwhile, his friend had waited outside and had been watching what was happening. As he was going back towards the exit he exclaimed with a clear show of annoyance: 'What on earth are you doing here, Dr James? The last person I expected to see! Are you following me around?' He hurried past but immediately stumbled into his dining companion who by this time was fully back inside the doors. I said, 'I'm certainly not following you around. Look, this is Bevan Clayton; he's getting an honorary degree at Encaenia. Bevan – Willoughby Morris, Principal of Holt College.' I turned towards the young girl as though expecting to be introduced. Morris responded rather ungraciously, 'Good. Congratulations, Clayton.' Peremptorily he thrust past us and, without introducing his friend, he took hold of her elbow brusquely and they went out hurriedly into the night. There was no doubt that Morris was embarrassed. He could not wait to get away from me. He knew that he had been observed in a compromising situation. I felt I now had a hold on him, a bargaining chip, a diplomatic tool.

Bevan commented as we made our way back to St James's Square, 'Strange man. He didn't seem very sociable. Couldn't wait to get away. Is he always like that? Who was his delightful-looking lady friend?'

'Yes. I'm sorry about that. You may very well ask. He's in a bit of a crisis at the moment. I think his wife might like to know who she is, if you see what I mean. You'll have to forgive him. He's having a tough time at Oxford at the mo. You might not see him on Wednesday. I think he'll stay away.'

I gave Bevan a quick summary of Willoughby Morris's difficulties.

Bevan commented, 'He doesn't have good judgement. He shouldn't be doing that job. It's not for someone who enjoys the exercise of power. He should have stayed in private business or headed a government agency; politicians love to leave matters to their executives.'

We parted at the East India and I caught my train back to Oxford after walking to Paddington station. I had promised to meet Bevan in the lodge of Holt on Wednesday morning at a quarter to ten. I would be his host until he was embraced by the university authorities just prior to the ceremony.

On Friday morning I saw Est. She went into college and was

mentally preparing herself for her broadcast in the evening. We met in the common room at coffee time and I told her what had happened at The Glasshouse.

'What a shock for Willoughby to find you there. Do you think it was the St Cecilia girl? Horrific! How embarrassing. Did you feel embarrassed?'

'No, not exactly – surprised, yes. Very surprised. I almost felt sorry for Morris; to be caught out in that way without in the least expecting it. But I quickly let that pass. He's got to go. It's outrageous that he's behaving in this way. He's a real fool.'

Later I met Donald and I told him about the chance meeting. He was preparing to go off to America in a fortnight's time; he was attending a conference of the Episcopal Church in Philadelphia and then going on to the University of Massachusetts at Amherst to teach on a month's summer school. That evening, before I watched Est on television, I rang Tony Gill and told him. His reaction was one of exasperation with Morris. He told me that he had set up a committee of inquiry into the misuses of expenses, which would consist of himself, Jane and Donald. It would issue a report for the whole of the governing body within a fortnight, before Donald's departure for the States.

Est performed most impressively in the discussion and debate on the contemporary novel and a recently released film. She was confident in front of the cameras, firm in her views and unfazed by confrontation with a radical critic from a left-wing national newspaper. I thought she was a natural for television debate and knew that if she wanted to she could turn herself into a popular, academic, intellectual TV commentator. She could have a parallel career in broadcasting; she might be yet another kind of A.J.P. Taylor or John Carey.

It was a quiet weekend. There was no sign of Morris. I gathered from Donald that Elizabeth had not left the lodgings since Morris had gone off to London. The domestic staff were keeping a wary eye on her. They said that she was drinking heavily and that in the mornings she was keeping to her bed and getting up late, around ten thirty to eleven o'clock.

On Sunday morning, after spending the night with Est in her flat, we read in the *Sunday Telegraph*'s gossip column that the Principal of Holt College, Oxford, had been seen dining in the company of a model-like young woman and on Saturday had been seen in the same young woman's company having drinks at lunchtime in the Shoreditch Club.

It struck me that the Shoreditch Club was not Willoughby Morris's usual sort of milieu; it was a convenient club for media, PR and IT techies. I knew it from my contacts with economic analysts in investment houses. It was close to the 'silicon hub' that extends from Old Street through the East End to Queen Elizabeth Olympic Park. Shoreditch was the leisure space for entrepreneurs and angel investors. Anyway, it was evident that the press was not losing interest in Morris.

Later when I went into college I met Donald. He had been assisting at the university church of St Mary's, acting as a sort of reserve curate. He was going to the chapel office to leave his clerical garb, his surplice and cassock, his bands and his doctoral hood. He told me that Tony was wasting no time and that the committee of inquiry was meeting that evening; he would let me know if anything important or momentous was discovered or discussed.

On Monday of that week Morris turned up. I learned from the head porter that around eleven o'clock a taxi arrived outside the college; it delivered Willoughby Morris with a small overnight suitcase. He had made considerable fuss of demanding a receipt for his paid fare and while the driver was writing it out, he blustered through the lodge and told the porter to take it from the man when he had done. Morris had gone directly to the lodgings. One of the maids had told him that there was quite a scene between him and Elizabeth. Elizabeth had quickly become hysterical and demanded to know where he had been and who he had been staying with. He had lost what little patience he possessed, shouted at her and isolated himself in his study. She had banged on the door but he had locked it. Elizabeth then retreated to the kitchen where she poured herself a large gin and tonic.

In the afternoon I took a call in my rooms from Susie. She said that she thought I ought to know that some time during the week the *Telegraph* would be running a story on Morris, either on his romantic liaison with the St Cecilia girl or further about the expenses scandal. 'Scandal' was her word; she said that was what the London journalists were now calling the Holt College story. I thanked her for the intelligence and said I would look each day at the papers. She promised to inform me of any other developments that she might hear of.

College life went on as usual except that there was a tense atmosphere that was almost palpable at times. Everyone was expectant; everyone was detectably nervous. Occasionally Willoughby would appear, come out of his lair and roar. He still clearly saw himself as head of college, as the boss, as the pre-eminent leader. He was not to be put down. He was like a dictator whose hitherto loyal ministers were rebelling against him. He refused to recognise that his power had evaporated, that his authority had waned. He thought, without any doubt on his part, that he could impose his will on those about him. He had forgotten long ago that he was merely 'primus inter pares'. It was sad to watch. In spite of Tony Gill's best efforts to dissuade him, on Tuesday he went into lunch in the senior common room. Tony absented himself. Morris took his customary seat. No one chose to sit next to him until Jeremy Eedes entered. Eedes sat next to him on his right. Even Eedes was embarrassed by Morris's presence. Little conversation passed between them but just before Willoughby rose to leave, he hit the table with the flat of his hand and said loudly to Eedes: 'What is the matter with this wretched college? My supposed colleagues are so damned uncivil.' There was no one who did not hear, and Morris marched out leaving Eedes by himself looking most uncomfortable.

That evening at my house Est and I were discussing Morris's appearance at lunch. We wondered if he would stay out of the way for Encaenia. 'He's not likely to be around,' she said. 'He knows the college feeling about his presence. He'd have to be completely blind if he didn't think the university's reaction would be the same.'

'That's the trouble,' I said, 'he is. He simply can't see what others see. He's lost his political sense. He should keep out of the limelight for the time being. He probably won't do it. He thinks he's right. He's like a wounded animal, beginning to bay and snarl. It's a pity; the hounds and terriers will soon have him by the throat. If I were him, I'd hide. I'd go off somewhere, say the Lake District or the Western Isles, and keep well out of the way.'

Of course, what he did was miles away from that.

24

Willoughby Morris stayed exactly where he was; and that was his ultimate undoing. It was not in his nature to withdraw. On Encaenia morning the following day, he was to be seen in the garden of the lodgings dressed in a formal suit and wearing tabs and a white tie. Those were the clear indications that he intended to attend the ceremony. It was reported to Tony Gill. He managed to persuade Timothy Knowles to ask Morris not to attend. Knowles took Brendan Naish with him to speak to Morris, but, Knowles reported, they were dismissed out of hand. Morris said that there was no possibility that he would not be taking up his rightful place in the procession and the subsequent proceedings as the properly elected Principal of Holt. Knowles and Naish should, to put it bluntly, mind their own business.

Tony decided on discretion. He would take his accustomed place as Vicegerent and see what happened. After all it was not a power struggle between two giants for leadership: it was, if anything, a contest between one man, Morris, and the collegiate body. Morris was challenging his constituency.

Eedes was nowhere to be seen. I commented to Est that he probably sensed trouble was brewing and since he played no significant part in the Encaenia ceremony, he had decided not to join in this particular year. Morris was very much on his own. It did not deter him.

The domestic staff who cleaned and serviced the lodgings reported to the head porter who relayed it to me that there had been a ferocious row between Elizabeth and Willoughby early in the morning.

Morris had been making himself some toast and coffee. Elizabeth had appeared in her dressing gown; she demanded to know where he had been, and who he had been with. He had replied brusquely that he had been in London on business. What sort of business incorporated meetings with a pretty young girl? Why had there been statements that were more than innuendos in the newspapers? She had been made to look an utter fool. She felt ashamed and diminished. 'You have betrayed me,' she was reported as shouting. In tears, sobbing, she had retreated to her bedroom. Morris, red-faced and fuming, looking as though he might be about to have a heart attack, sought fresh air in the garden.

When summoned by the porter at the appointed time, I met Bevan Clayton in the lodge. An assistant porter carried his suitcase and we went to one of the two college guest rooms. Bevan was impressed. 'This looks very comfortable. I see things have moved on in this ancient university. The last time I was here staying at Shrewesbury College, everything was still mediaeval, primitive toilet facilities; and I couldn't even make a cup of coffee.'

I explained that it was the visits of American guests like him who expected high standards of hospitality that made us change our ways. The guest rooms had been completely overhauled and could compete with any first class hotel. The rooms had en suite bathrooms, digital TVs, and Wi-Fi connections for personal computers. 'We don't want our guests to move across the road to the Old Bank Hotel. That wouldn't do. Anyway, I'm sure you'll be comfortable here.'

At a quarter to eleven I knocked at his door and we prepared to go to the Sheldonian Theatre where the degree-giving ceremony was to take place. I delivered him to the university authorities, the Vice-Chancellor's staff, at the Divinity Schools next door to the Sheldonian, and I returned to Holt just in time to join the procession back to the Theatre.

There was Morris intent on leading the Holt group. He wore his formal Principal's robes. Holt was one of the few colleges that invested its head of house with special gowns. The practice went back to the college's origin and Holt's Principal's gown was bright red; it contrasted brilliantly with his dark suit underneath and his white tie and tabs. As with every other member of the university he wore as headgear the traditional Oxford mortar board. Behind him in the procession was the Vicegerent followed by the rest of the fellows who were attending in order of seniority. Morris ignored Tony Gill and at the appointed time set off at a brisk pace for the Sheldonian.

There were about twenty of us and we took up our places on the floor of the Theatre. As I looked around, I could see other members of the university both on the floor of the building and ranged round the tiered seats of the classical arena, which had been designed and built by Christopher Wren. Behind the Vice-Chancellor's throne from where he presided over the proceedings, I saw Hugh Crammond among his guests who had already assembled and who were waiting for his entrance. A few minutes after our arrival the Chancellor, the Vice-Chancellor and the distinguished people who were to receive their honorary degrees entered in procession and took their places. Bevan Clayton was third in the line and looked to me as though he were an actor playing a bit part in a movie. He was slightly unkempt, otherworldly and seemed to have his mind on more important things than what was taking place.

The ceremony took its course. The university was celebrated in the Vice-Chancellor's speech and echoed by the Senior Proctor. The degrees were conferred and the speeches of achievements and congratulations made by the Public Orator in Latin. Finally the Orator sought permission of the Vice-Chancellor to speak in English and give the Creweian Oration: 'Honoratissime Domine Cancellarie licetne anglice loqui'. The Vice-Chancellor replied, 'Licet.' And so the Public Orator explained that Encaenia means renewals, and that the occasion was for looking back on the past with gratitude, rejoicing in the present with pleasure, and looking forward with hope. He emphasised that young shoots were always springing up in the university, cultivated by the rich, decaying, organic matter that lay around there; he joked that there was much of that spread out in the audience before him. He commemorated those of the university who had died during the previous year: 'Requiescant in pace in aeternum luceat eis Dominus Illuminatio Mea.'

Thus the ceremony of Lord Crewe's benefaction ended. Those who had been honoured were led out by the Chancellor and the Vice-Chancellor, and they went to Trent College for lunch. It was the turn of Trent College to host Encaenia that year, and afterwards, later in the afternoon, there would be the usual garden tea party with champagne, peaches, strawberries and cream.

Outside the Sheldonian everyone mingled. There were no formal processions back to individual colleges. The scene was a kaleido-scope of colour, academic gowns and hoods, predominantly the bright scarlet hoods of Oxford MAs that reflected the early afternoon sunlight.

While I was standing in a small group with Tony Gill, Donald, Est, Jane, and one or two others, I watched Willoughby Morris. He had come out of the Sheldonian and stood by himself. He shrugged in his robes and fanned himself with his mortar board. His face almost matched in colour his Principal's gown. Nobody seemed to want to talk with him. I noticed the President of Trinity and the Rector of Exeter College both walk past him without any acknowl-edgement. The only person who approached him was Brendan Naish. He was edging his way through the throng standing in the gravelled quad of the Bodleian Library; he saw Morris standing alone and greeted him. Willoughby looked around and for want of anyone else made some sort of conversation with him. Then Knowles in his MA regalia materialised from the melee of academics and guests and joined them. I noticed that after a short while Knowles touched Naish's elbow and indicated that they should move on. Once again Morris was left alone. It was a sad sight and Morris looked bereft and somewhat mortified. I could not bring myself to engage him in conversation. It was probably a defect in myself and yet while recognising it, I found it impossible to do anything about it.

I learned from Tony that the committee of inquiry was to meet again that evening after all the official engagements of the day had finished. I admired the conscientiousness of the committee.

At five thirty Bevan Clayton was going back to London. He had invited me out to Boston to give a keynote lecture at his university in the autumn. It was kind of him and a mark of honour and international recognition to enjoy the patronage of the man so important in the world of economics. If I had been ambitious I could have capitalised on my relationship with him. If you were one of his people, he could be an international fixer. If you desired a professorship, it was almost as if he could arrange the appointment within the month.

I had met with Bevan at the Encaenia tea party in the gardens of Trent College. We were lucky that it was a perfect summer's day. The lawns had been freshly mown; the herbaceous borders trimmed and tidied. Everyone was still in academic dress and university gossip bubbled and flowed. Again, I caught sight of Morris in the distance standing at the edge of the lawn of the large back quad. He was alone. Elizabeth was not with him. One of his old friends, the bursar of Magdalen, briefly spoke to him but then moved hurriedly on. He stood there for about twenty minutes. Then he sauntered over to a group that included the university registrar; it rapidly dissolved and once again Morris was left by himself. It seemed that there was a sort of ostracism taking place, and, once again, I almost felt sorry for him. Eventually I saw him remove his Principal's robe, put it over his arm and leave. Meanwhile I had joined Est and we mingled with various friends. I met an old colleague who had given up academia and was now head of fixed income research for the Far East and Asia at a leading investment house in the City. He tried to persuade me to do something similar; he thought I was a fool to stay in a poorly paid profession when there were these well-paid opportunities available. I listened to him but dismissed his suggestions. I was happy with my present situation. I was not interested in the huge salary, the suburban mansion, the ability to pay fees for three or four children at private schools. That was not my way of life, and besides there was now Est. I felt that our relationship was developing and maturing; she was now integral to my existence.

Once Encaenia was over, the university settled down and returned to its normal routine for that time of the year. Once again Willoughby packed his bag and left for London. The porter told me that without waiting for dinner the Principal had ordered a taxi and it took him to the railway station at seven fifteen.

Thursday was a quiet day. There was no sound or movement from the Principal's lodgings. Apparently Elizabeth kept very much to her room and started drinking in the late morning. Morris stayed in London. His secretary did not know exactly where he was. Everybody else went about their business.

A shock really made its impact the following morning around midday when Tony issued his report from the committee of inquiry. It was unambiguous and hard-hitting. Tony told me that he had stayed up late into the night writing it. He had checked it through with Jane and Donald early that morning and it was now ready for general consumption. He intended to release it to the press at two o'clock. All fellows had been circulated with a copy, which lay in their pigeonholes. I warned him that many would read about it first in the press; fellows were generally notoriously bad at keeping up with anything left in their pigeonholes. Tony said that the three of them realised that but it was thought better to have a speedy cleansing of the stables. The publication was part of that process.

Consequently there was a report in both the Oxford local newspaper and the *London Evening Standard*. Tony Gill's committee of inquiry endorsed everything that the finance committee had originally said and went further. It stated categorically, 'We do not have confidence that Dr Willoughby Morris always adhered to the college's clear policy on travel expenses.' The committee noted that it had 'issues' with expenses claimed by Dr Morris for six international trips, and it raised concerns over claims made by his wife who it said travelled 'routinely' with the Principal on college business. It commented that it was impossible for us to have confidence that on all occasions college and university rules were observed. In particular Tony's report drew attention to Willoughby's trip to India which the committee had scrutinised in detail and a special fifteen-page dossier had been compiled about it.

It had again been verified that the conference organisers had paid for economy airfares and hotel accommodation both for Morris and his wife; he had then claimed from the college upgrades to business class for Elizabeth and himself. There was no evidence that college authorisation had been granted for enhanced rates or for the claims made for the Principal's wife. The dossier raised serious doubts as to whether the trip was in fact made on college business. 'All the circumstances point in the direction that the trip was made for specifically external academic business.' It alleged that Dr Morris had 'tagged on some college business'; one arranged reception had been cancelled for lack of numbers in view of the short notice of the event.

What was also damning was that in one case for travel to the United States, authorisation for the trip by the Principal and his wife had been expressly denied but the trip went ahead regardless and expenses had been claimed and paid.

The report concluded that the purpose of the report was to expose the shortcomings of the past and to examine how the college could tighten up the way it policed its expenses. Tony's last emphatic point was that, 'The college policy on reimbursement of travel expenses explicitly refers to members of college or college employees obliged to travel because of their duties.' Anyone familiar with the college or the university immediately inferred that the Principal's wife was not a member of the college.

Naturally the Saturday *Telegraph* ran a detailed story about the expenses scandal at Holt. The paper wanted a statement from Morris but he could not be contacted. His wife occupied the lodgings but refused to talk to the press.

The weekend passed. Est and I enjoyed the summer weather and kept returning to the scandal. We, of course, wondered what Morris's next move would be.

On Monday morning all the national papers covered the Holt College scandal in one form or other and at different lengths. The tabloids were more interested in Morris's liaison with the pretty girl from St Cecilia's. I met Tony at coffee and he told me that, in the absence of Willoughby, phone calls from reporters were being put through to him. He tried to maintain a calm and reasonable approach to the problem of the Principal's behaviour and assured all questioners that the appropriate college authorities were continuing to investigate and put things right. His diplomatic skills, he said, were getting better and better.

There was a general heightening of tension in the college. Tony kept calm but almost everyone else was curious to know what was going to happen next. The question that was mostly being asked was about when the crisis would be resolved. A major shift in the order of things happened the next day. Willoughby returned to college and issued a statement.

He arrived again by taxi from the railway station in the middle of the morning. He went straight to the lodgings and after around twenty minutes he rang Tony. Tony told me that Morris informed him that he was going to issue a statement and he hoped that the college would accept it in good faith. He would distribute it as a press release.

That is what he did. It seemed to me that Morris was trying to negotiate his position, and make himself once again acceptable to his colleagues. He was trying to present reasons for misunderstandings and accommodate himself to new conditions. He wanted to explain himself and retrieve his position.

What Willoughby Morris's public statement said was that so far as his wife was concerned, the work she had done for the college meant that she was 'a very active member of the college'. Since his appointment, he contended, his expenses and his wife's had been dealt with in accordance with college procedures. If there was any fault in the way matters had been handled then it lay with the finance committee or the bursar's office. The statement continued, 'Nevertheless it is apparent that there is a need for simpler and more robust procedures about expenses claims and there is a general agreement about that in the college.' He complained that there were a number of unfortunate inaccuracies in the numerous newspaper reports that had appeared. His trip to India had included college and conference business on an equal basis. The allegation that a trip to the USA that had been widely reported as being unauthorised was a calumny; 'Explicit emails to my secretary authorised her to buy airline tickets for us to attend the alumni event. Reports otherwise are factually incorrect.'

That evening Est and I discussed the statement. We were having supper in her flat. She had cooked a cassoulet following a recipe by Raymond Blanc. The master chef had recommended slow cooking and it had rendered everything in the pot delicious, duck legs, slices of garlic sausage, pieces of mutton and haricot beans. A wide selection of herbs gave it a wonderful rustic taste. We shared a bottle of Madiran wine, Ode d'Aydie, 2009, which our wine steward said would complement the cassoulet; and he was right.

Morris's trouble was that he wanted to excuse himself. We decided that it was impossible for him to admit he was in the wrong, to apologise. He had to find justifications. That made his statement unsatisfactory. His political attempt to say that mistakes had been made and they must not happen again, that in the future steps would be taken to ensure this sort of thing did not happen again, hardly convinced. He made a salient point about his wife's position within the college community but what he had done in claiming expenses for her was at that time contrary to college rules. So far as the university went, it was a college affair; a university spokeswoman had told the press that. All in all we decided that Willoughby had not done himself any favours.

In the middle of that week as the summer vacation advanced, the *Telegraph* reasonably asked him to show his secretary's emails that confirmed his expense for the disputed American trip. They were not forthcoming. Wednesday afternoon I received a call from Tony. He told me two pieces of news. The first was that he was positively and actively being considered for the headship of Hereford College. He had been approached and asked if he would mind his name being put forward. Of course he did not, and eagerly agreed to his nomination. There would be other candidates but Tony did not hide his ambition. The second was that Hugh Crammond was coming into college that evening and would like to talk to him. Hugh had said that it was to do with making it easy for Morris to withdraw from the college. He said that Hugh had some plan in mind for a resolution to the present difficulties. Tony suggested that I might join them and Hugh Crammond had agreed. We were to meet in Tony's rooms at five thirty. I sensed that matters were reaching a climax.

25

It was a hot humid afternoon. I walked across the main quad to Tony's rooms towards twenty-five past five. The huge white globes of the Annabelle hydrangeas were shining brilliantly but dipping their heavy heads in the heat, desperately wanting water. Hugh Crammond entered the quad through an arch covered by spent wisteria, its seed pods beginning to ripen. To me it looked as though the scene had been choreographed and Hugh was making his entrance on to the stage or, even more appropriately, a film set.

'Evening, Johnny.' Hugh greeted me. 'We may have a solution for Willoughby. We might be able to mount for him the great escape. It would be a kindness.'

We had arrived at Tony's rooms and knocked on his door. There was an unusually long pause before he opened it, but when he did he released Eedes into the fresh air. 'Sorry,' he said when Eedes, having shaken Hugh's hand, moved off. 'Difficult to get him out of the door. He wanted to go on talking. He's worried about his future. He doesn't see what's to happen to him if Morris goes down. Will the college get rid of him? I told him that I couldn't answer the question. It would depend on our colleagues. Anyway, he's a worried man.'

As we settled ourselves into seats around a small work table, Hugh said, 'Well, at this stage we should not be too worried about the bursar; we have to solve the problem which Willoughby has given us. I asked to see you because I think we may have a solution. I was up in the Lords earlier in the week and I spoke with several people including some at Number 10. The Prime Minister is anxious to help in this matter. He doesn't like the adverse publicity that his old university is getting; and in any case it's bad for the reputation of higher education in general.'

Hugh paused and thoughtfully tapped his ballpoint pen on the tabletop. Tony broke the conversational silence. 'What's the suggestion? Is there a definite proposal?'

'Well, the idea, which seems generally supported by the great and the good, is that Willoughby can be found a London-based job as chairman of one of the big government quangos. There are two coming up. In fact one needs to be filled now and one becomes vacant in three months' time. As the PM said, Willoughby could easily do the job and he would from the start be closely monitored and subject to clear rules over his power and his expenses claims. The government is very careful nowadays about financial affairs after the recent public outrage over MPs' expenses. Everything is scrutinised and audited. It's a job the civil servants relish. Willoughby wouldn't be allowed to get himself into trouble and his proper abilities would be usefully employed. What do you think?'

I asked, 'How would it be put to him? Remember, he's a proud man, stubborn and pretty relentless.'

'That's what I want you to work out. Somehow he's got to be made to see that his present position is hopeless and what's offered is a dignified way out.'

We spent three quarters of an hour discussing all this and came to the conclusion that we, particularly Hugh, whose opinion would carry weight with Willoughby, had to present whatever offer it was going to be as a promotion. It had to appear better and more prestigious that being Principal of Holt. Hugh thought there would be no problem with that. He would be able to point out that many chairs of those committees and quangos were in the end knighted for their services. That sort of incentive would certainly appeal to Morris.

So it was resolved that Hugh would negotiate with Number 10 so that an immediate offer could be made to Willoughby. He would be mad to refuse it. Hugh said it would be quick. He had done all the ground work. The PM had said that all it needed was a general assent from all concerned. The college unreservedly welcomed it. Hugh said he would make necessary phone calls that evening and by the next day, Thursday, it ought to be possible to present the proposal to Morris. The trouble with that was that we did not know where he was, apart from being fairly certain that he was in London. Tony said he would call on Elizabeth and see if she had any clue as to where he might be; he reckoned it would be unlikely and we were inclined to agree. Hugh thought he might alert friends in London who might know. I said I was at a loss. I had no means of knowing where he was.

Yet, by chance, as I was passing through the lodge to go to Quod to meet Est, the head porter who happened to be on duty hailed me. 'Dr James. There was a call from the Principal an hour ago. He wanted to know who was in the lodgings. I told him that Mrs Morris was there so far as I knew. She hadn't been seen going out. I asked if he wanted to be put through but he said no. I asked if he wanted to speak with anyone else and again he said no.'

'Thanks. He didn't say where he was, did he? He didn't give an address?'

'No, sir, I'm afraid he didn't. But I did take the precaution of doing a call-back, 1471, to see what number he was ringing from. I can give that to you. It wasn't his mobile.'

'Brilliant. Well done. That would be very useful.'

So, having written down the London number, I went on to meet Est. About an hour later, when I calculated that Hugh would have arrived home, I rang him. I gave him the number and he thought he would try it and, with luck, speak to Morris. I rang Tony afterwards but he was not answering and so I left a message.

Over a light supper I told Est what we were hoping would happen. She commented that everyone would be happy if it all worked out as planned. I was right, though, in my prediction; everything was coming to a climax.

26

It was in Thursday morning's *Telegraph* that Morris's girlfriend was named. She was identified as a third-year undergraduate at St Cecilia's College named Deidre Lott, known as Dee. The report ran to no more than two short paragraphs; the second said that she had been seen with Morris on a number of occasions in London, including once at Sheekey's restaurant in St Martin's Court and another at Harrod's. It offered no comment. It was just plain reporting.

Est and I digested the news. What would that mean in the short term? We came to no conclusion. By the end of the day our question was answered. Donald rang me and told me the news that Elizabeth had announced that she was leaving Willoughby Morris. She had phoned him and asked if he could call to see her in the lodgings. It was in his role as chaplain that she wanted to speak to him. She told him that she could no longer stand the shame that Morris was heaping on her. Not only did his affair with the twenty-one-year-old Dee Lott make him look utterly ridiculous, but it also reflected on her and, she felt, made her look foolish. That was not all. She felt betrayed after such a long marriage, twenty-eight years, was it? She had put up with enough of Morris's self-important, self-centered preening. The only person he ever thought about seriously was himself. She had decided irrevocably to leave him.

Donald said he had an hour and a half's discussion with her but she was unmoveable. He told her he would speak to Tony and the bursar and he was pretty sure she would be able to stay in the lodgings as long as was needed to sort out her affairs. He noticed that she seemed not to have been drinking and thought that her decision had been made in a sober state of mind.

Est and I reckoned that this would be a heavy blow for Morris. Although he was happy to be a philanderer, we thought that it was in his nature to expect Elizabeth to go on suffering his behaviour. It appeared that he was wrong. Elizabeth was adamant according to Donald.

This development left the college in a difficult position, although if and when Willoughby returned it was possible for him and Elizabeth to live in the lodgings without much contact. The ancient house, one of the original buildings of the college, was large enough for the two of them to exist independently of each other.

I ran into Tony in the late afternoon as we crossed in the main quad. He asked me if the time had come when the college should demand Morris's resignation. He had just received confirmation from Hugh Crammond that he could offer Willoughby, on the government's behalf, the chair of a green energy quango. Tony thought he should sound college opinion on demanding his resignation which would then make Morris more inclined to accept the offer of the PM. I thought that a good idea.

Tony went ahead and emailed all the official fellows and explained the position that the college found itself in. By midday Friday he had replies from the vast majority of fellows who agreed with the strategy. The only fellow to oppose the move was the senior tutor, Knowles, who considered it unnecessary and thought that Morris would go without an ultimatum. We felt that Knowles failed to understand Morris completely, that he was stubborn and obstinate, and that he would need the extra incentive of an unequivocal demand for resignation to push him into acceptance of the very reasonable offer.

Again Tony rang me in the late afternoon. He apologised for troubling me yet again but said that he needed someone to talk with on these matters and I was the person whose views he trusted as well as being the fellow he knew best of all.

'It doesn't matter in the least bit. Of course I'm willing to be consulted. You must have someone to talk to.'

I knew, as well, that this whole business of Morris's abuse of position and power, and its resolution, was having a deleterious effect on Tony's domestic life. His wife, he told me, complained that the college was all he could think about and he was inevitably neglecting his children.

His call was to tell me that Hugh Crammond had been at work and that someone from Number 10 had managed to locate Morris in London through the phone number that our reliable and resourceful porter had discovered. Fortunately Tony had sent off an email to Morris saying that the governing body had agreed to ask him for his resignation and that a formal letter would be sent to him at the lodgings because no one knew of another address for him. Number 10's phone call was made a couple of hours after Morris might have received the email. We assumed that it had and we awaited Morris's response.

A terse answer came the following morning. Morris sent an email to all the members of the governing body. The burden of it was that he had no intention of resigning although the college should note that he had been offered and accepted the chairmanship of an important quango to do with green energy. He proposed to carry out both duties, that of Principal of Holt and the chairmanship simultaneously. He quoted other heads of house who doubled up with similar responsibilities. He stated categorically that if the college wanted to rid itself of him, it should sack him; that is to say, the fellows should vote him out and he would claim the appropriate compensation. Tony, as Vicegerent, would receive a letter from his lawyers in due course.

Est and I discussed his response. 'He's mad. Can't he see, the college has already voted? He's out and there's nothing more to it.'

'That's true, Est, but it's typical Willoughby Morris. He thinks he can still twist the situation to his advantage. He'll never give up. It's not in his nature.'

'Well, who's going to counter this one? Tony had better get Hugh Crammond to do something. Perhaps he'd better threaten cancellation of the PM's offer.'

'You're right. That's almost certainly what should happen. Willoughby won't want that. He's not going to miss that opportunity. Remember the knighthood.'

Est and I were in agreement and it was inconceivable that Tony would not think of the same solution.

'It still leaves the embarrassing little local difficulty of Elizabeth in the lodgings. In the short term it looks as though Willoughby's going to turn up and resume residence. The proverbial cat among the pigeons. Fur and feathers will fly.'

Naturally Tony did contact me; and he had thought of Hugh Crammond's possible political move in Morris's argument with the college. Apparently Hugh also thought he might be able to suggest to Elizabeth that she should as soon as possible move out. If anyone was able to persuade Elizabeth it was going to be Hugh. He was a man of immense charm, by nature considerate and good-mannered; and, in addition, he possessed the gravitas and gently disguised authority of someone used to high office.

Morris arrived that evening thus pre-empting any other move. Over the weekend most of us were out of college but the head porter told me on Monday morning that he wandered around college and was clearly trying to behave as though nothing had happened. The Sunday newspapers reported that the girl, Dee Lott, had renounced him. She told reporters that she had not realised that he was so corrupt. She had been flattered by his attention but did not want anything more to do with him. The *Sun* article headline ran, 'Dee Ditches Dirty Don', which must have enraged and humiliated Morris if he read it. Everyone I met in college thought it was time to call time on Morris with the exception of Eedes. He considered everything was getting out of hand and that the college should soften the treatment it was giving Morris. He had a point and made a good suggestion that might help to ease the appallingly awkward situation. 'What about also offering him next term as sabbatical leave? It would allow us to make a public announcement to that effect and for the Principal to make a diplomatic exit. He needn't ever come back. It is something that could be added to the other incentives. It would be a kind of vanishing trick. It might just help him to see that we're all trying to help him.'

I did not agree with his last point. There was a reason why we should help him more than we were doing already. He had brought the college into disrepute and made great trouble for us. Still, it might help to move him on without even more fuss. At least, that was my view and so I supported Eedes's suggestion.

As it happened, Eedes spoke to Tony about the possibility of Elizabeth moving into a vacant college house and using it as a stepping stone to her own independence. She could occupy it until she had organised herself and her new way of life. She had to be persuaded but Eedes and Tony both thought that she would quickly see that her presence in the lodgings was untenable with Morris back there. Throughout the few hours that he had been there since his return, there had been violent rows. They could be heard outside in the quad. The shouting travelled across the Principal's lawn into the quad. Already the porters had posted the wooden-board notices which instructed visitors not to enter the Principal's quad. Elizabeth's sense of betrayal was consuming her. She gave vent to it by railing at Morris whenever she caught sight of him; and from midday on she was not only angry but sullen with the effect of alcohol which she had reverted to taking, mostly in the form of red wine.

We decided that Donald and Est should approach Elizabeth with Eedes's suggestion. Donald had tried to keep in touch with Elizabeth as part of his pastoral mission within the college. He had partially succeeded and had seen her more often than anyone else. The trouble was that he was going off to the States at the end of that week. Est had always got on well with Elizabeth. Originally they shared the same interest in contemporary art and had gone to exhibitions together. As time went by the relationship foundered a little but Est was always able to talk to Elizabeth easily and in a relaxed way. Eedes said that there was no problem with the vacant college house. It was one that was usually used for distinguished visiting academics, was furnished and was not needed until the beginning of Hilary term just after Christmas. It sounded perfect to afford Elizabeth asylum from the main part of the college and from Willoughby.

Meanwhile I met Brendan Naish as I left the college and went out into the High. He was returning, coming back in. He was eager to tell what he knew about Morris. Basically he was a gossip, and although not a person with any official position in the governance of the college he liked to feel that he was at the centre of affairs. He was in rather an excited state. He hailed me, 'Good morning, Dr James.'

The formality grated on me. I decided to call a truce in my instinctive hostility towards him. 'Look, Brendan, drop the Doctor and just call me Johnny. I'd prefer that.' Although I did not like him, nor did I trust him, it just seemed ridiculous for him to be so formal.

'Oh OK, if that's all right with you.' He showed a respect for his seniors that was akin to obsequiousness. It was not attractive. 'I know it's not really my business, but the Principal was in a bad way this morning. He's in a self-obsessed mood. I passed him earlier. He looked very depressed, rather unusual for him. Nothing usually seems to get to him. I said good morning but it was as though he didn't hear me. He marched off with his hands in his coat pockets towards the far quad.'

'Where had he come from?' I asked.

'From the lodgings.'

'He'd probably had a row with his wife. That doesn't make for a settled mind.'

'Yes, I'd heard that she's leaving him. I think everyone knows that now. Anyway, I just thought he was acting uncharacteristically, and someone ought to know.'

'You're right, of course. Presumably you've told Timothy.'

He could not resist a tiny, teasing pout. 'I haven't. He's left me. I mean only temporarily. He's had to go to a meeting at the Department of Education in Whitehall. I'm supposed to be keeping watch at the office, fielding calls, logging problems. The Principal's the biggest for everybody, I think. But there we are, there's nothing I can do.'

'No, you're quite right. Thanks for alerting me.'

He passed on his way, and me on mine. I was unsure whether he was acting in good faith because he was concerned for Morris, or whether he was just interfering and causing trouble. Either way it did not matter. It was obviously going to be necessary to keep an eye on Willoughby, as well as Elizabeth.

27

I had never thought of Willoughby Morris being particularly vulnerable emotionally, but after the short exchange with Naish it suddenly struck me that the fallout of Morris's expenses fiasco might weigh him down. Was it possible that he would do something out of character? Might everything just mount up and crush him? I had no answer. I thought it unlikely. Morris was tough, obstinate, belligerent. He was the sort who would go down fighting. He would protest his innocence and justify his own position to the very end. Yet Naish's remarks had cast the shadow of a doubt across my mind. Nobody is entirely immune to the social and political forces that can build up around them.

Meanwhile the two immediate and major problems for the college simmered on; and they both concerned the Principal's lodgings. Elizabeth had to be persuaded to leave; and so did Morris himself. Donald and Est spent a long time with Elizabeth, around three hours of discussion and argument. They discovered that Hugh Crammond had already telephoned Elizabeth at length and talked to her. Hugh and his wife had invited her to stay with them for a long weekend in three weeks' time. So, already Elizabeth's mind, Est reckoned, was receptive to their discussion. Donald emphasised the spiritual side, which came naturally to him. He acted and spoke, Est said, more like a therapist. He told Elizabeth that she would feel happier putting a small distance between the college and herself. To stay in the lodgings for much longer would not help her. Apart from the fact that she had no right of residence, if she accepted the generous offer of the furnished house for a term, it would allow her to take an objective view of what had happened and what was continuing to take place. In every way it was better that staying put and eventually running the risk of being evicted. Est followed up on that and explained the college's practical point of view. A new Principal who would have to be appointed very soon, certainly within the space of Michaelmas term, would need to move into the lodgings. She appealed to Elizabeth to consider the implications of her continued occupation of the lodgings from the college's perspective and asked her how much could the college, as an institution, tolerate; how long could the present situation possibly last.

In the end, Est told me, Elizabeth agreed that she would move into the vacant college house at the weekend. That was the most satisfactory outcome in the circumstances because then Donald could go to the States and his pastoral duties in relation to Elizabeth, who was clearly vulnerable, would with any luck be over. Willoughby was, of course, another much more complicated matter.

I congratulated Est, and Donald, by text message, on their expert diplomacy. I knew it would come as a huge relief for Tony and the rest of the fellows. Elizabeth was one problem out of the way. Established for a term, tucked away and out of sight in the college house, she would become the responsibility, exclusively, of the bursar, Jeremy Eedes; he could deal with it.

The problem with the Principal was much more difficult. That was where Hugh Crammond was of crucial importance. At the time I did not realise the amount of effort and time that Hugh was devoting to the college crisis. He spent much time in London lobbying and persuading the government to help solve it. In all that he was successful. It was Morris himself who needed to be persuaded and convinced of a satisfactory resolution to the disaster that he had got himself into. Hugh visited the lodgings several times. Sometimes he saw Elizabeth on her own; sometimes Morris on his own. On one solitary occasion apparently, he had managed to speak with them together. He confided in me that it was one of the most difficult meetings with warring parties that he had ever experienced. No matter; in the end calmness had been restored and a sensible discussion happened. While he was able to leave Elizabeth to Est and Donald, it was necessary for him to concentrate on Morris. He told me that his main aim was to have Morris vacate the lodgings and maintain an absence from the college altogether. This he was extremely reluctant to do. Hugh, though, could enforce the conditions. As he commented to me, 'It was a matter of resorting to blackmail, disguised of course, but blackmail nonetheless. Underneath it all was the ultimatum, either you do what we want or the offer of the chairmanship and all that goes with it is withdrawn and you are on your own.'

'Did you put it to him bluntly or did you dress it up?' I asked.

'Not bluntly. But he could see the alternatives. There are diplomatic signals, ways of saying things that are polite but firm. Willoughby is experienced enough to interpret what is necessary when in negotiation with those he sees as equals or superiors.'

Hugh did not say that in any arrogant way. He spoke as a realist. He could not give a time or date for Morris finally leaving.

'The trouble is he's in a state of domestic chaos. OK, Elizabeth is moving out but she's not taking all her stuff with her. He's got to sort out his stuff from hers. He has to find a flat, a bolt-hole. Presumably he'll go to London. I suppose he'll have to put most of his stuff in store. Frankly I don't think Willoughby's capable of organising all that. He's used to having other people do those things for him. Either Elizabeth organised the domestic details or whatever position he was in gave him resources, and what's more important, manpower for him to have things done without personal involvement. He can't rely on the college helping him any more.'

Hugh saw the difficulties. 'Yes, it's going to be hard for him. I think we should help him as much as possible. It's in our interests as well. The sooner he has moved on and out the better. What can we do practically?'

I had no ideas. Not even Morris's secretary would be able to do much to help him. She was now almost fully occupied with work from Tony. Then Hugh had a brainwave. 'Why don't we borrow Brendan Naish from Knowles? It's the long vac. There's not so much to do in Knowles's office. Naish, if he's any good, can organise Willoughby's domestic arrangements. It'll be good for him; it will keep him really busy. And I fancy, if I ask him and arrange it with Timothy Knowles, Naish will regard it as a form of flattery and leap at the chance to do it.'

'I couldn't agree more. Brilliant. At last Naish will have something really useful to do. The college might start getting value for its money. And I bet he'll be good at it all.'

So, Hugh immediately went to Knowles who at first was reluctant but then apparently saw advantages all round. Hugh said he remarked that Naish was very efficient at that sort of thing and it would all be done quickly. Naish was adept at petty administration and had a developed eye for detail. 'Brendan will do well and he'll enjoy helping Morris. He's actually a really kind person. Whatever anyone thinks of Willoughby Morris, Brendan will feel sorry for him. If anyone is going to look after his best interests, it will be Brendan.'

Hugh was invaluable; he found Morris and told him. Naturally Morris grumbled that he was being pressurised and hustled out but in the end he was pleased that he would have help. He would not commit himself about when he would actually leave the lodgings. Hugh briefed Naish. He told him to search for a West End flat or somewhere close to Smith Square or in Pimlico. Then he was to assess what was in the lodgings and together with the domestic bursar's office sort out what belonged to Elizabeth and Willoughby, and what belonged to the college. Somewhere there would be an inventory, but Morris would have no idea where it was. Wendy Macklin, the domestic bursar, lent one of her office staff in the afternoons who efficiently found a copy of the inventory in the office files, and she and Naish worked together agreeably.

Morris moved about the lodgings in downcast mood. Naish who, given any sort of company, never stopped talking, chatted away to him whether or not Morris felt inclined to join in conversation. Later, Brendan Naish told me that he grew to like Morris a lot. When you got close to him and there was no need for a public front, Morris was a pleasant companion with a wide range of knowledge and an entertaining conversationalist. Still, Naish was no fool; he knew the job he had to do and he did it.

28

It all took some weeks. The long vacation proceeded. Brendan Naish spent some time coming and going to London. He found a couple of apartments that Morris felt might be suitable. One was in Pimlico, St George's Square, and a ten- to fifteen-minute walk from the centre of government. It was the middle floor of a large terraced Regency house, high-ceilinged, tall windows, with a balcony that looked out on to the road across to the Square's garden. The garden was lined by tall trees, bordered by flower beds and shrubs. The greater part of the garden was grass on which children could play and residents relax. In the centre was an ornamental pond with a fountain surrounded by rose beds. The garden also boasted a statue of William Huskisson MP, the first person to be killed by a railway train, dressed in Roman senatorial toga, which was distinguished by Osbert Sitwell when he described it as 'boredom arising from the bath'. It was one of the smaller lungs of London.

The other was in a new development, a modern, contemporary flat in a huge plate-glass and beige-brick five-storey building, on the south side of the river near London Bridge, overlooking the Thames. It was light and spacious but close to the rumble of traffic and undercurrent of noise from trains. It was farther away from Whitehall and parliament than Pimlico and in the end Morris, having visited both, decided to lease the St George's Square apartment.

It was difficult persuading Morris to cut his ties with the college and Oxford; it took time. It was not until the end of September that the lodgings were finally emptied. Until then, Morris was in evidence and a number of embarrassing incidents took place when he insisted on exercising his rights as Principal.

One example was at the annual prize-giving at a local secondary school. It was an ancient institution, as old as several of the original colleges of the university. It had its own extremely distinguished alumni list ranging over many years, from its foundation to the present time. At the annual commemoration it celebrated its founder and famous sons in a bidding prayer that went on at some length. There were bishops, among them London, Norwich, Winchester, one Archbishop of York, martyrologists, grammarians, epigraphists, historians, a president of Corpus Christi College, and a university printer. At the modern end of the list were theatre directors, novelists, poets and scientists including a Nobel Prize winner.

At this particular prize-giving ceremony, the headmaster and the school's governors whose academic members were in their academic robes, were assembled on the stage of the school's auditorium. Willoughby Morris was there in full regalia because the Principal of Holt College, whoever he or she happened to be, by right of the college being instrumental in the founding of the school, was ex-officio chairman of the governors. The prize-giver and speech-maker was a verbose Chief Executive Officer of a highly successful European-wide business consultancy company. He had been asked because he was high profile in the nation's press and he had sent his son to the school, and since a year ago, his daughter into the sixth form; the constitution of the school had been changed, in line with so many other boys' schools, so that it could admit girls as well as boys.

What happened was shocking for the audience of pupils and parents and for the teachers and governors; except one who was Willoughby Morris. Admittedly afterwards and in repose, the whole proceeding could be seen as distinctly funny; it was certainly not at the time.

The form was that the headmaster made his speech, welcomed all guests, and gave a report on the school's activities during the past year. He welcomed the guest speaker and prize-giver, gave a résumé of his career, and introduced him to his audience. The prizes were then presented, and one by one the recipients stepped on to the stage, shook hands with the giver, and retreated back to their seats. Then the famous CEO began to give his speech. He praised the winners and advised that they did not sit on their laurels, for everyone else in the school was snapping at their heels to emulate them. He stressed the admirable spirit of competition in the school community that he had detected. He praised the teachers; they belonged to a noble profession that was not sufficiently well rewarded financially as it ought to be. However, there were other rewards more valuable than could be counted in monetary terms. And so he went on. After about twenty-five minutes, there were stirrings of restlessness in the audience. Among the younger members there was a shifting of chairs and a general rustle of noise that became apparent. As the speaker finished a sentence and paused to prepare himself for yet another paragraph, Morris stood up, stepped forward, and usurping whatever authority the headmaster might have thought he had, said loudly and emphatically, pulling his red gown around him and gesticulating with his right hand, 'Thank you. Encouraging remarks, but we must get on. I think we all agree that we've had more than enough. Let's get on to the school song. Then everyone can go and enjoy their own celebrations.' With that he took two steps back and sat down, while looking firmly and expectantly at the headmaster. There was a long and terrible silence.

The prize-giver, clearly not used to being interrupted or over-ruled, looked both surprised and annoyed but adapted himself quickly to the situation and tactfully wound up his speech. 'Of course, you are right. I must not detain you all any longer. There are many better things to do than sit here and listen to me on such a lovely summer's afternoon. Congratulations to all the prize-winners and best wishes to each and every member of the school.'

The sixth-former who was head of school made a brief speech

of thanks, so obviously and noticeably written out beforehand, rehearsed and learnt. Yet it served its purpose and a babble of conversation filled the auditorium as the headmaster and the governors processed from the stage and out of the building. Many parents and their children were showing signs of amusement and ripples of repressed laughter were to be heard.

My source reported that Morris stood around for a short time afterwards but he was left alone. One or two people acknowledged him by a nod of the head or a brief gesture of goodbye, but mostly everyone shunned him. After some minutes when other governors and members of the teaching staff had clustered into groups before heading off to lunch, Morris took off his gown and left, making his way back to Holt.

The headmaster stood in a circle of his colleagues and apologised to the prize-giver for the unmannerly intervention of Morris. It was perfectly clear to my informer that he was furious with Morris. Apparently he said, 'I can't apologise enough. The man must have taken leave of his senses. What did he think he was doing?'

The school's guest speaker responded generously, 'Please don't worry. He was probably quite right. I'm sure I had been going on for far too long. You forget yourself on occasions like this. It was a healthy reminder to keep things short. Anyway, it's good to see that the school maintains its reputation for eccentricity. That's what makes it great.'

Although the speaker revealed himself as a tolerant and forgiving man, most of the governors were cross and offended by Morris's behaviour. They agreed that Morris was out of his mind. The speaker had added that he understood that Morris was under a great deal of stress. The deputy chairman declared firmly that he would bring a motion of censure before the governors at their next meeting. Somehow the remark got to the ears of the local newspaper's journalist who was reporting the prize-giving and it appeared in the late edition of the paper.

The annual prize-giving was always reported the following day. The account, as usual, recorded the prize-winners and gave a brief summary of the school's achievements but concentrated on the action of the Principal of Holt College who had brought the ceremony to an abrupt end. As the reporter wrote, 'It was something we would all often like to do on such occasions but politeness, consideration and good manners forbid us to.'

Brendan Naish told me that when Morris returned he was disturbed and angry. He muttered that the prize-giver was a fool and had no thought for the comfort of the audience. There was no sense of apology and no feeling that he had been rude or offensive. Brendan feared that Morris was losing his grip. We all agreed – Naish, who by now had become a sort of confidant of Morris, Est, Tony, and even Eedes and Knowles – that the sooner Morris was out of Oxford and settled in London the better it would be for him and the college. Tony said that he would do everything in his power to stop Morris appearing in public as a representative of the college and asked everyone else to do the same.

Yet it did happen once more before Morris's departure but it was more private. Eedes, for the sixth year running, had let the college facilities to the University of Texas, San Antonio for a summer school. It always lasted four weeks and students who attended were afforded the Oxford undergraduate way of life. They were given tutorials in the Oxford style and small seminars. They dined in hall each evening and were generally looked after by the college's domestic staff as students were during term time. At the inaugural, welcoming dinner, a formal affair, the president of the summer school, a distinguished woman professor from San Antonio who ran a world-renowned medical research group specialising in foetal medicine, took the chair. Next to her was Tony as Vicegerent substituting, in the circumstances, for the Principal. Just as the grace was about to be said, into the hall strode Morris in his Principal's robes and insisted on taking Tony's place. Tony gave way; the major domo quickly organised and laid an extra place setting and the dinner proceeded. Conversation was strained between the lady professor and Morris but both survived to the end when a couple of brief speeches were to be made. The professor succinctly stated how glad and grateful the Americans were to be present in college. They all looked forward to an invaluable Oxford experience. Morris then stood up at the same time as Tony to respond to the professor's remarks. Tony, in the cause of peace and tranquillity, gave way. Morris spoke a brief welcome but then started to rant against the college's administration that, to quote, 'I have been, in vain, trying to reform.' He raised his voice and started talking about matters that the Americans were completely mystified by. They knew nothing of the college politics of the moment. Tony decided that it was time to do to Morris what he had done to the prize-giver, but with entire justification. At a suitable pause, Tony stood up and said, 'Thank you, Principal. It's time to bring dinner to a close. We welcome you all to our college and look forward to seeing you at work and at leisure in our precincts.' He then said the short retiring grace, 'Benedicto, benedicatur,' let praise be given to the Blessed One.

Morris swirled his robe around himself and stalked out.

Est's comments on the proceedings were enlightening. 'He's definitely lost his grip. He's like Lear. Matter and impertinency mixed. He's a man of power whose authority is lost. He's flailing around. How bold, how right Shakespeare was. And it's why his works live on – because what they have to say is universal, for all time. Reduce the scale and Lear could be every man, any man. You'll find a Lear, to a greater or lesser extent, just down the street as your neighbour, in the office and even the pub. Morris will rage himself into the grave.'

'I can see why you're such a good tutor,' I said half-mockingly.

'Oh yes, OK. But I'm right.'

It was obvious that the reporters were keeping a close eye on Morris. His story began to run in every edition of the local newspaper. The printed items reported facts but reflected the general outrage at Morris's behaviour. Tony and the rest of us were more determined than ever to move Morris out and on to London as soon as possible. He had to be hidden from the watchful presence of the local journalists.

The deputy chairman of governors of the prize-giving school sent a very formal and abrupt letter to the college. It expressed deep concern over Morris's exhibition at the ceremony, wondered why Holt as a collegiate body could not keep its errant Principal under control, and told of annoyance and outrage shown by parents, teachers and governors. There had been a fundamental breach of etiquette and good manners which, he felt, was difficult to remedy; fortunately the speaker had publicly taken it in good part and, at least on the surface, was neither upset nor insulted.

Finally Brendan Naish told Tony early one morning a few days later that Morris would leave the lodgings and the college grounds at the end of the week. Quietly and efficiently, he and Wendy organised and accomplished Morris's exit. Naish even accompanied Morris up to London and helped him settle into his Pimlico flat. Naish stayed overnight and the following morning led Morris round the neighbourhood and showed him where various amenities were, a newsagent, a delicatessen, a small Italian café in Lupus Street. Just around the corner was Dolphin Square house with its gardens and restaurant. There, if he felt like it, he could have breakfast. Naish told him that at one time after the Dolphin Square complex had been built during 1935 and 1937, its apartments had been home to about seventy MPs and twenty Lords, so convenient was it for the Houses of Parliament.

Brendan Naish had met the occupants of the ground-floor flat when he had been prospecting for Morris. When Morris arrived he rang the doorbell but no one was in. It was later in the evening that he did so again and was able to introduce Morris to a young man who was a literary agent and his wife, a French girl who spoke perfect English, who worked in a large international advertising agency.

Naish's mission thus accomplished, he returned to Oxford and to Knowles.

29

Est's portrayal of Willoughby Morris as a modern-day Lear fascinated me. He shared with the mad king his intoxication by power but his inability to realise that he had lost it, his rants and rages, and his alienation from other people. A major difference was that Lear's wife was dead; Elizabeth was very much alive. My musings left me wondering if Morris recognised like Lear that he was slipping into madness.

Certainly until the time he finally left Oxford, he was unaware of his deficiencies. In London he gradually grew to recognise his failing control over an ordered and logical way of life. He almost stopped listening to anyone else. The only person he spoke revealingly to was Naish. Somehow Brendan Naish had gained his trust. Morris liked him, grew fond of him. There was, so far as we could judge, no sexual element to the relationship as there was with Knowles; it was simply that Morris knew that he could rely on Naish and was convinced that Naish was on his side. Knowles was not unhappy about the liaison. He saw that it did not affect his position with Naish. He was content to let him go to London every so often and help Morris sort himself out.

The newspapers both local and national noted Morris's departure from Oxford. The reports were straightforward. The scandal, corruption, the affair with the St Cecilia's girl, had lost their momentum. All of those things were in the past. Articles noted that the Principal of Holt College had been granted a term's sabbatical leave and during that time he had been asked to become chairman of the government's energy quango. The local Oxford newspaper simply reported the facts. The student paper, as soon as Michaelmas term started, called the arrangement a political rig that allowed Morris to make a graceful exit from the Oxford scene. It predicted that he would never return. Two of the nationals had said the same thing; one had given the story the headline 'Government and college ease Principal's way out'.

It was the *Telegraph* that rightly inserted the final thrust of the stiletto blade into Morris's ribs. After he had been in London for about a week, it ran a story that told of Morris trying to make off with two college pictures that had been hanging in the lodgings. One was a landscape of Oxford painted to show Matthew Arnold's city of dreaming spires viewed from Boar's Hill to the west of the city. The other was a portrait of a seventeenth century Bishop of Durham. Somehow one of the paper's journalists had discovered that the two pictures had been removed and had found their way into Morris's St George's Square apartment. She exposed what the newspaper described as the theft. In quite a long article she went on to draw a parallel with a nineteenth century Master of Magdalen College School called Christie who spent a short, disastrous spell at the school and then, forced to resign, made his way to London. On the way out of Oxford, the pantechnicon carrying his goods and chattels was stopped on Headington Hill and a number of paintings that belonged to the school were recovered; he had intended to take them to Christie's to be auctioned. A criminal charge was laid against him.

Nobody thought that Willoughby Morris wanted to do anything like that and Brendan Naish said that it was a genuine mistake on Morris's part. He had asked Morris about them when the report appeared and said that Morris thought they belonged to him and Elizabeth. He did not know the paintings at all well and believed that Elizabeth had bought them at some time during their residence in college. Since they were on the college's inventory of art works Naish organised their speedy return to college.

In conversation one morning in the main quad, Est, Tony and I wondered how Morris could really have thought they were his; but we decided that there should be no question of pressing charges against him. It was in the college's interest to bring the Morris era to as quick a close as possible. We did wonder, and discussed at length, how the paper knew about the paintings finding their way to Morris's flat. Perhaps someone watched the unloading of the removal van; but the pictures would have been well wrapped. Maybe someone, a college servant, in the lodgings had noticed the absence of the pictures and informed the press. It was impossible to know, and the newspaper would never reveal its source. Later that particular evening at home with Est, while we sipped a cool Chablis and listened to some Caprices of Paganini that had been recommended obliquely in a novel written by a friend and published recently, we concluded that there had been yet another leak. Someone must have leaked the information to the paper.

'But who would do that? Who could be bothered? After all, Morris was finished.'

'I know, Est, but it's odd. That journalist must have had inside information. She's good but she's not psychic and she doesn't know the inside of the college; it stops at the walls. There must have been someone inside who told her. Otherwise I don't see how she could have known.'

'Yes, OK, but apart from the cleaners and other domestics the only obvious culprit would be Naish.'

We were left with that curious conclusion; Naish as both confidant and betrayer. Naish had more or less supervised the packing of Morris's belongings in the van. Willoughby was quite incapable of doing that himself. He had always left that sort of task to Elizabeth. Elizabeth had made it extremely clear that she would have nothing to do with helping Morris move.

There was pause in our conversation. Paganini was performing a particularly impressive piece of scherzo virtuoso playing; it captivated and exhilarated both of us. When he slowed down and we relaxed, Est said, 'We could be missing the obvious, so obvious that it's been calculated that no one would notice.'

'What do you mean? The leak could be obvious?'

'Yes. I think we might have just touched on it before but dismissed it as ridiculous. Tony. Could Tony be the leak? Does he have motive?'

I thought for a moment. 'Umm, highly unlikely, I think, although possible. There might be something devious going on in his mind. The more discredit that falls on Morris and the more steadily and efficiently Tony runs the shop, the more the management, i.e. the fellows, would be likely to keep him on.'

'Yes. I'm sure Tony would prefer to be Principal here than anywhere else. He's still waiting to hear from Hereford. They won't announce until the third week of Michaelmas.'

We decided that it was not really credible that Tony would manipulate matters to that extent in his own favour but nevertheless we entertained the faint possibility that Tony was the leak.

The college settled down. The lodgings stood empty apart from the large downstairs room that had served as Morris's office. The secretary still went in there each morning and Tony spent most afternoons there sorting out regular college business. Morris was in St George's Square, Elizabeth was in her new accommodation. All was quiet in the ancient institution which, of course, had seen many vicissitudes of varied fortune over the centuries.

So the vacation approached its end. Est went off to visit her mother on the Suffolk border for ten days. It was, she said, an act of piety, her filial duty. It was difficult to part for so long but she did not want me to go with her or visit her; her mother was in the early stages of dementia. Est thought it best to be with her on her own. There would be short periods of time when she could, perhaps, work on an article she was writing for *Essays in Criticism*.

I decided to take a break and change scene. I needed sunshine. I borrowed a neighbour's flat in Naples. It was in the centre of the city, steeply high up overlooking the bay, in an old apartment block with access by so many flights of stairs that mostly residents took the old lift that only two people could squeeze into at one time. My neighbour said that it kept breaking down and that rescue times varied between fifteen minutes and two hours. It was not a risk that very often I liked to take. So, I became well exercised whenever I stayed there.

I was able to enjoy the warmth of both people and weather, do some work, and relax on the promenade, sitting and sipping a cappuccino in the mornings, an espresso after lunch. Sometimes in the afternoons or early evenings I would take the local railway service, the Circumvesuviana, round the southern rim of the bay to visit Vico Equense or Sorrento. There I would take a light evening meal and watch the westering sun reflected on the waters of the bay.

I missed Est, but I knew that we would be back together in a short time. The end of the long vac is always busy. Preparation for the next academic year, paperwork to do with the new intake of undergraduates, the first governing body meeting that is called in noughth week, that peculiar Oxford connotation for the week before the beginning of term; all those matters would occupy our time relentlessly in the seven days before the teaching term began.

When I arrived back in Oxford on the Saturday before the penultimate week of the vac, Est was still in Suffolk. She was to return on Sunday. It was pouring with rain. I had driven from Heathrow in my car. I had left it for the week away in Naples at an airport long-stay car park. The weather was foul all the way back along the short distance from the airport to the M25 and then along the M40 through High Wycombe to Oxford. The sky was black with dark clouds and the rain fell heavily and relentlessly. At the same time squalls of wind and rain buffeted the car and I had to endure driving through barrages of spray thrown up by huge lorries from eastern Europe, mostly, it would seem, from Poland, the Czech Republic and Hungary to judge from their number plates. It was not an enjoyable journey that rounded off my trip to Naples. Yet the hour and ten minutes of driving gave me a chance to reflect on what I was going back to. The college had to be restored to calm. Within the context of its history Willoughby Morris's aberrant behaviour was a tiny blemish. It was destined to be swept aside and in years to come would undoubtedly be laughed about. Morris was a fly-by-night, insignificant within the span of history. What was important was to appoint a new Principal as soon as possible and for us to ensure that he was reliable, conscientious and did not want to dominate the executive. Eedes had to realise this, and likewise Knowles. Both needed to know that they were servants of the college not of the Principal. All credit was due to Naish for accomplishing the removal of Morris from the lodgings but he was no more than a college employee. He was not a fellow and he should not have access to confidential matters to do with the fellowship; it was Knowles's duty to make the rules clear to Naish.

As I drove, it became obvious to me that for some time yet various people in college would want to discover where the leaks came from, who was responsible; but in a very real sense that was unimportant. The leaks had produced their effect. Corruption and deviousness had been exposed and the rot within the system got rid of. The college should not spend time on trying to detect the culprit. Everyone should be constructive for the future. And that mainly entailed the election of Morris's successor.

I left my car in the road outside my Jericho house in a residents' parking bay and ran in with my suitcase, laptop and document bag. Once inside I poured myself a Scotch and soda, put a Chopin Etude on the CD player and paced the room. Only then did it occur to me that we could not proceed with an election of Principal until Morris had actually resigned. Tony, or someone else if he were to be elected to Hereford, would have to be the acting Principal until that time. So, Morris's baneful influence was still going to affect us. We had to know what was in Tony's mind. I decided that when Est returned she and I would have to talk urgently with Tony.

30

Est arrived back late Sunday afternoon. She went straight to her flat, took her bags in, and then parked the car across the road in the college car park where she kept it. Later when she had somewhat recovered from her tiresome journey through Bedford and Milton Keynes, I picked her up and took her home to my place. We had supper together and talked about the days ahead. She reminded me that Donald would be back from the States by now, and that we would need his strategic thinking in our deliberations.

It was strange; we formed a kind of unofficial college sub-committee that safeguarded the interests of the college. As in many other institutions, particularly collegiate ones, as I have stressed, the majority of people did not concern themselves with day-to-day organisation and administration of affairs. It was left to the watch-dogs, the concerned few, and in this instance it all came down to Est, Jane, Donald, me and, of course, Tony. There were a few others who were interested, Frank Bradshaw, Bennet, JOB, but not sufficiently enough to be active. We constituted a sort of committee of public safety, the public being the college at large, all its staff, academic and domestic, and all its students.

I had not seen Donald but I knew he was around. One of the porters had told me that Donald had asked if I had been in college recently. Est said to me, 'We had better try to meet tomorrow or on Tuesday, before the governing body meeting on Wednesday. We should establish a clear direction that the college is to follow.'

I agreed. 'You're right. It's best if we are sorted out before term begins – anyway, so far as possible.'

It was wonderful having Est with me. We could both talk with ease about the mess that Willoughby Morris had placed the college in. We thought very much the same about what was good for the future of the college and increasingly we felt in every way that we belonged to each other. A profound intimacy had developed and we had become each other's consciences. Our relationship could not have been closer. We were, it seemed, what the therapists called 'compatible', in bed and out.

At coffee the following morning in the senior common room, luckily Donald was there and Tony. I outlined the idea that we should try to persuade Morris to resign officially immediately and that we should have some plan of how to achieve this. We decided to meet at five. Est said she would try to reach Jane, which she did.

Est caught up with Jane at lunchtime and explained what our thinking was. Jane said she was busy later; she was scheduled to have a brainstorming session with an American postgraduate student, a Fulbright scholar from Penn State University. Est managed to persuade Jane that our meeting was urgent and essential. Jane agreed to see if she could shift the meeting with her student to later in the evening. In the event she arranged to meet him for supper in Quod at eight.

We met at five in what was now Tony's room in the lodgings. It was all rather bleak. The lodgings unoccupied struck me as a sad place. It should have a welcoming, quite lavish, air about it; it should impress those who enter with a generous, even sumptuous, reception. It was desolate and dreary. At least you could say about Willoughby Morris and his wife during most of their tenure of office there, that they were most welcoming and hospitable. So far as being entertained there it was always a pleasure to enter, be greeted by the domestic staff, and, if after five thirty be offered a drink of your choosing. Morris always maintained that the yard-arm hour of six o'clock was purely arbitrary and he fixed it personally at five thirty. Tony's occupied room was functionally an office rather than a public room for entertainment.

We sat round a small conference table. Tony suggested that I chaired the meeting since the initiative was coming from our group. I looked round to see if that suggestion met with popular approval, which it did. I explained the dilemma that existed over Morris's present position. Officially he had not ceased to be Principal. We could not elect his successor until he resigned or knew definitely what his intention was. If he declared that he would resign at the end of his sabbatical, then we could proceed to a pre-election of the Principal; that would require a legal agreement. Either way the college would be relieved of uncertainty. It was inconceivable to all of us that Morris could ever regain his position in college; it was a matter of getting him to accept the position as we saw it.

Tony, of course, raised no objection. As he said, it would help him. The college could decide whether or not it wanted to confirm him in post, and possibly before Hereford College made up its mind about its own Principal. He added that, just between ourselves, he would much prefer to stay at Holt, a college which he knew thoroughly and loved dearly. From the chair I said that we all recognised that and agreed that speed was preferable to delay. Est quipped, 'I repeat Donald's quote, "Dull not device by coldness and delay."' She explained that she was using the term, device, kindly.

So, it was decided that Morris should be approached and appealed to in order to have him resign. It was recognised that he would enjoy his salary to the end of the already agreed sabbatical term. The question arose as to who was going to visit Morris and talk to him? The discussion was long but finally everyone thought that I should try. I was not very happy about this and suggested that Hugh Crammond might help me. That was accepted. I would represent the present college, Hugh the historic college. His diplomatic skills would complement my more direct and, sometimes perceived, abrasive manner. Tony would contact Hugh and find out if he agreed. The way ahead was clear; whether or not we would succeed was another matter.

Tony duly rang Hugh Crammond and went out to Fenmore. Hugh approved the idea and he rang me to arrange a meeting.

I assumed that the college would give its blessing to what we were doing. That would be apparent the day after at the governing body meeting. It was well attended and my supposition was right. Jacob Black was pessimistic; he thought that Morris would not cooperate. Why should he? He considered that he was being badly treated by the college. JOB said, 'If I w-were M-Morris, I'd be a-as awkward as p-possible. I'd st-string it all out.' There was no outright opposition. Both Eedes and Knowles kept quiet. They were edging towards the new order.

Hugh and I decided that he should phone Morris. He did but failed to get any response on about half a dozen occasions. Since he was going to be in London on the Thursday of that week, he decided to call on Morris early in the morning to be sure of finding him in. He discovered that Morris was getting up late. Hugh thought he might be a little depressed. Hugh called at St George's Square round about nine o'clock in the morning. Morris was still in his dressing gown, slowly having coffee and a slice of toast. Hugh, the ultimate diplomat, achieved Morris's compliance with our wishes without my presence. Of course, he was able to use the weapons associated with his close influence with the government. It was not outright blackmail but Hugh told me that he had pointed out to Willoughby Morris that everything in the future for Morris would be easier if he were to comply with the college's wishes; they were in effect the same as the government's. The scandal needed to disappear into the past as quickly as possible and be forgotten. Willoughby should regard his Oxford life as over, leave it completely behind, and concentrate on the challenges that lay ahead for him.

Morris saw the sense in that. He said it would be necessary for him to come to Oxford one last time in order to tie up some loose ends with his solicitor and to talk to Jeremy Eedes about his salary and pension. He wanted to do it face to face and anyway Eedes had been very supportive of everything that Morris had tried to do and it would be an opportunity to express his gratitude now that he was about to be out of office. Hugh was not sure that Morris's return to Oxford, and particularly to the college, would be salutary but he agreed to it, at the same time advising Morris that he should meet Eedes outside of college, perhaps in Quod. Morris said he would think about it. After a call to Morris's Oxford solicitor, they arranged that he should go to Oxford on the Monday of first week so that by the end of that week everything to do with Morris's principalship would be over.

In the event I was not needed. Hugh Crammond achieved everything brilliantly. What intervened was unexpected and disconcerting for all of us in college.

31

In the middle of Friday evening, Willoughby Morris ended up in the accident and emergency department of St Thomas's hospital. He was mugged in Lupus Street. He had come out of a newsagent's just opposite the Pimlico Academy School. He commented later to Hugh Crammond, quite amusingly considering the state of mind he must have been in, that he thought brutalism had been banished from the area when John Bancroft's late 1960s concrete and glass building had been demolished; it had stood as a prime example of the Brutalist architecture movement that belonged to those times.

Outside the newsagent's there was an automatic money dispenser. It was a no-fee ATM which Morris had begun to use. He withdrew a hundred pounds and as he walked away, a hooded youth swept up on a small wheeled stunt bike. The youth dropped it on the pavement, stood aggressively in front of Morris and tried to snatch his wallet, which Morris was putting in his pocket. The youth caught hold of Morris's hand and twisted the wallet from his grip. Morris resisted, and, according to the Bangladeshi woman who had served Morris in the shop, the youth slammed Morris in the face with his left fist. Morris staggered back, the wallet fell on to the path. The youth picked it up, grabbed the notes from it, and then hurled it along the street; he quickly retrieved his bike, pedalled furiously off towards Vauxhall Bridge Road and lost himself in traffic. Morris had tripped backwards and hit the side of his head on some house railings and had finished up lying on the ground with a swollen jaw, bleeding inside his mouth and a very painful, bruised temple.

A middle-aged woman who had been doing some shopping

farther along the road had tried to intervene. She had pulled at the youth's arm and had received a sharp jab from his elbow in the side of her neck. The Bangladeshi woman hurried along the pavement and picked up the wallet and found most of the contents which had fallen out, credit cards, library cards, a medical card and other oddments. There was certainly no money left in it. She returned it to a dazed and shocked Morris while another passer-by rang the police and ambulance.

All this was related by the Bangladeshi woman, and Hugh told me that eventually a shocked and traumatised Morris was taken off to St Thomas's. The paramedics thought it best for him to be checked thoroughly. It was ironic that the junior doctor who saw him in A&E was an old Holt College medical student; she recognised Morris immediately when she passed by him sitting in a corridor and made sure that he was treated promptly. Morris's face was patched up. The punch the youth had thrown at him had caused his teeth to gash the inside of his mouth. The injury was not serious although the impression made by the free flow of blood and saliva was alarming both for those who helped Morris and himself. He was made to wash out his mouth with an antiseptic solution and told to eat carefully until the small wound healed. The bash to the side of his head that he had sustained in falling was a little more serious, but after investigation and some cognitive tests, Morris was released and the ex-Holt girl had him taken back to St George's Square by taxi. He was lucky; but he was badly shaken and shocked.

Fortunately he had two days to recover, the Saturday and the Sunday, and, although Hugh thought he would pull out of the Monday meeting in Oxford, he did not. He was due to meet Hugh at twelve noon in Quod. He arrived at the college lodge at around eleven fifteen. The porter said he paid the driver and walked in through the lodge making a cursory acknowledgement to him. The porter mentioned that Willoughby looked in pretty bad shape. His face was swollen and bruised on the right-hand side; his complexion was grey. He commented that it looked as though he had not combed or brushed his hair. Hugh confirmed Morris's ill-kempt look when I saw him in the late afternoon when Morris had gone back to London.

Apparently Morris walked round the main quad and then into the next quad where he stood and seemed to contemplate the window boxes that displayed a glorious, fiery flowering of red geraniums which were set above border beds of fading pink hydrangeas. He sat down on a bench and remained there lost in thought until five to twelve when he went out through the lodge, crossed the High and entered Quod. Hugh, as always considerate, had made sure that he was there in good time just in case Willoughby should turn up early.

As Morris entered, Hugh rose to greet him. Hugh said to me that he was appalled to see Willoughby in such a poor state. It looked as though Willoughby was walking wounded from some war campaign. There was no doubt that Willoughby felt sorry for himself; and Hugh said it was difficult not to feel sorry for him. Yet, naturally, Hugh did not lose his sense of purpose.

Hugh had managed to take a table in a corner of the restaurant close to the double doors that gave entrance to the hotel reception. He was drinking a Heineken lager. Morris wanted a dry martini. Hugh ordered it from the bar and they sat down at the table.

Hugh told me beforehand that it was crucial Morris signed some form of letter that signified his intention to resign the principalship. He waited until lunch was well under way before making it quite clear to Morris that this was needed. They took the restaurant's express lunch; it had its own discrete limited menu. They both ordered a first course of chive and cheese omelette, and then Hugh had a minute steak and pommes frites while Morris ordered salmon with dill sauce. It was as they pushed their plates away and they were enjoying the remains of a bottle of 2004 Rhone wine, most of which had been drunk by Morris, that Hugh mentioned the letter of intent. At first Willoughby was belligerent but tactfully Hugh mentioned that it would ease matters with the Prime Minister's office if Willoughby was to cooperate and allow the transition from his rule as Principal to the election of his successor. In the end Morris capitulated. Hugh said it was a sad sight. Morris sat there with his injured face, his right eye weeping slightly which gave the impression that he might have been crying. Hugh was surprised that he came round so quickly; he thought it would take some time to convince him. Morris protested that he was furious with the whole proceeding and with everybody concerned; he had expected support from his erstwhile colleagues, fulminated against them and said that he was ashamed of them. Yet finally he accepted that there was no problem. He would resign from the date of the letter, which might just as well be today's date, provided that he could enjoy what had been arranged already, a term's sabbatical on full salary; then the college could proceed with the election of the new Principal without difficulty. Hugh reported that pudding was eaten and coffee sipped in a pleasant mood, which was more than he expected. Morris had obviously seen that there was no alternative. He had made his protest to Hugh. After that, together with Hugh, they looked to the future and discussed the prospects for Morris pursuing a happy life in London. Hugh was very good at describing an exceedingly optimistic picture. Willoughby would be at the centre of things, he would be admired for accommodating the wishes of the government, and he would be welcomed by the people working at the quango because they had been without firm leadership for over a year. There would be no risk of misunderstandings about expenses or anything connected with salary; government rules were unambiguous about that sort of thing.

Then what happened was most unexpected. Morris signalled a waiter who came quickly to the table. Morris asked him to fetch a couple of sheets of the hotel's notepaper. The waiter disappeared through the double doors to the hotel reception and returned immediately with the paper. Morris cleared a space on the table, pushing aside his coffee cup and wine glass. He took a black Bic biro from his pocket. He wrote his resignation letter. He addressed it to the

Vicegerent and the fellows of Holt College. It stated simply that from the above date he resigned as Principal of the college and relinquished all responsibilities of office to the Vicegerent; as a fellow of the college he would take full paid sabbatical leave until the end of Hilary term and then resign his fellowship. It was as brief and straightforward as that. He signed it and added that it was written in the presence of Lord Hugh Crammond and the waiter whose name he asked. They both signed as witnesses. Morris then gave the letter to Hugh, asked him to have a photocopy sent to him at St George's Square, and to give the original to Tony.

Hugh said he put the letter in his inside coat pocket, and with an expansive gesture and a sigh of relief Morris leant back in his chair. For a moment Hugh thought Willoughby Morris was crying; but he was merely brushing the tear that wept from his injured eye.

Hugh settled the bill and said he had better deliver the letter to Tony as soon as possible. Morris said he had to be at his Oxford solicitor's office at half past two. They rose and left the restaurant, parted company in the High and went separate ways, Morris up the High towards Carfax, Hugh across the road and into Holt.

That achieved, the college porter told me later that he did not see Morris again that day. In the late afternoon I met Hugh in the quad; he had given the letter to Tony who had been with Eedes. He was on his way to Knowles's rooms; he thought he should inform Knowles, as senior tutor, of the situation. We stood in the quad for twenty minutes or so while Hugh related what had happened at lunch. Then he suggested that I accompanied him to find Knowles.

We went into Knowles's office, which was an adjunct to his college rooms. The only person in the office was a secretary who was tidying her desk and was about to depart. She said Knowles was in his rooms. Hugh knocked on his door and after a little time, during which the secretary left, Naish opened the door. He was in his shirtsleeves, no sign of his coat. He was surprised. 'Oh, hello. Do you want Timothy? He's lying down, not feeling too well.'

He called out, 'Tim, it's Lord Crammond and Dr James.'

Knowles's rooms was a traditional set which consisted of a large sitting room that doubled as a study and for most tutorial fellows as a teaching room, and a bedroom. We went in. Knowles called out from the interior of the bedroom, 'Find a seat. I'll be out in a moment.'

Hugh stood before a bay window that overlooked one of the college gardens. He gazed out at a centuries old yew tree. I moved an upright chair from a table covered in papers and documents and sat down. After a short time, Knowles appeared. He was slightly awkward in manner for the first few minutes. I could not work out if he had been sleeping and was disoriented or if he felt that somehow he had been caught in a compromising situation with Naish. It was impossible to tell, except that as Knowles came out of the bedroom, Naish went in, retrieved his coat from somewhere inside and put it on. At the back of his neck, part of the collar remained up. Knowles stepped across to him, attentively turned it down, brushed the cloth across his shoulders, and patted Naish on the back. I thought at the last moment of the interlude he was going to embrace Naish. It did not happen. Knowles stepped back to the centre of the room. Hugh turned from the bay window. 'Very sorry to disturb you, Timothy. I've just been telling Johnny what happened at lunch with Willoughby. We thought you should be in the picture, in the loop.'

I was surprised by Hugh using such terms. It showed, I think, that he was a little disconcerted. He must have been thinking, too, that we had disturbed some intimate moment between the two of them.

Knowles said, rather stumblingly, 'No, no, no trouble, no disturbance. I haven't been feeling too well today.'

'You should know as well, Naish, since you've done such a lot for Willoughby recently. Anyway, he's officially resigned as Principal.' He continued to tell them both what had taken place in Quod at lunchtime.

Knowles digested all the information and finally commented,

'Well, significant news. I wonder what we'll do next. Wednesday's college meeting is crucial. Is Tony Gill hoping to take over? I suppose he is. Oh well, the king is dead. Long live the king.'

Hugh said, 'I'm sure you're right. Wednesday is important. You'll all have to make up your minds over what happens next. Whatever it is, it should happen quickly. Limbo is not a good state to be in.'

Brendan Naish was standing behind the chair that Knowles had sat in. He put his hand on Knowles's shoulder. 'I think poor Timothy should go back to his room. You should lie down. I don't think you're well.'

What he said signalled the end of the visit. Naish assumed the role of choreographer. It was as though he was in charge of proceedings. Yet it was impossible to upstage Hugh. He exhibited an effortless superiority. He dominated the occasion while simultaneously maintaining a quiet, powerful reserve. His presence in the room dictated whatever was going to happen next.

'Anyway, there you are, Knowles.' Hugh used the old-fashioned form of familiar address by surname, except in that instance I suspected that Hugh was putting Knowles in his place formally. It was obvious, too, that both Knowles and Naish were unsure.

The meeting then resolved itself. There was a knock at the door. Naish went and opened it. A girl student stood there. She was clearly in a distressed state. Knowles said wearily, 'Oh dear, come in. Gentlemen, I'd better see what the matter is here.'

Hugh reverted to Knowles's Christian name, 'Timothy, we will leave you.' Naish saw us out. As we left, he said, 'I think I'd better get Timothy into bed as soon as possible.' Hugh and I exchanged a smile.

32

Tuesday evening was a guest night in hall. There was an unusually good attendance. Many fellows decided to dine in because one of the guests, invited by Donald, was an American called Jason Modell. He was a potential benefactor. At home in the States he was the founder of what was now a multi-million-dollar computer software company, Modell IT Corporation based in California. One of his daughters had spent a year at Holt after her BA at Rutgers. Donald had met him one evening when he was in Massachusetts. Modell was travelling to London where he was to stay for a week. Donald took the opportunity of inviting him to the guest night.

It turned out that Modell was no fool. He knew why he had been invited. The bottom line was in his chequebook. When Donald introduced him to me, I asked him if he was enjoying his visit to Oxford. His reply was direct. 'Sure, though I'm not sure my bankers will be pleased I'm here. I'll have to talk to them seriously. They keep warning me about my present commitments and telling me not to make any more donations. But this is such a lovely place. I love it. It's so old, and my daughter just loved her time here. I'm so grateful.'

I had not mentioned anything about his possible financial support for the college. He just came out with those remarks. He added a little later: 'What do you want here, monies for buildings, for student scholarships, new teaching posts? You'll have to tell me.' Of course, what he was saying was the reason why so many fellows were there that evening. They all hoped to benefit in some way from his largesse, not personally but for their research, for facilities, for added teaching assistance. At the very end of the evening, when he was just talking to Donald, Est and me, unprompted he said to Est: 'Dr Treisman, I really appreciate what you did for Rachel. She wished she had been able to spend three years here. You really did help her. It was not to be. The homeland called her back.' And when Est and I said goodbye to him in the lodge, he told us that he would definitely make the college a gift. He had refused to stay the night because of business commitments in London on Wednesday morning; a chauffeur-driven Lexus picked him up and took him back to his London hotel. He was staying at Claridge's in Mayfair and was meeting for a breakfast conference at a London investment house.

Modell did not specify the amount of money he would give the college but he did say as he got into the car: 'Thanks. I'll work out with my money men what I can give you. It'll probably be spread over five years. That's the way I like to do things. Don't worry; I won't insist on anything being named after me. I don't regard a gift as a tombstone.' With that the driver closed the car door and the Lexus disappeared into the night.

'A good evening,' Est said to me.

'And a profitable one,' I added. 'Still we want to see the moolah in the bank. Many a slip between lip and cup, as they say.'

'I don't think we need worry. He sounds as though he's got it all worked out.'

She was right. Within six months the college was the beneficiary of a substantial gift to be delivered over five years that financed the building of a forty-unit student accommodation block on college land just beyond the river Isis to the south of the city and the endowment of two bursaries to help undergraduates from disadvantaged financial backgrounds, one for a girl and the other for a boy. The college did well that night.

Est and I went back to her flat where we spent the night. We were up early the next morning. We both had tutorials and it was necessary to think about the college meeting called for two fifteen. At breakfast, a rushed affair of coffee and toast, Est said, 'This is crazy,

232

Johnny, we should be living together properly. What's the point of two lots of outgoing expenditure? Either I should give up this flat or you rent out your house. I'm not going to want to be without you any more. I'm afraid I've got too used to you.' She walked behind me and gave me a kiss on the cheek. I shuddered with excitement and an extraordinary exhilaration came over me.

'Yes. I don't want to be away from you.' I could hardly bear to speak. What I said sounded so banal to me. I felt I could not fulfil her expectations. I was uncertain and lacked confidence in myself. Surely she would change her mind. I could not believe what I was hearing. It was so different from the dealings with Morris, our preoccupation with the succession of the Principal, the tawdry but necessary business of fundraising. Yet trying to listen to myself objectively, it all sounded like the script from a bad sitcom. I meant it though. I did not want to live apart from her. I would miss everything about her, even the things I did not particularly like, for instance the way she generalised about men. I knew not to argue with her; I just shut my ears and waited until she had talked herself out. Occasionally she would be so avid for an argument that I had to respond but I managed to control myself.

'Well,' she said, 'we must talk later and do something quickly. The way we're living is mad, completely mad. I don't know why you haven't spoken about it before.'

'Frankly, I've been afraid to. I don't know, I think I thought you would think I was presumptuous. I was too nervous.'

I got up from the table, took her hands and kissed her on the lips. 'But now it's fantastic. Let's do it. We'll discuss details this evening.'

Lunch was a hurried affair. I arrived late and sat next to the Bodleian Library's deputy librarian, who had been given membership of the common room because she was an Old Member of Holt, and the Grimmond professor of Inorganic Chemistry; his chair was an established one and not a personal one and belonged both to the college and the university. Neither of them were attending the college meeting, Bodley's deputy librarian because she was not entitled to, and the professor because he had to chair a meeting of the university's science division.

The governing body convened on time. Tony took the chair as Vicegerent and acting Principal. The usual preliminaries took place, the reading of minutes and apologies for absence. Tony then addressed the most important issue facing the college, the situation of Morris and the matter of his replacement. He spoke of the necessity of electing Morris's successor quickly and since Morris had pledged in writing his resignation and promised to sever all connection with the college at the end of his sabbatical term, it was time to set in motion the election process. He described the background of Hugh Crammond's moves to ease Morris into a position where he could with some face-saving resign. He stated finally that he should vacate the chair for the discussion on the next Principal since he wanted to be a candidate. The senior fellow, the fellow who had been in post longest, was Frank Bradshaw; he took the chair.

There was much debate and Tony himself offered various views and wise counsel. His contributions served his cause well. There was one unexpected obstacle that was presented. Jeremy Eedes stressed that it should not be a foregone conclusion that Tony was the best man for the job. Tony was there in the room. It was extremely embarrassing for him and before Eedes could go any further, Jane stood up and suggested that during any discussion of this delicate matter perhaps Tony should be asked to leave the room; he would be called back in when the subject had been fully discussed. Frank thought that a sensible idea and asked for a quick show of hands. Tony looked pleased at being released for the moment into the sunlight of the quad. Through the window I saw him stroll to the other side and sit on one of the far benches. Almost immediately a passing girl undergraduate spoke to him and sat down next to him.

I reckoned that Eedes's abrupt intervention did him no favours. It was rude and tactless and coming from a man so closely identified with the old regime must have prejudiced opinion against him. I don't think anyone realised that the bursar had ambitions to lead Holt. That sort of thing happened rarely. When it did, the bursar had also to be distinguished in his own academic field or to have presided over a particularly successful bursarship policy; for instance, a college had just elected its bursar to its Wardenship because she had followed a particularly lucrative investment policy. A rising stock market had helped her but nevertheless she was held in high esteem. Neither case applied to Eedes. He was not especially successful and he had allied himself too closely with Morris's attempt at autocratic rule.

In the discussion that ensued Frank let as many people speak as was reasonably possible. The weight of opinion was clearly against Eedes but finally Frank advised that the college ought to follow usual procedures and advertise the post; he thought too that the university authorities would try to insist on it. Certainly the government had made its position very clear over appointments to public positions; due process, advertisement of the job, applications, submissions of references, interviews, should happen. Frank said it made no difference to us having a preferred candidate, nobody could do anything about that, but the college had better follow the required path to the appointment. As senior fellow he would deal with the applications after advertisement of the post provided that he had secretarial assistance. Ironically Eedes was asked to make provision for that.

Tony was called back in and what had been decided explained to him. He saw that there was no alternative to this; the post had to be advertised. It was not very satisfactory for him. He needed to know what to do about his Hereford application. Naturally the fellows of Hereford knew all about the scandal at Holt and they knew that Tony was standing in as acting Principal and was doing a very good job. Tony had to make a crucial decision; should he let his Hereford application stand or should he withdraw and trust that Holt would confirm him in post as Principal. We knew he would prefer to stay at Holt. The Hereford election would take place within the next three weeks. Ours would take a longer time. Following advertisement, it would not be before the end of term that our appointment was made. After the meeting, which ended at four thirty, a longer meeting than usual, Est and I stood with Tony in the quad.

'I simply don't know what to do,' Tony said. 'I know I have quite a lot of support in Hereford but, as you know, I'd much rather stay here.'

Est was unequivocal. 'You should withdraw from Hereford. I can't see you failing here. You haven't any real opposition here. If we were able to elect today, it would be you we elected.'

I was less certain. 'Look, Tony, I don't give advice but I do have my own views. It's a gamble either way. You never know what might happen between now and our election. Some prominent, famous figure might emerge, and the majority might swing towards that person. Suppose, for example, the Director General of the BBC decided to retire and wanted to be considered or, even more dangerous for you, the editor of *The Times* who happens to be an alumnus, who knows what our colleagues would think. But I personally would take the risk. I'd run for Holt. I calculate that our colleagues have had enough of the bright boys, or girls, from the London scene or international arena.'

Est added, 'That's right, I think everyone is looking for stability. We want someone we know, who can be trusted, who we know will be around and not in London two days a week sitting on government committees or attending board meetings. You are ideal, Tony. You fit the bill. I think you should formally apply and let it be known that you would be pleased and proud to serve the college full-time.'

Tony looked towards the ancient sundial in the middle of a square plot of roses which were in second bloom beneath the chapel tower. He was lost in thought for a moment or two and then said, 'Yes, I think you're right. This is where I want to be. I should concentrate everything on trying to get the post. If I don't, then I shall think again. I shall withdraw from Hereford. There will be other heads of house becoming vacant anyway should this fail.'

I was pleased Tony did not prevaricate. It was typical. He was decisive. 'In the meantime, Tony, we'll campaign for you. Est, Jane, Donald and I, and JOB, I'm sure, in his own quiet way, will lobby for you, although I think there won't be much need for it. Judging from the mood in this post-Morris era, the fellowship will want you to succeed.'

33

The college settled down to its Michaelmas term routine. As I had mentioned to Tony, our small group, central to the college's interest, lobbied for Tony particularly among those of the fellowship who rarely came into college. They were mostly scientists who kept to their departmental teaching and research laboratories and others who spent most of their time in libraries. We judged that the general feeling was for Tony and as I had predicted not for some prominent figure from public life who might still hanker for the great metropolis. Rodney Bennet, the nuclear physicist, turned out to be a great supporter of Tony and was tireless and enthusiastic in his campaign among his fellow scientists. I rang Hugh Crammond and told him what had happened at the college meeting. He was naturally pleased with the way matters were developing and promised to use his influence on those present fellows that he knew personally.

Est and I decided that I should move in with her. Her apartment was large and convenient; it was in the High and a hundred or so yards from the college. I would let my house in Jericho. Most of my books were in my college rooms. It was an arrangement I looked forward to and I made the move within a fortnight of our decision. Needless to say I always slept at Est's place from the moment we had that discussion.

The term advanced into October. The evenings drew in, leaves began to drop, the heavy, decaying smell of autumn dominated and deadened the sweet scents of summer. Oxford took on once more its cloak of morning mist and evening vapours. Michaelmas daisies in the herbaceous borders did not allow those who wandered the quads to forget the gradual change of season. For weeks no one had heard anything of Willoughby Morris.

The only person in college to keep in regular touch was Brendan Naish. That was to be expected since he had helped him with his London move. Est had once described Naish in Shakespearean terms, 'A slight unmeritable man, fit to be sent on errands,' and for a long time I was inclined to agree. As Knowles's sybarite he was sycophantic, certainly towards Knowles but also towards anyone else whom he felt was in a superior position to himself. Over time I began to see him differently. After I had seen him give essential assistance to Morris, I saw him basically as considerate and kind. The nature of his character was to assert himself in an irritating, annoying way but that was born of insecurity and an over-developed fear of criticism and rejection because of his gayness. Anyway, during the vacation and the beginning of that Michaelmas term I had got on much better with Naish than previously. Est was still sceptical. She detected no change; he was exceedingly annoying for her, ambitious, pushy, presumptuous and sometimes impertinent. He did not regard his position in college as of less importance than any of the fellows. If that was so, in many ways he was right; too many of my colleagues had an over-inflated view of themselves, their importance, and their superiority. They were intellectual snobs.

I had reassessed Naish. I even began to realise what Knowles saw in him; I do not mean sexually, but what Naish presented as a sympathetic and compassionate person. What Brendan Naish said to me one day when we met by chance in the main quad was this: 'Willoughby was here yesterday. I don't mean here in college. I don't think he wants to come back here. But he was here in Oxford. He didn't tell me he was coming but Timothy saw him in the middle of the afternoon in Queen Street. I think he'd just come out of Marks and Spencer.'

I remarked, 'That's strange. I wonder what he was here for. I suppose he has people he needs to see here still. Anyway, a bit odd.'

'Well, I'll find out. I usually these days ring him two or three times a week – just to make sure he's surviving. In spite of his bravado he's been badly shaken by his removal from Oxford.'

'Yes, I know; it's sad. But he's only himself to blame.'

I felt a little cruel putting it all so bluntly, but it was true. I recognised that Naish would have felt considerably different. He had vested interests. Morris had been kind to him. At the time, if it were not for Morris, Naish would never have been allowed to enjoy so much of Knowles's patronage. In a sense Brendan Naish was repaying a debt. And yet, that was too crude; I had come to feel that Naish was quite kind and wanted to make sure Morris was all right in London.

'That's true,' said Naish, 'and I think he knows it now. I'll find out why he's been here today.'

'I suppose he's started work in London. Do you think he has?'

'Yes, but most of it is paperwork. The main committee meets twice a month. He told me his first meeting is Friday this week. He was looking forward to it. Otherwise it's meetings with other organisations and, as I say, paperwork which he does in his office in Victoria or at home. He doesn't like that. He likes to be with people.'

I experienced a slight feeling that I might have been too hard on Morris, but when I recollected what he had done and his unremitting arrogance in college, his disregard of the collegiate system and his detrimental effect on the reputation of the college, I had no regrets. Not convinced that I was being truly sincere, I said to Naish: 'Oh well, keep an eye on him. If there's any news, let me know.'

Again, I am not sure why I said that. I was not really interested in Morris's fate. We were well rid of him.

It was just a week later at the termly meeting of the senior common room that Knowles proposed that Brendan Naish should be made a member. Had it been at the beginning of the term before I had that conversation with Naish, I think I would have opposed the move. As it was, my view of Naish had changed. I now saw him as a useful tool in the management of college politics. He was certainly useful in looking after and keeping an eye on Morris. So long as he did not get beyond himself and presume upon his position, it seemed good that he should share the facilities of the common room; it would make it easier to stay in touch with him. He would be there at coffee time and for lunch. The idea was that he should be given rights to lunch and a right to dine in twice each week. Those privileges were provided at the college's expense and were usual for someone who was not a fellow but was considered to be performing useful work for the college.

There was some opposition. Part of the fellowship thought that there were more deserving members of the administrative staff who should precede him to election but in the end Knowles succeeded and Naish was elected. When I next saw him, which indeed was next day at coffee, he was very pleased. We spoke more easily to each other and I really began to like him.

I discussed my change in attitude to Naish with Est. She was quizzical. She did not see what I saw in him now. For her he was still Knowles's rather pushy little placeman, the sybarite provided with a convenient job by his older lover. So far as she was concerned that was it. Nevertheless she did not have any fierce objection and when she registered my support for Naish she did not block his election. 'I'll take your word on him. You vouch for him. That's good enough.'

'OK, we'll see; but I think I'm right. At base, I think he's all right. Quite a nice guy.'

That was what most people thought. His relationship with Knowles was irrelevant. He did his job and was apparently good at it. One doubt remained in my mind but I suppressed it; perhaps it was Naish who was responsible for the leaks, or at least some of them. At that particular time, that too was irrelevant; the leaks were in the past.

34

Michaelmas term moved towards its climax. The last week approached and all the usual Christmas preparations were under way. Donald rehearsed the great Christmas carol service, which for years now was always televised and rivalled that of King's College Cambridge, and planned the now three-hour-long Christmas vigil that he had introduced when he was appointed. The college kitchens prepared for the festival feast on the evening of the last college meeting of term. The late afternoons and evenings were dark and dank. There were heavy frosts which descended in the night and were in evidence until midday, gradually disappeared and then reappeared after a few hours as soon as dusk fell. In the older buildings the college heating system rattled away, pipes vibrating, all day long and most of the night. In the dining hall at dinner time a huge log fire burned under special dispensation from local council rules. Most college members, the teaching fellows and the undergraduates, concentrated on keeping warm and there was a general air of expectation and excitement about looking forward to the Christmas vacation.

Naturally the most important matter on our minds was the election of the new Principal. Various candidates had visited the college and been interviewed. A short list of three had dined in, Tony, of course, a professor of Law from University College London, and the woman dean of an arts faculty at an enormous American university, an old Oxford graduate who reckoned she had experienced enough of the States and wanted to return home. In the event the last college meeting of term decided to postpone the election to the first meeting of Hilary term after Christmas. That would be in noughth week before the undergraduates in their mass returned. A significant number of the fellows wanted more time to consider the election and one or two of them, both arts people and scientists, wanted to find out more about the candidate from America.

Tony was both annoyed and disturbed by the delay. He had planned to move into the lodgings at the beginning of January. It would have suited his family circumstances, his children, at the beginning of the new year and the fact that he would have liked to let his house for the Hilary term. There was little we Tony loyalists could do about it. We were effectively blocked by the small quorum of fellows interested in the American university candidate. It meant that the Principal's lodgings were to continue unoccupied for a few weeks more. Tony had to delay his plans.

I said to Est as we walked past the chapel that evening: 'I sense danger.'

'Oh rubbish. We've done our lobbying. We know the strength of opinion. Tony doesn't have to worry. It's a done deal.'

I was not so sure. I remembered a saying of my old friend, an administrator in a Scottish university; he always advised against trusting anyone to do with university life. 'Never forget, my friend,' he said, 'all academics are shits, and all university administrators are arseholes: the two are made for each other.' Yet Est was right, we had done our lobbying and we should have been confident.

We paused outside the chapel entrance. The music coming from inside was magnificent. The choir was rehearsing the Christmas service of nine lessons and carols. The hauntingly beautiful melody of the old New England carol 'Jesus Christ the apple tree' soared out of the chapel, the leading boy soprano in his solo reaching the highest, purest notes with practised ease. I knew the hymn; it was my favourite carol. The setting was by Elizabeth Poston. It was the best and I had listened over the years to all the notable recordings of it, the King's College Cambridge one, Eton College's and many, many more. It was sublime. Est and I stood there, both of us enraptured by the music. What a privilege.

Clear and bright, the words resonated in every sense:

For happiness I long have sought
And pleasure dearly I have bought.
I missed of all; but now I see
'Tis found in Christ the apple tree.

Est said, 'What a contrast; such rare beauty and the banality of the provincial politics that we've been discussing. That amazing music puts things into perspective. Let's leave things to take their course and not waste time worrying about the outcome.'

I agreed. 'As you say, everything's assured.'

35

The Christmas vacation passed. Est and I parted for a short period. We both had family commitments, she with her parents, while I went off to visit my sister's family in Washington DC. I did not particularly enjoy the trip. I missed Est and desperately wanted to be with her all the time; we were separated by the mighty Atlantic. I phoned her every day; we spoke for an hour, an hour and a half. Time and expense were not important. My sister thought I was stupidly infatuated and warned me, in her wisely perceptive way that she had been the mistress of since childhood, that all would end in disappointment and failure. It annoyed me that she could not be positive and indulge my passion for Est. She lived in a fine apartment within the Kalorama Triangle of central north-west Washington; she lectured at the School of Advanced International Studies and her husband worked for the International Monetary Fund. They had a small baby boy and Christmas was wholly for him. Christmas Eve and the day itself were both enjoyable; friends came from out of town and others from apartments in the same block. Their friends were cosmopolitan, urbane, witty, of different nationalities and diverting conversationalists. I was reminded of how isolated Oxford was compared with the US capital.

For two days after the festival I spent my time thinking mostly of ways to withstand the cold, and sat in the coffee shops and bookshops of Dupont Circle. After those few days I was released and flew back home to Britain.

Est and I met again at her flat in the Oxford High. My house was let from the beginning of January. We now shared her apartment and most of my personal belongings were with her. We had both survived Christmas without each other and were immensely glad to be back together. The satisfaction and the celebration were both spiritual and physical. My life had changed much for the better and I was confident that hers had too.

As the crucial vote for the principalship approached in noughth week, our lobbying continued and intensified, although I was disturbed by a decline in enthusiasm from one or two of Tony's supporters. I had heard even Frank Bradshaw extol the virtues of having an academic from outside the college, someone with a completely fresh view of the college and the university; the fact that the someone might have experience of a famous and highly successful Ivy League university would be more to the point. In days when finance was difficult and fundraising of paramount importance, it meant that an academic from an American university, who was accustomed to private money coming into the system of higher education, was attractive to many people.

So, Est, Jane, Donald and I worked particularly hard to rally support for Tony and we strove to maintain that support in the face of a developing opposition and defection to the American candidate. Our straw polling still showed that we had a considerable majority.

Then, on the Sunday of noughth week, I met Brendan Naish in the High. I was coming out of our flat, we now termed it our flat, and as I closed the door I almost backed into him.

'Oh, sorry. I wasn't looking. How are you, Brendan? Did you have a good Christmas holiday?' I knew that, like all other college officers and admin staff, Naish would have been back at his desk on the second of January.

'Yes. Fine. Timothy and I went to the south of France. Beaulieu-sur-Mer. Very pleasant, warm, sunny. We were lucky.'

'I envy you. I was frozen in Washington.'

'Tim is very good. He inherited a flat on the seafront at Beaulieu. We went down to Cap Ferrat. Drinks in the Grand Hotel. Lots of celebs to be seen. Then along to Antibes. We met fascinating people. Actors, directors – Mendes was there. Wonderful time.'

'You certainly had a better time than I did.'

'By the way, good job I bumped into you, almost quite literally. I phoned Willoughby a couple of times. He didn't sound too good. The second time he sounded drunk and depressed. He complained about his loss of power. He has no direct executive power. He's been used to it from a very early professional age.'

I commented, 'He'll probably be OK now that the new year has started. Christmas can be a terribly depressing time if you're on your own; but once things get going, he'll be all right. I've known him for quite a long time. He's tough, I reckon. He'll snap out of it and be all action.'

Naish was not so sure. 'Well, I hope you're right. He was really down. I said I'd go up to London and see him on Thursday, after we know who the new Principal is. Mind you, I don't think he'll want to discuss that.'

In fact, Naish told me later, he went and saw Morris on the Monday of that week. He had been phoned on his mobile late on Sunday night by an extremely distressed Morris. Again Morris had drunk too much and was barely coherent. He seemed to be losing his grasp on reality. He could see that he had made mistakes, taken wrong decisions, followed a course that would lead to a form of personal destruction, and now it was too late to redeem himself. He seemed not to know what to do, who to turn to; he could not appreciate that there were still one or two people who were his friends. According to Naish it made him sound at times self-pitying, and self-obsessed, and at other moments defiant and aggressive. Naish added that at the end of the phone call, Morris said tearfully that he wanted to come up to Oxford; he needed to exorcise some persistent ghosts.

'He didn't quite put it like that,' Naish said to me, 'but that's what he meant. I think I've dissuaded him at least until after the election. I don't think it would do anyone any good if he were to show up before. You never know what he might do in his present state. He might start beating his breast and rant and rave in the middle of the college quad.' Naish laughed uneasily.

'Let's hope you're right. Afterwards he has to get used to it.'

What happened next came as a complete shock.

Morris did appear in Oxford. The consequences were terrible, for me, for Est, for anyone who had ever been involved with him.

Brendan Naish had been truly worried by Morris's state of mind. Morris had rung him early on Monday morning. It had sounded as if Morris had not been to bed that night. He said that like Churchill, he was trying to dismiss the black dog from his consciousness by drinking cognac before breakfast. Once again he was a peculiar mixture of self-assertiveness and self-pity. He was determined to travel to Oxford. Naish told him to stay put; he was going to London and he would visit him. They would go out to lunch together. Where was he working that day? At home as usual in St George's Square. Knowles was very understanding and released Naish to catch the first available train. The battle with Morris's moods and depression took all day, but at least Naish kept him occupied and stopped him appearing in Oxford.

It was different on Tuesday. In the early afternoon I was in my room. Est had called in on her way to her rooms; she had been shopping in town. My phone rang. The head porter, Archie Rook, reliable in every detail of his work, told me some startling news. He had tried to get hold of Tony but he was out of college. Jeremy Eedes was at a university meeting. He thought I should know, as an official fellow of the college, that when he came on duty at two o'clock, one of the assistant porters had reported that Morris had arrived round about one thirty and asked for a key to the lodgings. The lodgings were locked because the secretary was part-time and worked only in the mornings. Tony was away. Morris was insistent. He had been quite cross with the porter. He maintained that he was still in fact the Principal of the college and would be until a new Principal was elected.

The porter was reluctant to hand over the keys but could not hold out against the dominant Morris. Morris had gone off, across the quad and disappeared into the lodgings. When Archie came on duty and after the assistant had left, Archie had gone across and found that the lodgings had been locked. Either Morris had gone away with the keys or he had locked the house from the inside. Rook thought it best that a fellow accompanied him into the lodgings in case Morris had to be confronted in some awkward situation. I agreed with Archie and told him I would go with him. Est said she would come too.

Est and I struggled across the quad against blustery winds that descended in surges and whose chills made us shiver. Rook was in a dark raincoat and wore his uniform bowler hat. Est greeted him; I nodded. As we approached the lodgings we looked more like a bailiff's party than a small band of anxious people on a possible mission of mercy.

Rook produced the master key from a bunch that he kept in the porters' lodge. The lock of the old oak, iron-clamped door shifted but it was soon obvious it had been bolted. So, that indicated that Morris was inside.

'What on earth is he doing?' Est tried to peer in through a window. She saw nothing but the empty, rather gloomy unlit interior of the reception hall. No one could answer her question. Rook said we should go round to the back of the lodgings and try one of the other doors. In order to be quick we stepped across a flower bed; we avoided some clumps of snowdrops whose green shoots were just beginning to appear. The back door, more modest and modern than its front-of-house counterpart, was not bolted and opened with Archie's key. We went in.

I called out, 'Principal Morris. Dr Morris. Are you here?' It was odd. I could not think how to address him appropriately if he were in fact there not wishing to be disturbed. It was Est who was more familiar. 'Willoughby. Willoughby. Where are you?' Archie stood and listened. There was no response.

We started looking round on the ground floor. Tony's admin room was locked. We thought it unlikely that Morris would be in there. No sign of him was in the other downstairs rooms. We continued to call out. Our voices were absorbed and muffled by the high-ceilinged rooms. We went upstairs. There were three bedrooms and two dressing rooms, two bathrooms and one separate lavatory. All the doors bar the one to the master bedroom were open. Archie was the first to notice that there was a cord tied round the door handle; it went up the door and over the high top and presumably hung down the other side. His voice was dry and hoarse: 'What's that doing there?' Est and I looked, and then looked at each other. Fearful I went quickly to the door and tried to open it but the handle with the cord attached was difficult to turn; with Est's help, our hands touching, and with me feeling the electric thrill of her physical presence, we managed to turn the knob. The door was exceedingly heavy to move open. It was as though something had been propped against it and yet there was not sufficient resistance and gradually it swung open. We went in. A library stool, one used for standing on to reach books on a high shelf, was on its side across the floor. Rook pulled at the door and to our intense horror we saw the sagging figure of Morris hanging suspended by the thick nylon cord which once must have served as a sash or belt for a dressing gown. Morris was a stocky, thickset man; the toes of his outstretched shoes missed the ground by a couple of inches. He must have calculated exactly what length of cord and what clearance of the ground he needed for his grisly task, stood on the library step, and then kicked it away. There was the pungent, acrid smell of urine in the air. His head drooped at an unnatural angle as if his body had been broken, crushed by some giant's hand. He was quite obviously dead.

Est was aghast, shocked. She sat down on the side of the made-up bed. I said to her, even though I was as upset and horrified as her: 'You'd better sit outside. In fact I think we all should. I'll call the ambulance and police. This is just awful.'

Rook who had not removed his bowler hat when we entered now did so. He stood in front of the appalling sight of the hanging man. He held his hat, clasped in front of him, bowed his head and under his breath, whispered, 'Oh Lord, let now your servant depart in peace according to your word.' I knew Rook was an evangelical Christian and I recognised his prayer as a modern rendering of the Nunc Dimittis from the Book of Common Prayer.

Rather than sit down again, we all went outside. Rook hurried away to the lodge and alerted other college staff that the police and ambulance paramedics would be coming to college. Est and I, in spite of the wind and cold weather, sat on a bench in the quad for a few minutes. We then went to the lodge and told Archie that we would be in my room. There, I rang Tony on his mobile. He was shocked speechless and it took him some considerable time to comprehend what I was saying. Eventually the full extent of the crisis registered with him and he said he would immediately leave his colleagues in the labs where he was and come straight into college. I also rang Hugh Crammond who, likewise appalled, said he would come in from Fenmore.

Gradually the news of Morris's suicide spread. In the early evening the reporters turned up. Est and I avoided them. Everyone was referred to Tony. Poor Tony had to be the college's mouthpiece. How, in the end, he must have regretted being the prime mover in the first place for getting Willoughby Morris elected Principal. Morris's death made an item on the local television news at half past ten. Otherwise it became public news the following morning in most of the national newspapers. The background story to his severance from the college was mentioned briefly and his subsequent suicide featured. There were photos of the college prominent in most of the papers while the story ran to no more than two or three paragraphs.

Thus the life and ambitions of Willoughby Morris, sometime Principal of one of the oldest and most distinguished colleges in Oxford, came to an end.

36

Est and I were extremely upset by the experience. We comforted each other. It was all very sad that such an able man could descend so swiftly into a moral chaos that would lead to his suicide.

'It was just so awful seeing him hanging there. It was unreal. I couldn't believe it. I still find it difficult. It's almost as if it were an illusion.'

'I know,' I said to her. 'I know exactly what you mean.'

'It's just awful. Almost exactly the same happened at Pembroke in the early years after the War. The namesake of the great poet Robert Browning who was an English don hanged himself from the back of a door. A truly awful upset.'

What was especially odd was that I experienced a powerful feeling of sadness for the death of a man I did not like and certainly did not respect; in fact, it would have been true to say that I despised him. And yet when I witnessed that hanging corpse of the man I knew and realised what he had been driven to by, I suppose, his inner demons, I was infinitely sad. It was not just his mortality that struck home to my soul but the mortality of all of us. Naturally I shared my thoughts with Est.

At last it was Est who brought us back to ourselves in the contemplation of the future. 'I fear what Morris has done is in the nature of certain people. It's what they will do with no deflection of purpose. They're mad, like Lear.'

'At least Lear did not kill himself.' I quoted one of his lines, '"And, to deal plainly, I fear I am not in my perfect mind."'

'That's true,' she said, 'but you might say that he died of a broken heart, and in some sense that might be true of Morris. After his arrogance and consequent failure, he must have seen that he was in love with the college and Oxford. After all he came back to take his life in the surroundings that he loved best.'

'You say that but there might have been a more malign motive, something about revenge, and making as much trouble for those who got rid of him as possible.'

'Who knows? It's impossible to conjecture.'

What did transpire was malign. The ancient foundation of Holt, its scholars and fellows, because of Willoughby Morris's willfulness and thoughtlessness in choosing the college as his own personal sacrificial altar, ruined Tony's career. Gradually the fellows grew to feel that the college did not need an internal candidate, someone somehow blighted by the events leading to Morris's death. They felt a new, fresh academic mind from the New World was preferable to any other contender. Support for Tony's election as Principal fell away.

At the college meeting the day after Morris's suicide it was proposed by Donald that a decent interval should pass before the election took place. A strong movement of opinion from mostly science fellows and the historians contradicted that view. It was necessary for the college to have a new head at once. Strong leadership, a firm guiding hand, someone who enjoyed everyone's confidence was needed in the Principal's chair. The consequence was that Tony lost the election, even Jacob Black voted for the academic from America. 'I-I d-did not v-vote against T-Tony, I-I s-simply voted f-for the A-American c-candidate.' The voting figures stood at fourteen votes for Tony and seventeen for the American academic. Frank Bradshaw who had sat in the chair for the vote wanted us to present the election as a unanimous vote but Doanld, Est, Jane and I refused to accept that misrepresentation of the facts.

It was a very bad day for Tony. He was utterly devastated. We urged him to consider other options. Donald knew that the Rector of Exeter was going to announce her retirement shortly; Tony should consider applying for that post. Anyway, we knew that he would survive. His family, his wife and his children, were more of a comfort to him than the negation of family life and career that Willoughby Morris had suffered in his dismissal of other people's feelings.

And, of course, the great college of Holt would survive. Morris's tenure as Principal and his unfortunate death would be as a speck, a tiny blemish, a mote *sub specie aeternitatis*, on the records of the institution. In the dining hall the majestic portraits of Walter Grimmond and many other benefactors would continue to look down, some with serious demeanour, others with beneficent and tolerant smiles on fellows and undergraduates alike. The old Archbishop's family motto was mounted under his portrait, carved from oak on the panelling above and behind the Principal's chair, 'Stryke out corruption, and doe alle that is goode'. What an irony!